THE TRIANGLE

Teresa L. Cannady

Dedicated to my parents, Verlon and Martha Cannady, who not only believed in me, but taught me how to believe in myself.

Special thanks to my brother, Joey Cannady, and dear friends, Carlene Howe and Bill Hallock, for reading the manuscript and providing thoughtful recommendations.

CHAPTER ONE

Otis flipped through the ten channels available on the bar's television, thanks to a small satellite dish he'd recently installed. Before the satellite, there were only three. Not that it really mattered, the drunks didn't pay much attention to what was on the television. They came for the hooch, especially his local brew, made of rice and a few other secret ingredients. Otis had the only bar on this remote island, aptly named Otis's Bar and Grill, thanks to his obsession with re-runs of Andy Griffith. He'd always loved the Mayberry town drunk, Otis, who had the good sense to check himself into the jail when he went on a bender. If only his customers were so wise.

Otis wasn't his name. Of course he couldn't use his own, that's how it is when you are on the run. Not so much running, as hiding, at least now that he'd found this great escape. No one would ever look for him here.

"How about another one?" Jake said, throwing his glass down, hard, on the bamboo counter. Jake didn't need another one, but who was Otis to judge. He was in the business of selling alcohol so he wasn't going to refuse anyone. He had to make a living after all. Jake, not his name either—it dawned on Otis that he didn't even know his real name—didn't have a car so there was no danger of drinking and driving. Otis poured him another, but with a bit of a warning.

"There you go Jake, but you might want to take that one slow, it's only 3:00 p.m."

At three in the afternoon the crowd was pretty slim, a few regulars, a couple of guys playing some pool, and one guy he'd never seen before sitting in a corner both. They didn't get many strangers around here, they stood out like a sore thumb, and folks were quick to ask questions. This place was not only, *not* on the beaten path, it wasn't on any map he'd ever seen. Otis liked it that way, actually needed it that way, and the locals didn't mind, they didn't want the gringos dropping by and ruining a good thing.

Otis clicked through a few more channels, a Spanish telenovela, re-runs of M.A.S.H, a documentary on whales. He yelled to the guy in the corner and asked if he needed anything.

"Sure, bring me a beer."

"What kind?" Otis asked, as if he actually had a selection.

"Doesn't matter, whatever you recommend, as long as it's cold."

Cold was relative, but he wasn't going to do any better, so Otis took a slightly chilled Budweiser over to his table. "Anything else?"

"Yeah, could you find a news channel on that big screen television of yours?" He asked.

Otis should have been offended. This guy was mocking his 1980s cathode ray TV. Sure, it was a relic, but it was the only one around. Obviously this guy wasn't "from here." He needed to learn some manners.

"Are you looking for something in particular?" Otis asked, trying to make conversation.

"Just curious as to what may be happening out there in the big bad world today," he replied, very confidently.

"Nothing ever happens out there, or in here, for that matter. Some days I wish it would." And with that Otis was gone, leaving the stranger to wonder what he meant.

Otis flipped through a few more channels and managed to pick up CNN International. There seemed to be no escape from the reach of the 24-hour news cycle. Nothing interesting was happening so Otis decided to check his inventory and clean the place up a bit before the happy hour crowd rolled in.

There wasn't a lot to clean, it was an open air building, a thatched roof held up by bamboo poles. Rusty ceiling fans scattered around the place kept the temperature tolerable, their creaking and whining drowned out by the golden oldies Otis played on his IPod and portable speakers.

The guy in the corner continued to watch the news, and drink his beer slowly, a little too slowly for Otis's taste. He was a businessman after all. Otis asked the guy if he wanted another, or something else, perhaps a taste of his rice liquor. But he declined and continued to sit alone, watching the "big screen" television, while Otis struck up a conversation with Jake about his favorite college football team. Jake was a University of Michigan man, which was very telling; now, Otis knew where he was from. Otis was skilled at getting that kind of information out of people, although it wasn't that difficult, given that most of them were drunk. Otis always told people that the University of Alabama was his team, which usually brought a stunned look, if they were sober enough to put two and two together. Otis didn't have a southern accent, probably because he wasn't from the South. He played his cards a little closer to the vest.

Otis poured Jake a glass of water. He wanted to slow him down so that he wasn't asleep on the bar during the dinner hour. It was a bar *and* grill after all. People didn't like to dine with drunks. The place wasn't Chez Francois, it was only burgers and fish; nonetheless, Otis tried to maintain some decorum.

The cuckoo clock over the cash register crowed five times, the regulars would be here soon. He decided to check the television again. It was the top of the hour, there would be headlines, which was about as much news as he could handle. What appeared to be a mushroom cloud covered the screen behind the pretty blond reporter who had caught his eye. But that mushroom cloud caught his eye in another way, he had to find out more.

Otis grabbed the remote — the television was old but not that old — and turned up the sound. He didn't get the entire story but apparently there was an explosion in some remote place in Taiwan, speculation was that it was nuclear but the cloud looked different. No one was sure what caused it, whether it was toxic, or what was being done to contain it. It would take some time to get the truth, Taiwan wasn't hurrying to offer up any details. Not willing to wait around all evening for what might or might not be the truth, Otis decided to look for another Andy Griffith re-run.

To be polite, and to maintain some semblance of customer service, he turned to ask the guy in the corner if he could change the channel, but he wasn't there. Otis thought perhaps he'd gone to the restroom, or worse, maybe he'd skipped out on the tab, but then he saw a five dollar bill on the table. As Otis walked over to pick up the cash, he saw the guy walking away, heading down the one road — if you could call it a road — that existed on this island. Perhaps he'd had enough or else he got what he came for, either way Otis figured he'd never see him again.

CHAPTER TWO

As the airplane took off from Honolulu after a five hour delay, Amelia could hardly believe she was on her way to an island in the middle of the Pacific Ocean. An island that, until a few weeks ago, she'd never known existed. Even though she fancied herself fairly well informed on geography, she had never heard of Panzau. But, it was only twelve miles long and eight miles wide, with slightly less than 8000 inhabitants, so not exactly a well-known tourist destination. She'd traveled to Europe, the Caribbean, even to Machu Picchu, but the Pacific region had not been on her radar until a few weeks ago when she received an intriguing and somewhat disturbing call from a marine biologist. He described some rather odd occurrences with marine life washing ashore, dead and severely deformed, likely the result of some contamination, in his opinion; although, he hadn't been able to pinpoint the source. Given Amelia's work at the Environmental Protection Agency, especially with oceanography, she was eager to find out the cause, and besides it was a chance to visit an island, go to the beach, something she'd always loved.

During her five hour layover in the Honolulu airport, she had seen enough of duty free shops complete with perfume, muumuus, and leis, of course. It was a shame she didn't have time to see the real Hawaii, she was sure it was perfect. But there wasn't enough time for sightseeing now and besides she was already exhausted from the fifteen hour trip from New Orleans via Los Angeles. Hawaii's coconut and palm trees, blue skies, and even bluer water would have to wait for another day.

As the plane ascended to 30,000 feet, the city of Honolulu disappeared beneath her and Amelia wondered what she was getting herself into. From her online research, Amelia knew that Panzau was mostly inhabited by indigenous Polynesians; although, there was a small ex-pat community, perhaps a hundred or so, mostly Australians, some Americans, and a few Europeans. She'd checked out all of the websites, including the very limited Panzau visitor's bureau site, and looked at every picture she could find. There were inviting shots of long white beaches, mangroves, and coral. But she wondered whether that was the real Panzau. Pictures don't always reflect reality and visitor bureau websites are notorious for highlighting the best features, often exaggerating them.

When Amelia heard someone ask "would you like the chicken or the lasagna?" she was reminded it was an eight hour flight to Guam. Guam was another place she'd never been. She assumed it was an insurance policy for the U.S. given its strategic location in the Pacific. Dinner only added to the unpleasantness of the trip—lasagna, stale bread and wilted lettuce. It should come as no surprise that air rage was on the rise. Between the lackluster food, tiny seats, and being cooped up for all those hours with people you don't know, it is no wonder people get upset. Not to mention the crying babies and rowdy children, usually kicking the back of your seat.

After dinner, the flight attendant dimmed the cabin lights so passengers could watch their choice of movies from the on-demand system. That was a fabulous advancement in air travel. At least now you weren't stuck with one movie, one you probably had already seen or didn't want to see. Amelia thought life would be complete without one more movie under her belt, so she pulled up her blanket up and tried to get some much-needed rest before touching down in, what she hoped would be, her island paradise.

Just as she started to doze off, they hit turbulence, quite a bit of turbulence, and the fasten seat belt sign blinked on. The pilot announced a rainstorm, which he hoped to fly around, but it was likely to be a bumpy ride for fifteen to twenty minutes. She wanted to raise the window shade and have a look for herself, but she feared the flight attendant "police" or her neighbors might claw her eyes out. Somehow the airlines managed to transform broad daylight into darkness, in the hopes of tricking a barrel full of sleep-deprived people into quiet submission and probably, to keep them from attacking each other.

As the pilot predicted, they soon flew out of the storm and life was good again, as good as it gets at 30,000 feet. When Amelia could no longer keep her eyes open she thankfully dozed off, but not to restful sleep. That wasn't anything new, she had annoying dreams almost every night, often dialing a telephone or operating a calculator, getting numbers in the wrong order and having to start over. Amelia was curious what the dreams meant, if anything at all, and why she kept repeating the same, or remarkably similar ones. But, she wasn't convinced she wanted the answer. I was likely that stress played a big role, and tonight, today, whatever it was now, jetlag was adding to the effect. Whatever the cause, it was extremely frustrating, during, and after, when she would awake feeling exhausted, as if, she had been running all night.

In this particular dream she was being chased by a man with a gun, a high school classmate she hadn't known very well. She dashed into a twenty story building running from floor to floor and room to room trying to escape. Amelia was growing exhausted and afraid, he was closing in on her. When the police surrounded the building, she made her escape, running through the lobby and out the front door, to the sound of a ticking bomb. On the street, she looked left, then right, not sure which way to go, knowing the building was about to explode. Amelia headed right, but as she ran, almost in slow motion, she could see the shadow of the building chasing her, challenging her, managing to escape just in time to avoid being crushed. Amelia was safe, but the high school classmate was dead inside the building.

The dream took an abrupt change. Amelia safe and serene, was walking down the street, hand in hand, with a gorgeous blond guy who looked as if he just escaped a soap opera. They stopped in front of a sea foam pastel cottage, complete with a lattice porch, a white bichon dog was yapping in the yard, under a Japanese maple tree in full bloom, its deep red leaves rippling in the light breeze. Just as he leaned in to kiss her, she was awakened by the unwelcome sound of a flight attendant shouting "duty free", "duty free". Although, her dream, and more importantly her dream man, seemed to have lasted only minutes, when she checked her watch, Amelia had been asleep for over two hours.

The flight was still three hours away from Guam, where she had another layover before traveling on to Panzau. Amelia would've preferred to spend a few days in Guam sightseeing, taking in the Chamorro culture and trying to figure out what really went on in this U.S. territory. The one odd fact she knew about Guam was that there were no birds. They had been driven out by brown tree snakes, which were not indigenous to the island, but had managed to invade as stowaways on flights from other parts of the world. Amelia was trying to remember where she heard that tidbit of information when her thoughts were interrupted by the guy sitting next to her, who had been completely silent, and mostly asleep, for hours.

"Going to Bali?" he asked.

"Oh no, to a much lesser known place I am afraid, what about you?"

"Yes, it is my first vacation in several years and I am looking forward to a week of fun in the sun. I hear that Bali is awesome. The travel agent recommended it highly."

"Yes, so I've heard. Are you traveling alone?"

"Oh no, a buddy of mine is going also. He is a few rows back. We figured we have a whole week to hang out so no need to sit together all the way there."

He looked to be about twenty-five years old and spoke with a New Jersey accent. She asked what kept him so busy that he hadn't taken a vacation in years.

"Computer business," he replied. "Every day there is something new. You have to keep up, can't seem to turn your head for a minute."

"Do you work for a company or do have your own business?" Amelia asked.

"I wish I had my own," he sighed. "Maybe one day, it is kind of a dream, you know, but for now I am just in the rat race with all the others. I work at a regional operation known as NetScan — ever hear of it?"

"No," she said, "but I am afraid I am from Louisiana and my line of work is quite different than yours."

"Really, what is it that you do?" He asked, appearing at least mildly interested or perhaps he was trying to flirt with her. He was actually cute with a great smile, lots of shiny white teeth, and dimples. It wasn't unrealistic that he would flirt with her; she was only thirty-two and not quite an old maid, yet. Although, her mother certainly feared that was where she was headed, especially given the recent break-up with her boyfriend of two years.

"I'm an environmental engineer for the U.S. Government, for the EPA," she replied rather proudly. In fact, she was proud. She worked her way through college, maintaining a 3.0 grade point average. After graduating, she worked for an oil company in Texas but wasn't satisfied, feeling she was on the wrong side of this game. She wanted to prevent damage to the environment, not help companies find ways to subvert government regulations, so Amelia took the job with the EPA almost seven years ago and, most of the time, she liked it. Her real passion was protecting the oceans. As a child, she'd spent many happy days in the sugar white sands of the Gulf, enjoying the beach and playing in the water. She wanted to be sure generations of children could do the same.

"Uh, that's interesting," he said, unconvincingly. Like most people, he probably didn't even know what the EPA — Environmental Protection Agency — was. "So, is that what brings you to the Pacific?"

"Yes, it is," she replied. "There is a small island where some unusual things are happening, environmentally that is, so I'm going to check it out."

"Very interesting. Sounds like Gilligan's Island. Did you bring your formal gowns? You know that Ginger was smart to think ahead like that, especially *for a two-hour tour*." He giggled furiously as he sang that last part from the show's theme song, reminding Amelia how silly men can be. Given his age she was surprised he had ever watched Gilligan's Island. Thank goodness for re-runs.

Amelia laughed politely and said, "Yes, you never know." Thankfully he chose that moment to find his buddy in the back of the plane and she was grateful to be done with this inane conversation. Most of all she wanted to get out of this metal tube and into a real bed. Amelia was looking forward to the day when travel would be like the Starship Enterprise — beam me up.

Amelia couldn't get back to sleep and began analyzing why she was headed to this obscure island to help some guy she didn't even know. It was a good excuse for a vacation, a break not only from work but from life, and she was never one to turn down a challenge, especially when it came to work. About a month before, Justin Gibbs, a marine biologist, contacted her at the EPA, after a referral from the Pacific Environmental Safety Department, and explained his growing concern about the fish, crabs, and other marine animals washing up on the shores of Panzau. He was passionate and persistent and Amelia, despite her busy schedule, wanted to figure out the problem, and more importantly, a solution.

When they talked, Amelia wasn't aware of a similar situation, but promised to conduct some research and get back to him within a week or so, even though she had a full plate trying to combat pollution in the Gulf. The oil companies claimed that their rigs were safe, but she wasn't convinced. Two times during the past month she had flown to the Gulf for on-site inspections, but so far the pollution levels had not exceeded EPA standards. She would keep watching and waiting for the day she could prove otherwise—a day she knew would come, eventually. The oil companies couldn't keep us this façade forever and when they faltered she'd be there to catch them.

Between keeping the oil companies at bay and handing off work to colleagues so nothing would fall through the cracks while she was away, Amelia's research time was pretty limited. She had managed to track down some formerly classified information through her contacts in the government. She had printed a few research papers to read on the plane but had conquered those in the first six hours of this seemingly never-ending trip. Serious information on toxic chemicals wasn't that easy to come by, especially recent information. Amelia was fascinated by reports of the biological and chemical testing on humans and animals the U.S. conducted in the 1960s. It was hard to believe such things happened and not that many years ago. She was glad that era was over, or was she just being naïve?

CHAPTER THREE

At a small lab on the outskirts of Zhushan, Taiwanese workers were enjoying their oolong tea. Zhushan was famous for its high quality tea, grown in the mountainous regions near the tropic of cancer where the climate provides the ultimate growing conditions. A day never passed when the workers didn't enjoy several cups, one of the few, small pleasures they were afforded for their work in this remote place, and for their silence. But then few people in Taiwan were willing to speak up, it wasn't worth the risk. Taiwan had experienced a tumultuous history from Dutch settlers to the Qing Dynasty, Japanese rule, the Kuomintang and now a strained relationship with the Chinese mainland. By all accounts, their relationship with the U.S. wasn't going all that well either. The official U.S. position was one of encouragement and dialogue between China and Taiwan, but secretly there were other motives at play. The U.S. feared China and its growing financial capability, especially in this era of ever-expanding deficits and trade imbalances. With China holding such huge chunks of U.S. debt there was clearly cause for concern. But did it really matter, weren't we all just citizens of a global marketplace, a marketplace that determined its own rules? Some would say so, many didn't really care. The real truth was that a lot of people didn't even know where Taiwan was, but some — particularly those in the defense business — were gravely concerned.

When it came to Taiwan, U.S. relations were pretty tricky as well, especially where China was concerned. The U.S. maintains a policy of strategic ambiguity, trying to maintain the status quo without saying what the status quo actually is. The U.S. doesn't have full diplomatic relations with

Taiwan, operating instead under the Taiwan Relations Act. China claims Taiwan as a part of their territory, while the U.S. doesn't acknowledge that fact, they also don't dispute it, trying to maintain peace between all three sides of this triangle. But the indigenous people inhabiting the mountain village weren't interested in politics or diplomatic relations; they were interested in making sure their families could survive.

The tea was particularly smooth this morning and the workers took their time. Why get in a hurry when no incentives existed, no one really cared whether you gave your all. They'd heard about the competitiveness in the U.S., the climbing of the corporate ladder, and workers who toiled in overtime to earn a few extra bucks. But they couldn't understand it. What was their motivation? Money has its limitations after all, it only buys things and there's a limit to how much one needs. Life was simple in Zhushan and they liked it that way. Do your job, keep your head down, and enjoy the luck the earth gave you.

The employees at the lab weren't really sure what their job was. They were given instructions, chemicals to mix, tests to run, a kind of experimental kitchen for reasons they didn't know, or care to know, for that matter. Occasionally there were explosions or bad reactions, people got rashes or were burned, but there was no Taiwanese version of OSHA or an FDA to keep a check on their safety. And even if there was, they would never come to this lab. The only folks who knew it existed were a few folks at the Ministry of State Security. The wages here were good compared to most factory workers, so the employees didn't complain, they did as they were told and told no one. Why did they care what was happening here? Whatever it was, wasn't any of their business; their business was to feed a family and enjoy their quiet and simple life, the way they enjoyed their morning tea.

Lin had often wished her work room had windows so she could look out at the rolling mountains, which brought her a great sense of peace and harmony. This must be the most beautiful place on earth, she couldn't imagine living anywhere else; but, she didn't have a clue what other places were like. Each morning as she walked the two miles to the lab she took in the tranquility that surrounded this remote mountain village. She often wondered about the origins of this village, it wasn't exactly in a convenient location. Was it men who were lost and wouldn't ask for directions, dissidents escaping one of the many oppressors who had inhabited their island over the years, or naturalists who sought an oasis of tranquility? All she knew for sure was that she was glad that she was born here and thankful for the natural beauty that brought so much joy to her life; otherwise, there was little joy to be found. At least she had a job with a steady income. Her husband, Gang, didn't and without her income the family would be in dire straits. Gang did a bit of farming, occasionally doing home repairs for a bit of extra cash, but he didn't have regular employment and hadn't since the clothing factory closed and moved to China. Life was hard, but it was all so normal that Lin believed she had a great life. She had a husband, son, parents who lived on the same plot of land and most of all those beautiful mountains. The job wasn't particularly interesting, though, it was steady work and provided a decent life for all those she loved.

Lin wondered what kind of miracle cure they might be concocting here. She hoped it was a cure for cancer or some other terrible disease; she wanted to believe their work had some kind of meaning. But no one told them anything and the actual testing was done in another, very isolated, part of the facility so she couldn't even hazard a serious guess as to what might be going on here. In any case, she was more interested in keeping her job and collecting her paycheck than trying to find out information she didn't need anyway.

Lin worried about her son, Bingwen, and what kind of life he might have, particularly if she lost her job. She had named him Bingwen, it meant bright and cultivated in Chinese, in hopes that his name would inspire his future. She was less inspired by her husband's prospect of finding work anytime soon, so Lin bore the responsibility of taking care of the family. Lin was putting aside her own stash of money, a little each week from her paycheck, hiding the money in an old tin she had buried in a secret place, just in case. She didn't like keeping secrets from her husband but she knew his limitations, and it was up to her to make sure they family could survive. Gang wasn't very observant, he didn't realize Lin got a raise last year, but that made it all the easier for her to squirrel away that extra money. Even though she loved Zhushan and would never leave, she was sure there was something more, something more important, that Bingwen would want to do, deserved to do. She wanted to give him that chance — he was her only child and this was her only chance.

Already, Lin recognized the talent in her young son. He was a whiz with math, sitting for hours with his lesson books trying to solve every equation, so much so, that she had to force him to go outside and play. He wasn't nearly as interested in baseball or even taekwondo, which was very popular in their little village. But Lin pushed him to participate, wanting him to have friends his own age and understand about balance in life. Most people in the village followed the Mahayana branch of Buddhism that focused on the universal liberation from suffering for all beings. One should strive to possess a mind of great compassion and transcendent wisdom and eventually achieve six perfections. Lin, in an effort to achieve those perfections, often visited the many Buddhist temples that dotted the mountainside, and participated in the various festivals and holidays, such as Vesak and Avalokitesvara's Birthday. She always brought Bingwen to the temples, trying to be a good influence in his life, hoping that he would achieve complete enlightenment and enjoy all that this life could offer. But in this, too, he showed little interest.

Although Bingwen liked visiting temples, it was more of an entertainment venue than a spiritual journey. He liked investigating the Buddhas, searching for the unique qualities of each one and using his math skills to determine the dimensions of the temples. The fat happy Buddhas were his favorite. It was no wonder that children flocked to the fat happy Buddha, since they believe he has candy in his sack. The Budai, as he is known in Chinese, represents the concepts of good health, wealth, happiness, prosperity, and longevity. Who didn't want those things for themselves and even more so for their child? Lin was convinced that if he was to have any happiness and prosperity in this life, Bingwen must fully understand Buddhism and seek spiritual enlightenment. But she also realized she couldn't force this spirituality on him; Bingwen was very young, there was still time.

Tea time was over when Lin's boss, Mr. Kao barked at her, "Here is the list of chemicals, please prepare four liters of the new solution and send it to the testing center before noon today." Mr. Kao was an incorrigible man with no sense of humor and little respect for his employees. "Well, what are you waiting on, do you want the Buddha himself to ask you, you silly girl?"

Lin took the list, with no verbal reply, and began to locate the necessary ingredients. Her boss, also silent, went to his office to drink tea and await further instructions from high level officials he had never met and never would. Mr. Kao was often bored here, he had no real work to perform, but he knew what a honey hole he had fallen into. While he didn't know all the details, Mr. Kao had his suspicions, more than suspicions, but he would never discuss them with anyone at the factory. The only person he discussed his work with was his wife, who not unlike Amy on the other side of the world, also thought her husband had an overactive imagination.

According to Mr. Kao's version of the story, they were developing some magic substance that would grow corn or wheat in a matter a days. This project, at least by his account, was at the direct behest of Communist Party officials in Beijing and outside of a small group of three or four, no one else knew about it. If there was an information leak, should others find out the truth, the lab would immediately be shut down and the project moved elsewhere. But in a place like Taiwan, especially in this remote village, it was still possible to keep a secret, or so he believed.

Mr. Kao's wife, like all good Taiwanese wives, listened with feigned interest to his talk about work. He'd tell her about visitors to the lab, officials he was sure he had seen on CCTV. His wife had learned to smile and nod, continuing with her sewing or cooking, with an occasional "Really, are you sure? Well, that is indeed fascinating. I know you'll be famous one day." And Mr. Kao knew she was right, he would be famous one day and then he'd move to a fabulous house on the ocean, have loads of servants, and eat cookies and candy imported from Europe. This mountain village couldn't hold him, he had big ideas and one day he would be rewarded for them, but until then he'd be very careful about who he shared them with. For now, his wife would remain his confidant and more importantly his support. Even though he never realized it, or if he did would never admit it, he'd be lost without her — incapable of taking care of himself. She was a quiet woman who didn't contradict him, tradition had taught her that, but she knew how to manage his life and most importantly, how to keep him out of trouble — a skill that would prove invaluable to Mr. Kao's survival.

At least the employees at the lab only had to endure him during the work day, unlike Mrs. Kao who had to cook for him, wash his clothes, and clean his house. Besides Mr. Kao was mostly bark, although, he did plenty of barking, usually in an attempt to belittle someone in front of the rest of the staff. He needed to show his authority, needed to feel like the big man he deluded himself into believing he was. Once, he had blamed Lin for a severe allergic reaction to employees in the testing department, claiming she had not properly followed the mixing instructions; he threatened to fire her. In his mind, fear was the key to good management; otherwise, employees would lose all respect and do as they pleased. In reality most Taiwanese, especially those in a subordinate position, were adverse to personal conflict. They weren't going to challenge him.

Lin did her best to avoid trouble, she didn't want any complications and she was in no position to jeopardize the family's livelihood. It wasn't just about avoiding trouble, Lin felt it was important to do good work, no matter what that work was. She carefully measured each chemical, checking the type and proportions against the written orders. She didn't want to be blamed if something went wrong—if it did, it was truly going to be an accident and not human error. Lin often worried that someone, her included, could get seriously injured. The accidents so far had been fairly minor, but that didn't preclude a major explosion one day. None of them knew the danger of the chemicals they were handling—were they safe, could they be toxic when mixed, did they cause cancer? She had noticed markings on some of the bottles that clearly indicated danger. Lin saw the names of some of the chemicals—potassium cyanide, chloropicrin, tabun—but that didn't mean anything to her.

Lin and her co-workers began gathering the various chemicals and equipment to mix the latest formula. Some of the items were located in the storeroom beneath the lab, so Lin went down there herself. It was the only way she could ensure inventory control, which was one of her responsibilities. It required careful attention and record keeping, lest an employee be accused of stealing. If something went missing she was going to be held responsible no matter the circumstances. Lin couldn't imagine why anyone would want most of this stuff, she wouldn't know what to do with it, but it might prove valuable to some people.

It took about three hours to finalize the mixture, adding ingredients and waiting for them to react before adding others. But by lunchtime, they had managed to complete the batch and two of her co-workers delivered the concoction to the testing department. Mr. Kao himself was nowhere to be seen, probably on one of his extended lunch breaks. As they did every day, Lin and her coworkers, lunch pails in hand, headed outside to have a picnic on the grass, taking in the beauty of the mountains while enjoying their bowls of rice. It was a welcome break, if only for a short thirty minutes, and one of the few tranquil moments in their day. Some days there was conversation, usually about family, other days they sat in silence observing the natural beauty.

Today the topic of conversation was the local school. None of them were satisfied with the programs or the quality of teaching available to their children. They understood that the teachers were poorly paid, but so was everyone else in this village. It was no excuse for not doing your job. They had high hopes for their children to get professional jobs and not have to be the lackeys of a Mr. Kao for the rest of their lives. They didn't want that humiliation for the next generation, but without a proper education they would never see the other side of this mountain. Lin suggested they approach the headmaster as a group, but others didn't think he would listen, they were afraid of the repercussions, especially for their individual children. The group resigned themselves to self-study at home utilizing materials, mostly from abroad, which they'd managed to collect from friends and family. One co-worker had a sister in Taipei who sent books that were newer and more advanced than those the local school offered. But, it was difficult to convince the children to do more lessons at home, taking away the few hours they had for fun. After school and chores around the house, they inevitably wanted time to play games or watch the few television programs that were available. Lin was discussing a plan to encourage the children when she was drowned out by a loud explosion from inside the lab.

People were yelling, employees were running outside, and nearby villagers began to gather to see what was going on. Lin didn't see any fire and the smoke was fairly minimal, so hopefully no one was injured. She saw Mr. Kao begin running up the hill, just as he was returning from his "power lunch." The local fire brigade, such as it was, wasn't far behind Mr. Kao. Public services weren't well developed in Zhushan and the community had to take matters into their own hands. The fire department consisted mostly of volunteers — or otherwise unemployed men — who sat around all day playing mahjong. They weren't trained in the art of firefighting, but rather a rag tag group who could barely handle the hoses from the one, early 1950s, fire truck the city owned.

The men jumped from the sides of the truck and began rolling out their hoses as Lin tried to make sure all of the workers were safe and accounted for. She saw all three of the testers sitting on the ground outside, coughing and wheezing, their faces covered in soot and their hair filled with sticky goo. Mr. Kao didn't even notice their existence, he was too busy slinging his arms in a dramatic flair and complaining that his staff was a bunch of imbeciles who were ruining his good reputation. He grabbed a mask from the "firemen" and went inside the building, trying to give the impression of being a hero, the first to enter the building in an alleged rescue attempt despite the fact that all the staff were outside. He ran out quickly enough when he was almost overtaken by the vile smoke that had filled the testing room. Try as they might, the staff couldn't avoid getting a laugh out of his misery; although, they were discreet about it. This would be great fodder for their conversation on the walk home this afternoon.

"Don't laugh at me, you'll all be fired. Besides what are you doing lounging around outside?" yelled Mr. Kao; never mind that their break time wasn't even over. The firemen went inside to assess the damage — the mahjong game could wait — and make sure no one was injured. Although this incident was fairly minor, there was always the potential that one day they wouldn't be so lucky. This place could well be blown to bits taking most of the village with it, but no one wanted to discuss that possibility, so they pretended it would never happen.

"You ok Mr. Kao?" asked one of the fireman.

"I'm fine, don't I look fine? Get away from me you buffoon."

"Sure thing, Mr. Kao, no problem. We'll finish cleaning up here and go back to the station house."

"That's right, go back to your mahjong and tea and quit meddling around here. This is a serious place of business and we've got work to do," Mr. Kao, always trying to win friends and influence people with his notorious charm.

After providing some basic first aid for skin burns, the firemen quickly loaded up their equipment and headed back to the village, they'd had enough of Mr. Kao's thanklessness. Mr. Kao rinsed his eyes and his arms in the mountain stream and went to his office to recover with a glass of tea. But that wasn't enough to stop the burning and itching of his eyes and skin, so he decided to go home and let Mrs. Kao, as usual, solve his problems.

"I'll be back in twenty minutes," he shouted so everyone would hear and not slack off, fearing his return. He wasn't going to return today, but they didn't need to know that. Mr. Kao wanted to keep that fear factor going, he needed to get a full day's work out of them. He didn't give them much credit for understanding human nature; they could see right through him, they knew he wouldn't be back.

Even though they knew Mr. Kao wasn't going to return today, he would be back tomorrow, and if this mess wasn't cleaned up there would be "reassignments," so they all pitched in to help make sure everything was spic and span. Not to mention the potential health hazards they'd been exposed to, so the sooner they got rid of this stuff the better. Lin and the others put on their protective clothing, found some mops and cleaning supplies, and headed for the testing lab. Most everything was covered in dust or goo so the clean-up took longer than expected. The floors and counters had to be thoroughly scrubbed, all the instruments washed and sterilized, but they managed to get the place back in decent shape before quitting time.

Mrs. Kao was surprised to see her husband home in the middle of the day, especially looking like he had been part of one of the experiments.

"Are you ok, dear?" she asked.

"No, I am not ok. I've inhaled who knows what and I'm covered in soot. I've been embarrassed in front of my staff. I am sure they are all laughing at me and no doubt not the least bit of work is getting done Those imbeciles are going to be the ruin of me," he roared loud enough for most of the village to hear.

Mrs. Kao knew the employees didn't like him, but she couldn't imagine that they would be so cruel as to laugh at a man who could've been seriously injured. She washed his face and arms and put some local herbs on his skin to stop the itching. This was one of those rare occasions when she felt justified in pulling out the rice liquor; a few hits of that stuff and they would both be feeling a lot better. For sure, it would stop the pain and, hopefully, improve his mood as well. After two cups of the wine, Mr. Kao was ready for a nap in the shade of the bamboo trees behind their meager, but very comfortable, mountainside home.

While Mr. Kao slumbered away in his liquor induced sleep, the workers were walking the two miles, more in some cases, back to their homes where no nap awaited them. It was just the beginning of the second shift for most of them. Lin had clothes to wash, dinner to cook, and lessons to complete with her son. As usual, his father had allowed him to run wild since returning home from school, without any thought of his homework. Bingwen was so full of energy it was hard to keep up with him. He'd run for miles into the mountains, play in the streams, catch butterflies, and still come home with energy to spare. Lin wished she had some of Bingwen's enthusiasm to help her make it through the day. Even though he was a very rambunctious boy, she enjoyed his eagerness, his smile, and the laughter he brought to their house. She couldn't imagine her life without him.

Lin worried what might become of Bingwen if she were gone. Today's explosion made her think about her mortality — she knew the lab wasn't safe, she was rolling the dice by working there. The question was, did she need the money enough to take the risk, but Lin didn't have the luxury of considering that question, she had no choice but to keep on working.

CHAPTER FOUR

Flying into Panzau, Amelia was spellbound by the lush green view from her window seat on the crop duster — well crop duster was a bit of an exaggeration. This airplane was too small for comfort. As they approached the island, Amelia gave a careful look and was left wondering where the runway was. All she could see was a blue ocean, white sand, and very thick greenery. She was beginning to wonder whether they might land on a dirt road, barely avoiding a couple of cows and a herd of goats out for their afternoon stroll.

As the airplane descended further, she could see that a fine ribbon of white sand rimmed the entire archipelago, like the border on a 4 x 6 snapshot. A beautiful vibrant coral reef wrapped almost the full length of the island. Through the ice blue water you could almost see the fish cleaning their teeth on the reef. Amelia even spied a fin prominently protruding from what, she assumed, must be a shark. Just as Amelia was sure they were about to crash into a long line of palm trees, a short, but fortunately paved, runway appeared below them. As they barreled along the bumpy pavement she feared they were heading directly into the ocean. But suddenly the plane came to a screeching halt with three to four feet to spare; obviously, the pilot had done this before.

There was no jet bridge for exiting the plane, just a set of stairs that flipped down as part of the cabin door. All twenty-four passengers de-planed in five minutes, onto a scorching black paved tarmac, saved only by a cool westward breeze. Luckily it was a short walk to the terminal. As they made their way towards the building, Amelia noticed two large silver garbage cans, one filled with umbrellas, a critical accessory during the rainy season. As passengers departed the terminal they could take an umbrella from the garbage can and then deposit it in another one just before boarding the airplane; a simple but effective system.

The terminal consisted of a single open-air building, with a thatch roof, including one baggage carousel, a set of rest rooms, and a check-in counter. The only obvious security was a metal detector, which wasn't plugged in. Amelia got the distinct feeling that security wasn't a big issue here. In a place this small, any suspicious character would almost certainly stand out; no need for security equipment with all those prying eyes.

As they headed towards, what could loosely be referred to as baggage claim, Amelia noticed a man eagerly scanning the arriving passengers, as if he were trying to find someone in particular. She wondered if he was expecting a mail order bride; though, from his looks, which were better than average, he wasn't likely that desperate. At first glance she could see he had a boyish charm, sandy hair—a bit unruly, was slender, and tanned. She wanted to sneak a better look, but just as Amelia turned his way, the waiting crowd flooded onto the runway and she was caught in the counter flow of the traffic. When she got clear, he was nowhere to be seen.

Amelia headed into the baggage area to wait as the ground crew, all two of them, unloaded the suitcases and packages from the airplane. What Amelia first assumed as a lack of funding for the terminal actually turned out to be an effective design. A cool breeze wafted through the open air terminal, pushed downward by numerous ceiling fans, maintaining a fairly consistent seventy-two degrees, which was necessary to combat the extensive humidity. So much for customer service—the luggage arrived at the building entrance in the back of a truck and that's where the ground crew left it, job done, time for a drink. The veteran travelers knew the system and were first to grab their bags and be on their way. As Amelia headed towards the luggage truck, she heard her name being called and feared she was having a heat stroke. But when she felt a tap on her shoulder, she realized someone actually was calling her. Much to her happy surprise it was the good looking guy she had spied earlier. Perhaps he was confused and thought she was his mail order bride; clearly, she was delusional from the heat. He was probably a driver Mr. Gibbs had sent to pick her up. Whoever he was, he had a beautiful smile, lots of white teeth, and baby blue eyes.

"Are you Ms. Santon?" he asked.

"Yes, well Amelia, how did you recognize me in this crowd? "

"Well, you look a bit lost and, in fact, you're the only person on the plane I don't know. It's a small place; everybody knows everybody. Sorry, where are my manners, I am Justin Gibbs. Thanks a lot for coming all this way to help me out."

"Nice to meet you," Amelia replied. "Glad I could come. I hope I can actually help. You presented a situation too intriguing to pass up. Anyway, I really need to get away more, and this is pretty far away."

"A bit off the beaten path," he correctly noted.

"More than a bit, especially for me, but at least from the airplane, it looks so beautiful that I think it may be well worth the trip." Amelia noted, brushing her jet black hair away from her heart shaped face and out of her green eyes. At least there was a breeze to make the humidity tolerable, even if it did wreak havoc on your hair. "You might want to reserve judgment until you see your accommodations. We don't have a lot to offer." It sounded as if was afraid she might take one look and run, but Amelia was no shrinking violet. She was used to hard work, standing up for herself. That's how she got this far with the EPA, and physically she was stronger than most, she'd recently ran a half marathon.

This place wasn't too likely to scare her off, it was a tropical island. How bad could it be?

"I am sure it will be fine," she replied confidently, but actually wondering what she was in for, given that comment.

Justin grabbed her suitcase from the luggage truck, and offered to take her carry-on as well, but she assured him she could manage it herself, especially since it had wheels. He threw the bags into the bed of an old red Chevrolet pick-up truck. She wasn't sure if it was red from the paint or red from rust. Amelia opened the door and jumped in the cab just as Justin rounded the passenger side. Apparently he was planning to open her door—ah ha, a gentleman, a rare find these days. So as to not completely offend him, she let him shut the door, which was a wise move since apparently it was a trick door. This salty climate had taken a toll on the moving parts of his little red truck.

As they pulled away from the airport Amelia noticed a group of local, elderly ladies staring and pointing at them. Justin explained that so little happened here, most of the locals went to the airport every time a flight arrived. It's the highlight of their day. Besides they all want to know who is coming and going, spread the local gossip, and in some cases, pick up a few bucks helping people with luggage.

"It'll be all over the island by sunset," Justin informed her.

"What will?" Amelia naively asked.

"Rumors that my mail order bride arrived today," Justin laughed.

Amelia went white as ghost. Was he joking, surely he must be. Her overactive imagination seemed to be getting the better of her today. Justin started laughing when he saw the startled look on her face, a bit afraid she might actually think he was serious.

"No way, I'm not that desperate, "he replied.

Amelia laughed and said, "Don't worry, I knew you were joking. Well, now I do," laughing even harder. "I grew up in a small town. I understand the rumor mill."

They proceeded through the usual first meeting pleasantries—home towns, colleges, first jobs. Seems he grew up in a small town in Iowa, went to a local junior college and decided to take a break before going on to university. He'd always wanted to learn to surf so he moved to Hawaii for a year, taking a job as a life guard, and falling in love with the ocean. After the year was up, he knew what he wanted to do, be a marine biologist. He had his heart set on the University of San Diego, Scripps Institution of Oceanography, but his less than stellar grades made that impossible. He managed to get into the program at the University of South Florida, where interestingly enough his grades improved immensely. After graduating, he worked for the government for two years at NOAA—the National Oceanic and Atmospheric Administration, at their main office in Maryland. But he didn't consider himself a G-man, so to speak, and figured out pretty quickly that working for a bureaucracy wasn't his cup of tea. He'd done some part-time teaching and lucked out by getting a special research grant to work in Panzau a couple of years ago. He knew it was temporary, he wouldn't want to live on this island forever, the place was just too small and the social life very limited. Besides, it got a little lonely here. He'd tried to maintain relationship with a girlfriend back in Maryland, but it was just way too long distance—information Amelia didn't need to know, at least not yet. For the time being, Panzau offered interesting work and a laid back lifestyle, and he'd made a decent life there.

This dirt road, if you could call it a road, wasn't the smoothest ride. Potholes and mud puddles made for slow going, some were almost big enough to swallow an entire automobile, not to mention the children playing soccer and the young women braiding hair as if the road were their own front yard. Amelia wanted to know more about this roadside beauty shop business. Was there a reasonable explanation or were they just bored?

Thatched roof huts lined the roadway near an area known as Lewalu, the downtown or city center, such as it was. As far as Amelia could see the downtown consisted of a bank, a school, and a two story concrete office building that housed the post office, a restaurant, and a dollar store. The concept of the dollar store was particularly interesting given that dollars were not the local currency.

"Are you hungry?" Justin asked.

"Huh?" she replied.

"I was just asking if you were hungry. We could stop at the Jesus Saves Diner," he said.

"Jesus saves—saves you from what—not the food I hope?" Amelia asked.

Turns out missionaries ventured to Panzau in the mid-19th century, fueled by their desire to convert the un-churched. Fearing that the islanders' souls might end up condemned to hell these well-meaning missionaries promoted their religion. Although Christianity wasn't widely accepted, it had left its effects, apparently on the owners of this café. From the looks of the place, not to mention the sketchy quality of the food, a more apt name might have been God-Forsaken Diner.

The selection of food was pretty limited—fish and chicken, of course, both grilled and fried, as well as hamburgers, but she wondered about the source of the meat. There were also local favorites like taro and breadfruit, and fresh lime juice, no doubt the healthiest item available. All the entrees were accompanied by french fries, fried in the same grease as the chicken. No matter what you ordered, it did, in fact, taste like chicken. The menu also listed lobster and crab, in season. It turns out that "in season" means whenever the local fishermen decide to actually check their traps. Amelia made the only sensible choice and ordered the grilled fish, with the greasy fries and a glass of the fresh lime juice. It was a big improvement on airplane food, not that it took much. Justin insisted she at least try some taro, so she could say she had when the islanders started asking, and they would be asking. It wasn't so bad, not much flavor, just a lot of starchiness.

Everyone in the café dropped by their table, apparently curious to find out about Justin's new friend. Amelia suspected the gossip mill would be rampant. By sundown they'd probably have the two of them married and headed to Guam for their honeymoon. Justin had a great rapport with the locals, who were obviously very fond of him, and with the few ex-pats who had chosen to make this exotic place their home. Some of the ex-pats came looking for paradise, others running from something or someone—the IRS or an ex-wife—and perhaps a few were in the witness protection program. This would certainly be a perfect place to hide; no one would think of looking here.

In between the frequent visitors, Justin updated Amelia on his research. There had been some limited success. Some of the specimens had tested positive for Tabun, a nerve agent originally developed as an insecticide, but one that hadn't been used, at least to his knowledge, in many years. Although, it was alleged that Iraq had used it against Iran during the wars in the 1980s. A bit of research had confirmed it was used in some experiments by the U.S. Government in the 1960s. Tabun, which mixes easily with water, can be used as a water-poisoning agent, as well as for contaminating food. The fluid form can also be absorbed through skin. He had a hunch that there were other chemicals involved, but he hadn't been able to pinpoint them yet.

His technical update was interrupted by the arrival of Panzau's illustrious governor. He made a bee line for their table and introduced himself, in one long breath, as Harry Lingowe Governor of Panzau. Governor of Panzau—how does one get that job? — Amelia wondered to herself. A short stocky man, around fifty, with a great deal of charisma and a wicked sense of humor, he seemed to have the respect of everyone in the restaurant. Governor Harry, that's how the locals referred to him, immediately slid into the booth next to Amelia and began to ask questions. Justin warned Amelia to keep her eye on this guy and told the good Governor to back off. "At least let her get her bearings before you start harassing her," Justin told him.

Justin explained that Amelia was in town to help him investigate the deformed marine life that had been washing up on the island over the past few months. Harry said "Oh, yeah, that. This guy has a suspicious mind. It's no big deal, maybe some gene pool gone bad, maybe even the work of some pranksters. I think those guys over at Laulu-Laulu are trying to yank your chain."

Justin replied, "Could be, but better to check it out and see what's up. It's part of my job to protect the islanders and the marine life from possible toxic exposure. And it'll be good to have a professional, second opinion from Amelia."

"You're right about that one, especially when the second opinion is a professional looker," Harry added, causing a disturbed look on Amelia's face.

Justin chuckled and clarified, "A professional who is such a looker." Seems Harry's command of English wasn't quite perfect. Amelia wasn't sure whether to be offended or accept it as compliment, which it was apparently meant to be. She was too tired and jetlagged to care much either way and apparently it showed. Justin suggested they get the bill and head over to the hotel.

"Staying at the Venus and Mars?" Harry asked.

"Where else? It's not like there are any other options. Until the Ritz Carlton opens up, I guess we'll have to make do with it," Justin replied.

"I'll be fine. I'm not high maintenance, really. Anyway, it's a short visit, I think I can survive," Amelia replied, trying to ease her own fears more than theirs. She noticed a look pass between them, one that wasn't reassuring, but maybe she was reading too much into it. Justin graciously covered the tab and said, "Let's get you to your temporary home for the next two weeks."

Back in the rusty truck, the sun was starting to set. Shades of pink and purple streaked across the evening sky and faded into the ocean. Amelia wanted to ask Justin to stop so she could run to the beach and take it all in, but she was just too exhausted. When she mentioned how breathtaking it was, Justin didn't seem nearly as impressed. But he'd had this vantage point for a long time and had apparently grown immune to its splendor. The cloud formations appeared so real in her imagination—a castle, a horse, a dolphin jumping and playing, eventually falling into the ocean and swimming away to the other side of the world. Between Justin and the sunset, maybe this was paradise after all.

CHAPTER FIVE

Lieutenant Ansley liked his work at the Pentagon, mostly because he didn't really like working that hard, so this job was perfect for him. Today was not that different than most days, except for the amount of activity and a palpable sense of nervousness. There was always some nervousness in the halls of the Pentagon and it made him wonder what these folks were up to behind all those locked doors. But to know those secrets, he'd either have to get paid a lot more or be looking over his shoulder for someone wanting to kill him. Sometimes ignorance is bliss—if you don't know anything, people can't expect too much of you. The good Lieutenant was sure that ambition was highly overrated. Just do your job, keep your mouth shut, and don't make trouble—that was his mantra.

The Lieutenant was prone to day dreaming. He had a lot of time on his hands so he concocted stories of spies and covert operations in faraway places he'd never been and would likely never go—places like Turkmenistan, Tuvalu, and Togo. Sometimes he even invented imaginary countries, but never planets or galaxies. He didn't believe in aliens, was sure they didn't exist. He worked at the Pentagon after all; if such things existed he would know. The whole Roswell thing was a hoax, the media made it up. The greedy capitalist press would do anything to sell newspapers, trying to entice poor little grandmothers into spending their social security income to read the latest gossip. It was truly shameless.

Already this morning he'd been on a boat trip down the Mekong, looking for communists who were plotting to take over Burma. Some would say communists were an improvement over the military government that had long prevailed there, but any intelligent person knew that communism was bad. It didn't work, plain and simple. It just brought corruption and the poor Burmese had lived with enough of that.

The Mekong was a beautiful place, lush and green, water buffalo cooling themselves all along the river, their heads barely visible, as they surveyed their surroundings. He imagined the fishing here must be great, except for the effects of DDT sprayed during the war which had probably contaminated the place and made the fish inedible. In any case, he didn't have time for fishing. He was a man on a mission—literally. Mission Papaya Fire was the mission code name. The Lieutenant wondered how they came up with these names. Was there a guy, kind of like him, in one of those locked rooms, sitting around all day doing nothing but inventing code names?

It never dawned on him that halfway around the world, working in the Chinese Ministry of Defense, was his mirror image. Some poor sap that also did as he was told and hoped for the best. But the Lieutenant didn't know anything about China; he hadn't even been there in one of his imaginary adventures. The Chinese were the enemy. They were out to get the U.S. and that was one of the reasons he never went to Chinese restaurants—that and the fact that he didn't like rice. Even though he didn't know much about the Chinese, they knew plenty about him and the U.S.

He waved his badge over the hallway door and headed down the corridor, long and slender like a shadow reflecting on the ground, colorless and drab with only black block letters on the doors. They must have saved a bundle on decorating this place, that's probably where the money went for some of those $10,000 toilets. The Lieutenant realized this wasn't a museum, but perhaps a little color wouldn't hurt, at least a picture or two to cheer the place up and divest it of this prison atmosphere. He checked the number, verifying he was at the right place, then stepped up to the retinal scan and presented his baby blues. Once inside there was another shorter hallway, where he parked the cart of reports and pressed the intercom button to announce the delivery. The Lieutenant departed by the same route, without ever having seen anyone or having any clue as to what he'd just delivered.

Back at his desk, the Lieutenant returned to his little boat, creeping along the Mekong on this sunny day. He was constantly on guard, never knowing who or what might pop out of the jungle. But he was ready, he had the latest assault rifle, the RF2—Rapid Fire times two—a gun twice as fast as anything on the commercial market. He was soon to put it to the test. As they approached the Laos border, they came under fire. One man went down, but not the trusty and talented Lieutenant. He single-handedly saved the day, using the crafty new rifle to take out ten bad guys and throwing a grenade that destroyed their boat. These guys wouldn't be bothering anyone else. The Lieutenant carried the rest of his crew safely across the border, mission accomplished. Just in time, thankfully, since it was 5:00 p.m. and time to go home. Laos would have to wait, he docked the boat and headed for the metro.

There was only one exit for employees in his part of the building, so he left by the same route every day, where he walked to the Pentagon Metro Station. It was an easy trip home, only a few stops to Alexandria where he lived with his wife, Amy. They'd been married for five years and she was a 4th grade school teacher at the local elementary school.

Since it was July, Amy was home for summer break and spending a lot of time cooking, trying out many new recipes. Every summer he put on a few pounds as she tried to cook her way through the Julia Child cookbook. Amy was a pretty good cook and with all this practice, getting better all the time. The problem was that many of these recipes were a bit rich for his simple palate. He'd grown up in Missouri eating farm food. The family hardly ever went to restaurants, not so much because they couldn't afford to, but because there were only two eateries to choose from. On the rare occasions when the family trekked to St. Louis, his mother insisted on trying the newest restaurants. She preferred French or Italian, he preferred meat and potatoes. But he never complained about Amy's meals, he wouldn't dare hurt her feelings, he was much too nice of a guy for that.

He wondered what she was serving tonight. The Lieutenant almost missed his stop contemplating the menu, jumping off just before the doors closed, which almost chopped him in half. Another guy did the same thing, making a quick exit at the next set of doors. He'd notice the guy get on behind him at the Pentagon station. He didn't look familiar and the Lieutenant was getting a strange vibe from him — that feeling of being followed.

In typical fashion, the escalator was out of service, but never mind he needed the exercise. He wondered how Metro managed to raise fares three times in one year and yet never repair anything. The Lieutenant found it embarrassing that the transportation system in the nation's capital was in such poor shape, especially given the hordes of visitors who come to see the nation's history, to visit their forefathers and be inspired to greatness. The Metro certainly wasn't inspiring, except maybe to inspire you to take a cab.

Pressing his smartcard to the turnstile, he was released from the metro and decided to walk the rest of the way home despite the sweltering heat. The bus wouldn't get him there any sooner, with all of its stops and turtle-like speed; although, it did offer the advantage of air conditioning. The Lieutenant took a right at the top of the platform and when he turned the next corner he noticed that same guy behind him. The hair on the back of his neck began to rise and he decided to make a couple of unneeded, but telling, turns to see if he actually was being followed. At the next corner, the

Lieutenant gave another look back and the mystery man was nowhere to be seen.

It must be my active imagination, he thought to himself, deciding that he probably needed to stop the day dreaming before he landed in the mental ward. What interest would anyone have in following him? Sure he worked at the Pentagon, but he didn't know any great secrets and even if he did, he'd never consider disclosing them — not for money, not out of fear, not for any reason, at least not any he could imagine. But it's easy to say that when you aren't confronted with the temptation. For sure, he was no Benedict Arnold, he wouldn't commit treason; he was a true blooded American.

While the Lieutenant and Amy were enjoying the Chateau Briand on tonight's menu, one of the reports he had delivered today was causing indigestion back at the Pentagon. Eyebrows were raised, heads were scratched, concern was growing. This wasn't the plan, assurances had been made. What were they going to do now? The two military analysts debated whether to report it to the General. This could get out of hand, well, even further out of hand. They debated whether it could be contained. Perhaps it wasn't so serious, the information could be wrong. They certainly hoped it was wrong. But what if it the information was, in fact, correct, or even worse than described. The analysts argued, decided to go for some dinner — no Chateau Briand for them, just a quick stop at the Burger King in the food court — and revisit the report later.

During their all-too-brief dinner, they chose to ignore the report and instead discuss college football. The big question was who would win the NCAA championship this year. Sure Alabama was great, they had a winning history and once again a great coach, but Florida was hungry for revenge after what happened last year. Both of these guys had played in high school with aspirations for scholarships to one of the top universities. But the competition was just too stiff and neither had the luck, or the actual talent, to make it happen. They considered walking on, but knew chances were slim and it was a lot of work for an unlikely reward. Girls and fraternity parties were more interesting at that age. Besides they were nerds at heart and went on to major in tough subjects—chemical and computer engineering. Their fields couldn't match NFL salaries, but that was a pipe dream that came true only for a very few, the very best. At least, engineering paid their bills. If they wanted to make some serious money they needed to quit the government and work for a defense contractor. Maybe go overseas to one of the hot spots, like Iraq or Afghanistan, where the danger pay and allowances could quickly add up to a lot of dough in a few years. That is, if you were willing to take the risk, which was no small risk given the dicey security situation.

French fries finished, the two analysts returned to the locked room and read the report again desperately hoping that in the brief interim the story could have somehow changed or that some revelation would have come to mind. But they were faced with the same dilemma and no new wisdom to make the decision with. It was a decision they didn't feel they should make. People might get hurt, but then again they might get lucky—nothing would happen, no one would know. A gamble no doubt, but one they decided, in the end, that was worth taking. At least for a few days, maybe the news would be better tomorrow, ignore it and hope it goes away. Americans really are internal optimists. But optimism is one thing and acting with stupidity is something else. This decision was like dancing on a thin wire between two buildings; they hoped they wouldn't fall off.

But thankfully none of this was the Lieutenant's problem, as he polished off the chocolate mousse Amy had prepared for dessert. He wondered how anything could be so smooth and creamy. It was truly scrumptious and never mind the calories he'd have to work off during tomorrow morning's run.

"How's that dessert?" Amy inquired.

"Honey, it couldn't possibly be better. You'll soon have to give up teaching to work for the food network," he said.

"Oh, don't be silly. It's just mousse, anyone can make it."

He knew his Amy and while she feigned modesty, she knew that she was a good cook. She was pretty much good at everything she tried; she had the Midas touch. But she craved praise, needed that extra affirmation, and wanted to be the best. Despite her superior skills and healthy ego, Amy still carried a twinge of self-doubt, but then who doesn't. It wasn't as if she held out false hopes of being the next Julia Child, but she did like that feeling of superiority, the joy of success. It was probably her greatest fault, save only for her belief that the Lieutenant was a talented, high-placed official in the cog of the national defense machinery. But why would she believe otherwise? Amy didn't understand the ins and outs of the military world and it was easy for him to convince her of his imaginary achievements. And she loved him so, she always believed the best about him.

They had first met at a speed dating event in Alexandria. She'd been very reluctant to participate, hanging on to the belief that her White Knight would one day be waiting on the playground as she left from school or just around that next corner, perhaps in the cereal aisle of Whole Foods. But her girlfriends finally managed to convince her this was how it happened in the 21st century—five minute musical chairs and Mr. Right was at your disposal. If not Mr. Right, then at least Mr. Right NOW. She blushed at the suggestion and refused for months to give it a whirl, but finally gave in after having no success in her own Cinderella land. The first time yielded two dates with two different guys—one an accountant and one an artist. They weren't really compatible with her interests and nothing came of either.

But on the second attempt, she'd met the Lieutenant, who attended only at the behest of friends who convinced him it was at least worth the entertainment value, if nothing else.

He went along for the ride with no expectations, and certainly no hope of meeting the love of his life. When he landed at Amy's table, he knew she was different. Maybe it was her tender eyes or the way she wrinkled her tiny button nose, but he knew immediately that this had potential.

At first it was difficult for them to find time for dating. He was busy with specialized training, traveling around the country to attend. She was away caring for her sick, elderly mother every other weekend, providing much-needed relief for her sister who has shouldering the burden of this enormous challenge. Her sister had generously moved their mother into her house, a place already full with three kids, two dogs, and a husband.

On those rare occasions when the Lieutenant and Amy were able to schedule time together, they both knew it was special. In their shyness and awkwardness they weren't able to express their feelings for many months, leaving each other to wonder whether there was really anything there. Their friends were beginning to give up hope that anything would become of it, despite feeling sure they were a perfect match, time seemed to be their enemy.

Amy was a home-body with a care-taker mentality; he was a thoughtful guy who needed to be taken care of. Ambitious in his own way, the Lieutenant wasn't a ladder climber or worried about being the top dog. Looks weren't that important to either of them. Neither were runway material, but that didn't matter since what they loved about each other was truly on the inside. And based on the Lieutenant's spreading waist line, you could truthfully say their love was growing. He wasn't overly concerned about the weight, when Amy's school was back in session, the gym would be also. He ran every morning, four miles, but it wasn't enough to completely ward off the calories from the Julia Child cookbook or worse, Southern Living. Now there was the real taste, never mind the copious amounts of fat, butter, and fried foods—everything from chicken to dill pickles. But, oh how he loved those dill pickles. That wasn't something he'd confess in this part of the world, lest people think he was crazy or at the very least, a bona fide hillbilly. The Lieutenant knew he was neither, he was a superhero — well at least a hero, and one day, maybe soon, he'd get a chance to prove that fact to the world. Perhaps then he'd be one of those guys on the other side of the locked door. This time it wouldn't be day dreaming or imaginary trips around the world, it would be the real deal.

"Do you want seconds?" she asked.

"Huh?" he replied, not paying attention.

"Where is your head today? It's as if you are a million miles away, instead of your usual, half million. Anything interesting happening at work?"

"Nah, just the usual stuff, though, on the way home, I thought I was being followed," he proclaimed with a slightly troubled look on his face, realizing how it sounded once he'd said it out loud.

Amy just laughed and shook her head. She never knew when he was serious. If anything ever did happen to him, she'd never believe it. He'd had so many suspicions, so many wild tales, she'd learn to take it all in stride. What was the harm, she knew he had an overactive imagination, but he always seemed to know the difference. She handed him another serving which he didn't really want, but he didn't like to hurt people's feelings, especially hers.

Every year he visited her class and explained to the students what an honor it is to serve your country. Time permitting, he'd tell the kids the personal story of a particular soldier — perhaps a civil war soldier at Gettysburg or a marine who stormed the beaches of Normandy. His favorite was the story of John F. Kennedy and his PT boat, but much to his dismay, many students had never heard of JFK. How could anyone not have heard of JFK, even if you were eight years old? The Lieutenant could understand their lack of knowledge about his military service, but why didn't they know he had been President and a great president at that, even if he was a Democrat. But the Lieutenant didn't care that much about politics, he wasn't really a party faithful. He was about God, honor, and country.

The Lieutenant's world was a world of rules, he wouldn't think of disobeying any of them—not unless it was to ensure the safety of this country. But then he had never been put in that situation, never had to make the difficult decisions. Most days his most difficult decision was what to have for lunch or perhaps on a more taxing occasion whether to sneak a peek at documents that came across his desk. Though he never did it, well almost never, the temptation was always there. After all he was just a human being, except when he was daydreaming as a superhero.

The Lieutenant connected well with the students. In many ways he truly was a kid at heart and despite having a very grown up job, there were experiences in life he had missed out on as a child. He longed for the opportunity to re-live them. Amy saw that side of him and understood the need, even though it went unspoken between them. She didn't know a lot of the details of his childhood and didn't want to pry, she just took it as a given that it was less than perfect. But then whose childhood was? She wanted him to be happy, to protect him, make up for lost pleasures so she gave into his daydreaming and childish whims.

Inevitably, there was an over achiever in the class who wanted to take over the presentation and explain the entire military structure. Sometimes a kid who had seen too many M.A.S.H. re-runs would ask who gets to be the mess chef or does dressing up in "pretty lady clothes" get you a quick release. But the class always enjoyed having outside speakers. As much as they truly loved Amy, they tired of listening to the same person every day, and besides, these kids needed to expand their horizons, open their minds, and realize there was life beyond these United States. Though

Amy knew many of her students would never leave the state of Virginia. She tried to make sure they traveled the world, if only in their imaginations, hoping that one day some of them would actually get the opportunity to see places like the Egyptian pyramids, the Taj Mahal in India, the Registan in Uzbekistan, or tropical islands so remote no one had ever set foot on them.

The Lieutenant brought a new perspective to their world. Even though some came from military families themselves, most really had no concept of how the military was organized or operated. Most saw the military only as a fighting machine, they had no clue about counterintelligence or the clandestine ventures that were masterminded at the Pentagon While he fancied himself an important national defense figure, there was so much he couldn't imagine. If he knew, he wouldn't be able to maintain his respect, let alone his duty, to the military he loved or to his country. In this post-911 world there were easy excuses to justify security at any cost. One look at those sweet children and the Sergeant knew he would do almost anything to make sure they grew up in a safe world.

Now that the Lieutenant had polished off the rest of that mousse, he found himself stuffed and ready for bed, even though it was only 9:00 p.m. He helped Amy clear away the dishes, though she insisted it wasn't necessary. The Lieutenant was a modern man — he understood that it wasn't the 1950's — and even though Amy certainly had plenty of time on her hands these days, he was going to do his part of the household duties. That's not how it was in the house he grew up in, but he wanted a different life, a better life, a relationship of respect and support.

Their conversation turned to the upcoming street fair, an annual event in Alexandria; one Amy liked to participate in each summer, always entering the cooking contest with a special recipe. She always said it wasn't about winning, that she just wanted people to enjoy her food, but the Lieutenant knew better.

"Did you hear that?" he asked.

"Hear what?" she replied, sure that it was only his imagination, and in any case, she was never afraid when he was near.

"I'm going out for a look, there's someone in the alley, I'm sure of it." Grabbing a knife on the way out, he remembered the guy, from earlier, on his way home. Could it be him? Was the guy even real? Of course he was real, but was he really following the Lieutenant or was that just his imagination. As he rounded the corner of the row house, headed for the alleyway to the back of the building, he almost ran into his neighbor, Mrs. Heverstein and Gepetto, her Corgi — the breed of dogs that Queen Elizabeth is so fond of, out for their evening walk.

"I'm sorry ma'am, didn't mean to startle you, but Amy thought she heard someone in the alley behind our kitchen." He thought it sounded more legitimate that Amy was scared and wanted her big strong man to check it out.

"I didn't see anyone out here Philip," she replied, "but lately there have been some cats getting into the garbage cans, maybe that's all it was. I think I'll call the city dog catcher, you know, animal control officer or whatever they're calling them these days or maybe there's a shelter. Do you know if there's a shelter?"

"No ma'am I don't know, but I am sure there must be. Don't worry Mrs. Heverstein, I'll call them tomorrow. Are you sure you didn't see anyone around here, a man, anything suspicious?"

"Oh no, nothing at all, just those naughty cats. You worry too much Philip. Go on back inside with your bride."

It was funny how she always referred to Amy as his bride, but it was a nice reminder of how lucky he was to have someone special in his life. Poor Mrs. Heverstein had been alone ever since he had known her. They'd met shortly after he and Amy married and moved into the row house a few doors down from her, five years ago. The Lieutenant wondered whether there had been a Mr. Heverstein, but he realized he didn't know anything about her family or her past. They were neighbors, they chatted occasionally but didn't really socialize, they were from different generations and he wasn't one to pry into family history. He only knew that since he and Amy moved to the row house, it had just been her and the Corgi.

"Let me walk you back to your apartment ma'am." The Lieutenant offered.

"You army fellows are always so polite and helpful. Do they teach that stuff over at the Pentagon?"

"No ma'am, it's just common courtesy, anyone would do the same."

"I don't know Philip, folks around here seem too busy to even notice me, let alone take the time to help."

"Well that's too bad. But you know you can count on me. If you ever need anything just give me or Amy a call, we'll be glad to come right over."

Mrs. Heverstein thanked him profusely as she went inside to her small, but ample, one bedroom apartment determined that tonight would be one of her good nights — one where she didn't wake up crying about her beloved Mr. Heverstein. He'd been gone now for ten years, but it seemed like just yesterday he brought the Corgi home and they had laughed and played with the cute pup, not realizing that in a few short months he would pass away. It was cancer. How she loved him, and missed him, but she found peace in the belief that he was in heaven and no longer suffering. Gepetto had since been her constant companion, a great source of friendship and strength, but now he too was getting old and tired, like her.

As the Lieutenant was opening the door to the row house, he got an eerie feeling that someone was near, that sense of presence you sometimes feel. He turned to take one last look before heading inside and there, at the corner, just under the streetlight he thought he saw something, someone, but in a flash he was gone.

Amy was already in bed reading the latest Janet Evanovich novel. She wasn't worried, confident that it was either his imagination or a sense of chivalry, wanting to prove himself as her great protector.

"Did you find anything dear?"

"Just Mrs. Heverstein and Gepetto. I walked them home."

"Well, that was very thoughtful of you. I hope she is ok."

"She's fine I suppose. Seems a little lonely, but I guess that's to be expected for an elderly lady living alone."

Amy reminded herself, and the Lieutenant, that Mrs. Heverstein had Gepetto, but she knew what he meant and it made her hope that she'd never be alone. She couldn't bear the thought of being without her beloved husband.

The Lieutenant couldn't shake the feeling of being followed, but he tried to convince himself it was just his vivid imagination, that subconsciously he wanted to add some intrigue to his otherwise dull life. Maybe dull was good, at least it was safe and there was something to be said for a sense of security.

CHAPTER SIX

Once checked into her home away from home, Justin promised to pick Amelia up at 8:00 a.m., which by his account was late. The bungalow had a thatched roof, giving it a more tropical, spa-like appeal, though she soon learned the downside. Thatching sheds, a lot. After a quick shower, Amelia fell into bed, and although she was exhausted, now underneath the flowing mosquito net and the whine of the ceiling fan she found herself suddenly wide awake. As the clock ticked she grew more frustrated at the contradiction of being too exhausted to sleep. Her mind wandered, understandably to Justin. What was his story, was there a wife, girlfriend, someone waiting at home for him? She wasn't normally so easily rattled by a nice smile and a few muscles, well more than a few in Justin's case, but maybe she was just feeling alone and vulnerable after her recent break-up. Amelia knew the relationship wasn't forever, that was the main reason she finally broke it off with him, but she was losing hope for a relationship that would last.

Even above the hum of the ceiling fan, Amelia could hear the gentle sound of the waves, rolling back and forth, as the ocean moved toward high tide. Amelia loved the beach, the feel of the sand on her bare feet, the moon rise, the sunset. It brought back happy memories of childhood vacations spent on the Gulf coast chasing tides and catching sand crabs in paper milk cartons. Another 30 minutes and sleep was not in sight, the waves were calling her name so Amelia decided to have a walk down to the beach.

The moon was low in the sky and only at one-quarter so the visibility was pretty dim, but she managed to see a small boat tied to a short rickety pier. She thought someone was inside but couldn't be sure. Uneasy about being in a strange place in the dark, potentially with someone lurking in the boat, she decided it was best to return to the bungalow. When she opened the front door she immediately saw a young guy, short, dark, going through her computer bag. There were pages of research inside and for some reason he seemed interested in them. Startled by her return, he grabbed the bag and its contents and made a bee line for the back door. Instinctively Amelia screamed, rather loudly. She lunged and managed to grab the shoulder strap of the computer bag, causing him to drop it as he ran for the beach. She stopped at the door, thinking twice about pursuing an intruder. In minutes she heard the hum of a motor, she presumed the boat, making a get-away.

Amelia tried to call the front desk, but no one answered. She was afraid to go back out again so she locked the doors and got back into bed, wondering how this guy got inside. There were no signs of forced entry at the door, but when she looked up at the window she saw the screen and slats of the jalousie window had been removed. This guy was small enough to crawl through. Amelia was thankful she saved her computer, but he managed to abscond with all of the research on chemical and biological warfare she had completed, including reports on the MKNAOMI and MKULTRA experiments conducted by the CIA and Department of Defense from the 1950-1970s. Allegedly, they were attempting to develop lethal and incapacitating biological and chemical materials. It seems a deadly shellfish toxin was obtained by a CIA scientist. MKULTRA purported to test chemical and biological substances on humans. Amelia didn't know whether there was any connection, but she had to start somewhere to solve this mystery in Panzau. Most of these materials she only had in hard copy so they would be hard to recover.

An attempted break-in and the loss of many hours of work was certainly not conducive to sleep. But Amelia was completely exhausted and jet lagged, so eventually she managed to drift off only to be awakened by a loud banging noise at her door. She awoke to the sound of Justin yelling her name and asking if she was awake. Who could sleep with that much noise? He was better than a wakeup call, apparently much better, since she obviously didn't get one. Amelia opened the door, blurry-eyed, hair standing on end, and eyes almost swollen shut from the effects of jetlag.

"What happened to you?" he asked.

"I'm so sorry, seems I overslept," adding "I had a late night visitor."

"George Clooney in town?" Justin quickly retorted.

"Clooney — in my dreams. This was not a welcome visitor, I'm afraid. Do you think I'm that fast? I only arrived last night."

"It's not *you* that I think is fast. These island guys can be quite aggressive," he politely informed Amelia. "For some reason they feel inclined to offer their services."

"If that was the intent, I assume he would have knocked on the front door rather than trying to come through the window."

"What?" now Justin looked seriously worried. "Someone tried to break in? What did you do? Did you call the police, or at least the front desk?" He peppered her with questions not even waiting for answers.

When he finally gave her an opening, Amelia responded with a bit of annoyance, "Hold on, big brother. I wasn't hurt. They only got away with some documents; although, they tried to steal my laptop. "

"What do you mean tried? Did you stop him?" he asked with great surprise.

"I grabbed the strap of the bag as he was running and he didn't bother to fight for it, thankfully."

"Yes, thankfully. What were you thinking? You could have been hurt. What did he look like? What did he say? Where did he go?" Justin asked, again with the questions.

Amelia didn't know the answers, nor did she want to think about what had happened. Otherwise, she might just want to get back on the plane and leave; although, she felt too bad at the moment to even consider that option.

"How should I know, it wasn't exactly daylight, and I wasn't thinking about needing details for a police sketch," Amelia shouted in her defense, not realizing the tone of her voice, which drew the attention of staff working nearby.

Justin called the front desk and threatened to move her elsewhere. Amelia was wondering to where exactly since this was apparently the only hotel.

No one at the Venus and Mars had seen or heard anything or at least they wouldn't admit to it. Justin scared them with his reaction, no one was going to speak up now. Amelia did her best to reassure everyone — a bit of a crowd had gathered in her room now — that she was no worse for the wear. At the moment her goal was to get them all out of her room so she could get properly dressed; she was still in her pajamas. After managing to convince them she was fine, everyone cleared. Everyone, except Justin, who didn't seem to be catching on. Or, did he? Well, she could dream.

"Do you see what I am wearing?" Amelia asked. That's when Mr. Observant realized she was still in pajamas and began to blush. Justin made a quick departure, mumbling something about getting some coffee and promising to come back in thirty minutes. Alone at last she tried to pull herself together and start this morning over. This trip was getting off to a memorable start and not the kind of start she had in mind. Amelia feared the attempted break-in would be the highlight of today's gossip and probably on the front page of the local newspaper before noon. She only hoped that no one got a picture of her this morning in her pajamas. That wasn't how she wanted to appear in the headlines of the Panzau Press Journal.

By the time Justin returned, Amelia was practically a new women. A quick shower and a little makeup went a long way. She wasn't ready for the runway, but she'd pass muster for a visit to the lab, which was exactly where they were headed in Justin's rusty red Chevrolet. The humidity was rising, it's stifling effects easily felt with the truck's air conditioner on the fritz. Fortunately the lab, a small block building with a flat roof, had its own generator and air conditioning. It was painted a shade of blue, remarkably similar to the blue in the Panzau flag, a color that seemed extremely popular for local buildings. Amelia didn't think the prevalence of blue buildings was the result of national pride, and Justin, in fact, confirmed it was actually because of a big sale last year on this particular shade.

Justin's staff included a research assistant, a lab assistant, and an office manager, all of which had attended the local community college. None of them had ever left Panzau and probably never would. The staff obviously felt a great sense of pride in their lab. Most of all they were thrilled to have a steady job, one that paid a decent salary, something that wasn't so easy to come by on this island. What they were doing here wasn't rocket science, but their work was no less important to protecting the local environment. Over the past two years they'd conducted serious research on the ocellated dragonet and mandarinfish, and developed long-term strategies for marine conservation. Amelia had read some of their research reports and it was part of what inspired her to come to Panzau. They'd accomplished a lot with their limited resources and small staff. She felt sure with some extra support they could also figure out what was maiming and killing the marine life and, hopefully, find a solution to stop it.

Charts and posters littered the walls of the small lab, everything from the periodic table of elements to topographic maps to pictures of volcanoes erupting. Despite the meager accommodations, it had a quaint charm. It obviously had a man's touch, but how much glamour does one need in a marine biology lab. Besides they had a very glamorous lapis blue pool outside—the Pacific Ocean. The building had the necessities and plenty of modern equipment including radio frequency identification, the latest microscopes, and laptops; although, the internet access was patchy with low bandwidth, making web-based research and communications a challenge.

Justin's research assistant was a young man, probably twenty-five years old with a big smile and an amazing crop of jet black hair. There seemed to be a lot of good hair on this island, no need for Rogaine here. The assistant introduced himself as George, to Amelia's surprise. George didn't strike her as a traditional Panzau name, she had imagined something a little more exotic.

Quickly picking up on Amelia's puzzled look, George proudly responded, "My mom was a huge Beatles fan."

Amelia gave a little laugh and said, "I completely understand, my mom loved Joni Mitchell—that's my middle name." George talked vividly about his keen interest in sharks, reef sharks mostly, not the great white or tiger sharks, usually seen on the big screen with some unsuspecting diver in their clutches. He was especially interested in preserving the island's vibrant coral reefs, an interest he wished more islanders shared. They didn't appreciate the dangers of plastic, Styrofoam, and raw sewage, not to mention the overfishing in the region. George drilled Amelia about the work of the EPA, eager to know more about their projects, their authority, their funding. He wished Panzau had a similar agency, they needed regulation and a watchdog to protect their beautiful island home.

Justin, eager to move on with the tour and, more importantly, the work Amelia came for, was trying to find a polite, but effective, way to extract her from this seemingly never ending conversation. George finally picked up on the cue, those impatient Americans, and ended the conversation with a word of warning for Amelia, "Watch out for Justin, he's the most eligible bachelor on the island and I don't see a wedding ring on your finger."

Justin obviously wasn't good at hiding embarrassment, turning as red as a beet and losing his train of thought. He made a brave but awkward attempt at recovery, quickly nudging Amelia outside for the nickel tour of their outdoor lab, which included a somewhat rickety wooden pier about 100 feet long. Justin couldn't hide his obvious pride, giving an impassioned history of their research, the community awareness activities they'd conducted, and their work to garner local support. Given the limited funding for the lab, he wanted to be sure someone carried on after he was gone. But all of that was taking a back seat at the moment to the urgent situation with the deformed and dying marine life.

Justin's tour was interrupted by a couple of dolphins putting on quite a performance only a few hundred feet away. Molly and Golly, that's what Justin had named the dolphins, were regulars around here and according to him they wanted to know who the new lady was.

"Do you see the dolphins often?" Amelia asked

"Pretty much every day, I think they are keeping tabs on me. We're old friends now and they bring me all of the ocean gossip. It's like a 'telenovela de mare' out here. If only I could speak dolphin, then I'd be well informed." Justin responded with a laugh.

Molly chose that opportune moment to get a better look at the new visitor, swimming close to the pier, jumping into the air, and making quite a splash on impact, leaving Amelia soaked and surprised. Molly was soon joined by Golly, who made of splash of his own. Either he didn't want to be left out or he was trying to impress Molly.

"They like you," Justin said.

"How can you tell?" she asked.

"They want you to play with them. If they weren't interested they would have swam away or just flipped you off, ha ha."

Amelia thought Justin better stick with marine biology, his comedy was pretty weak, but she giggled nonetheless, even more aware of her attraction to him. But why not, he was a good looking man with a sense of humor, obviously passionate about his work. There had to be a catch. Despite George's earlier assertion he was an eligible bachelor, Amelia suspected there was a woman somewhere.

"Hello, anybody home?" At first Amelia thought it was the dolphin talking, but then she realized it was Justin. "You zoned out on me, are you ok?" he asked.

"Sure, I'm fine, just enjoying the view," Amelia replied, which was true, just not the view he suspected, or did he.

"Sorry, those naughty guys got you all wet," he said.

"Actually it felt nice, a good reprieve from this heat," Amelia noted.

Justin took that as a cue to head back inside where the air conditioner was keeping things cool and where he could give Amelia a full debrief. He wanted to show her some of the deformities, explain the tests they'd completed, and see if they could formulate a plan on how to solve this mystery. That was why she was here after all, wasn't it? His physical attraction to her seemed to be blurring that reality.

CHAPTER SEVEN

The Ministry of National Defense building in Beijing was nothing special. It was large with a sense of foreboding, clearly conveying a sense of power to those who entered there. But very few people every entered its door, only those employees with the appropriate security clearance and high level officials. It was a very secretive place.

But isn't that what one expects from a Ministry of Defense? After all, what kind of defense would it provide if there weren't plenty of secrets? Sometimes what we don't know won't hurt us; unfortunately, sometimes it will. The secrets of the Chinese MND had the potential to hurt a lot of people in a lot of places, but the likelihood they would be caught was almost nonexistent. That's another thing that ministries of defense are good at, hiding their mistakes, and even better at denying them should they ever be caught.

On that particular Friday morning, General Peng was reviewing the latest reports on some important projects. He was responsible for monitoring and reporting to the appropriate authorities on at least five ongoing projects, allegedly designed to better defend and protect the Chinese people. Not unlike the Lieutenant back at the Pentagon, he considered his position one of great honor, always serving proudly and giving his full measure of talent. He was supporting his country in a noble and important way that only a few could truly claim, especially in China. He felt sure his devotion was superior to most, it was a devotion that came easy for him. He was from a long line of military men. His father had been a decorated general and his grandfather before him. While the MND doesn't exercise command authority over the People's Liberation Army — the Central

Military Commission does that—the ministers have typically been active military officers. And so it was that he came to be working in the MND. The General spent many years in the PLA and had developed quite a knack for languages, speaking four fluently, including English. Coupled with his excessive discipline and deference to higher authorities, he'd done well, rising through the ranks to a coveted position. Unlike the Lieutenant, he wasn't a polite and thoughtful man, the needs of others didn't interest him.

The General was troubled by what he read in this latest report from Operation Red Panda. Not because of any concern for harm that might come to civilians, that was just par for the course, one had to accept that prospect; but because the project wasn't going as planned and he might be blamed. He had never failed and he wasn't going to start now. He certainly wasn't going to be the fall guy if this operation went south. Already he was devising a scheme for who could be blamed, who might have done something, anything, wrong that he could point the finger at. His career, and his life, was too important to be put in jeopardy over a project that he considered unlikely to succeed in the first place. Although if it did work, the balance of power, the longstanding rivalry between East and West, could potentially shift, giving China the upper hand.

Not unlike the analysts at the Pentagon, he pondered over the need to take this higher. Was this a minor setback, a serious flaw, the death knell for the project, or just another in a series of bumps in the roads? He had more important fish to fry. So after reading the report a second time over a cup of green tea, he decided to bury it, metaphorically and literally, in his secret files. He'd hold out hope that next week's report would be more positive and so what if it wasn't—a week's delay was a risk worth taking on this one.

A knock at the door interrupted that train of thought. His assistant Lt. Liang was there to remind him of his appointment at the Second Department of the PLA General

Staff headquarters. This Department was increasingly responsible for scientific and technological intelligence in the military field; although, traditionally they had been responsible for military intelligence only. Times had changed, the world had changed, and General Peng didn't care much for it. He was accustomed to a rigid way of life, he didn't like change. The Second Department now had its own research institute known as the International Institute for Strategic Studies. General Peng grudgingly cooperated with the Institute. What choice did he have? There was a pecking order to follow. Even though they had no authority over him, his superiors were more forward thinking and planned to use every possible avenue, technology, or weapon to make the world respect China, as it well should. A nation with more than one billion people, 10 million square kilometers and a history that dates back to the Peking man almost 500,000 years ago is a force to be reckoned with.

Lt. Liang didn't care so much about respect, for himself or China. He just wanted to live a quiet, simple life with this wife and young son, Fu. He chose that name, which means wealthy, with high hopes that his son would have a different and more prosperous life than himself. His was a decent job with average wages and his wife also worked, so it wasn't as if they were living in poverty. But Beijing was expensive and they both worked long hours. Lt. Liang, like most parents, wanted more for Fu and if China couldn't give that to him then he hoped Fu could go elsewhere where his prospects were better. Lt. Liang would never leave, he'd lived too long in this country and couldn't abandon his parents—it wasn't the way things were done in China—but Fu's was a new generation and the rules had changed. Even though the communist government controlled many aspects of their life, they couldn't control everything that went on in his home. So the good lieutenant tried to open up his son's horizons by teaching him English and French, going to extreme efforts to get videos of faraway places and studying the history of other nations. The Lt. was sure that the history of a country was a window to its future. He'd seen plenty of Chinese history and in his opinion it didn't bode well for the future, at least not their immediate future.

Lt. Liang, along with his wife and son, lived in a small one bedroom apartment on the outskirts of Beijing, traveling for more than an hour each way to get to work. His parents lived even further outside of the city on a small parcel of land where they were able to grow a garden and provide both families with fresh vegetables. On most Sundays, Liang took his wife and son there to visit the family and work in the garden, enjoying a meal with his parents and giving Fu an opportunity to play outside. The pollution of Beijing, not to mention the lack of space, made it difficult for Fu to get fresh air. Childhood asthma problems were rampant in China's biggest cities with little that parents could do to mitigate the effects, short of locking their children inside. Times had changed in China, people used to see the land as sacred, but now making money was clearly the priority, so pollution reined and health was a minor consideration. The government might be communist, but the market was definitely capitalist.

Liang enjoyed those visits with his parents. It reminded him of the freedom of his youth — playing with friends, enjoying the open space, walking to school. While they didn't have many material possessions, no one did, and he never wished for more. Now all he could think about was buying one of those new ubiquitous Chinese Chery cars, maybe a red one, so he could drive to work and to his parents. His wife thought it was a foolish idea. Traffic was so congested it was faster to use public transportation, not to mention the added expense of parking, gas, and insurance. He dismissed her beliefs as old fashioned and provincial. She'd grown up in a small village hours away from the city and would have been happy to remain there, but when her parents arranged this marriage there wasn't much she could do to stop it. She'd been happy with Liang, they had a good life and the city had its advantages, but she found it exhausting and longed for some fresh air. That was the reason she didn't mind spending her Sundays with his family, both for herself and for Fu. She knew they needed some time outside. It also gave her a much needed respite from parenting. The grandparents were so happy to have Fu, they devoted their full attention to him and, on the pretense of doing a little shopping, she could wander about the village on her own for a few hours. Even working in the garden, unburdened by her everyday tasks, she found some peace.

Lt. Liang was glad it was Friday. Tomorrow he would spend time playing with Fu and watching baseball and then on Sunday they'd go to visit his parents and their garden. Tomatoes were in season and he loved tomatoes.

"What time is it?" the General asked, but when he didn't get a response, he raised his voice significantly and asked again, "What time is the meeting?"

Lt. Liang had let the tomatoes get the best of him. His mind was a million miles away, well at least the 100 miles to his parents' house. The tomatoes were almost as large as melons and nearly as sweet, not acidic or tart like lots of tomatoes. He guessed the soil there must be blessed. His predecessors must have done something right to end up with this fruitful plot of land. If he didn't start listening to the General he was going to be living on it full time, after he was fired.

"Sorry, sir. I meant to tell you it's at 2:00 p.m. I've reserved the car to take you there. Will there be anything else, sir?"

"Yes, Lieutenant, there will be. I expect you to keep your mind on your job and out of the clouds or wherever you were moments ago. I need an assistant who is focused and always at the ready. If you can't be, I am sure there is someone who can. Do I make myself clear?"

"Perfectly clear, sir. Again, I do apologize. It won't happen again General Peng. I promise. Will you be returning to the office today?"

"Why is that any business of yours? Are you hoping to leave early and get started on your weekend?"

"Oh no sir, I never leave early. I just wanted to know if the car should pick you up and bring you back to the office or elsewhere, wherever you like General," The lieutenant nervously replied.

"The car will wait and I will instruct the drive where I need to go. You go back to your desk and put in the day's work you are paid for," the General tartly retorted. The Lieutenant made a quick getaway out of the office and back to his post.

The nerve of these young folks, the General thought, always wanting to know everything, no respect for authority, no respect for their elders anymore. He enjoyed keeping people in the dark, especially his staff, it made him look more important than he was. Speaking of important, he realized the report was still on his desk. He stored it away in the hidden space in file cabinet number five—five, being a lucky number in China because it is associated with the five elements—fire, earth, water, wood, metal —and with the Emperor of China. The Tiananmen gate, as the main entrance to the Forbidden City, has five arches. He imagined himself as the Emperor of China. What a grand country it would be, led by a man with such purpose and discipline. He was what China needed, especially with this large and ever growing population. If someone didn't maintain order, chaos was soon to take over and their great history would go to ruin.

Of the more than 400 Emperors in Chinese history, the General most admired Kublai Khan of the Yuan Dynasty. A Mongolian and the grandson of Genghis Khan, he ruled over an empire that stretched from the Pacific to the Urals, from Siberia to Afghanistan in a total land mass that was one-fifth of the world's inhabited area. He especially identified with the relationship between Kublai and his brother; although, the General's rivalry with this brother was hardly as tumultuous. No civil war or destruction of cities had occurred, though they had come to blows on occasion. That was probably the reason they only saw each other at the Chinese New Year and, even then, they seldom carried on a conversation. For the sake of the family, the General tried to be civil—well, at least he tried to avoid a confrontation—when he did find himself in the company of his brother. His brother was a capitalist, a rich one at that, with no regard for China's future as a military power. He thought money could solve all problems, he was truly selfish.

Most of all, he hadn't shared any of his wealth with the family and the green-eyed monster of jealousy was the real problem here; although, the General would never admit as much. For him, it was all about duty and service. His brother couldn't understand these concepts, his only service was to himself. He lived in a lavish villa in Beijing and traveled often throughout China and the world, for that matter. He wanted for nothing. They had been close once, in their younger years, but after their father passed away a dispute arose about inheritance, they fought vehemently—even taking their claims to court, which the General lost. His pride wounded, his name dishonored, he lashed out at his brother and despite their mother's valiant and prolonged attempts to reconcile them, things had never been the same. They lived in different worlds and as far as the General was concerned he hoped it remained that way. But sibling rivalries have a way of re-emerging and sometimes at the most inconvenient moments.

It was 1:45 p.m. by now, so the General grabbed his coat and his files and headed for the door. In reality, he could walk to the meeting, it was in the same compound. But how unseemly for a man of his stature to be seen walking about in the open. The car and driver was just another one of the perks that added to his increased perception of self-importance. Besides, it was hot today and the pollution was unusually thick, even by Beijing standards, so why bother to expose himself. This wasn't his own personal driver, he wasn't that important. But his position did afford him access to the pool of drivers for high level staff. Today the driver was Guozhi, who seemed to appear a little too often. Often enough to make the General suspicious that he was actually a spy, reporting on him to the Communist party leaders. But then that would be a very odd twist of fate, given the knowledge General Peng had about some of them. Interesting how names define what we become in life, Guozhi, meaning "the state is ordered," seemed somehow apropos.

Guozhi said nothing to the General, as he had been taught. There were strict rules of protocol here and violating them could cost you your job in short order. Open the door, drive, wait, wait some more, open the door again, and most of all, if by chance you did hear any conversation it was to be forgotten immediately. Even if the conversation was benign—a conversation with the dry cleaner or the wife—it was taboo to mention to anyone. Guozhi was more careful than most, he would never even tell his wife who he had driven, let alone any conversation that had taken place. But his wife wasn't very interested in these things or in anything about his work for that matter. Theirs was a marriage of convenience and she knew it—she was there for his convenience and resented it very much. It was not the life she had dreamed of. Though a poor peasant with few amenities in her life, she grew up hoping that she would move to the city and become an actress. Now she was playing the role of a subservient wife, a role she never expected and there was no understudy to bring relief.

Guozhi rather quickly and quietly whisked the General away to the building in the compound which houses the

Institute, arriving exactly at 2:00 p.m. at the office of the Director. He was always on time, never early, never late. It was bad form and inefficient to do otherwise. How easily chaos might set in if schedules weren't adhered to. Of course, not everyone in China, even in the military world, was so orderly. This was one of the many things he despised in the Director—he always kept him waiting, whether by design or incompetence he had never been able to ascertain. The Director was a short man, much shorter than the General, with round wire glasses that gave the impression of intelligence; although, the General felt sure it was the wrong impression. His limited experience with the man had proven that while he might be knowledgeable about certain things—mostly the nuances of military operations and counterintelligence in other countries—he didn't understand the vision for China. But then there were only a few people who truly did, only a few who were willing to do whatever it took to make China the vanguard of the world that it should be.

Today, the Director was being completely obnoxious. It was already 2:10 p.m. and the General was growing antsy. Who did this man think he was doing, keeping a General, especially one with such importance, waiting in his damp and dusty reception area? The walls were lined with photos from his travels around the world, mostly pictures of glad handing with dignitaries alongside a few decent shots of the Eifel Tower and Chichen Itza. The office was dismal and unbefitting a Director of such a high level institute. He wondered what this man had done to deserve such disrespect.

"Good Afternoon General, so sorry to keep you waiting," the Director announced.

"Good Afternoon Mr. Houng, a pleasure to see you, as always," he did have some measure of diplomacy. Although, truly he wouldn't care if he never saw this man again. He didn't bother to accept the apology, for this there was never a reasonable excuse. Time had been wasted already, he was ready to move on, the sooner they got started the sooner he could be on his way.

Mr. Houng's reports always sounded as if he had the world by its tail. He was just one step short of discovering all the greatest secrets of the world's finest intelligence agencies. According to his latest information Israel's Mossad had a new short-range missile, the CIA had infiltrated an Iranian nuclear site, and the Japanese had hacked into the MI6 website. Sure, he had a lot of information, but unfortunately it was mostly mis-information. The General occasionally pondered whether the Director might actually have valuable intelligence, real information that he could work with, but like many of his counterparts he clung to that information as currency and instead fed others dated material. Surely, someone at this level in an intelligence institute must know more, heaven help China if he didn't. Sharing intelligence outside of an agency is fraught with difficulties in every country. Look at the FBI, CIA and DOD in the United States, never let it be said that the right hand knew what the left was doing. The General wondered why he bothered with this man—oh right, he had been ordered to by his commanding officer. After all he was a soldier at heart, a good soldier, one who knew his place and knew how to follow orders.

But today something different happened. After the General reported on his ongoing projects, Mr. Houng, without even looking up asked, "What's the latest on Operation Red Panda?" much to the surprise of the General. He'd never been asked before about this operation. In fact, he didn't think they were aware of it, very few people were.

Although it wasn't in his nature to lie, General Peng replied, after pausing briefly to consider his options, "I'm not aware of an operation by that name."

Looking up from his reports the Director said, "Really? I thought this one would be right up your alley and I only ask because I'm sure the Institute could be of assistance to you."

The General knew a bluff when he saw one and he wasn't falling for the bait. He doubted that the Director had any knowledge of this operation, it was "off the books" and the circle of people involved was indeed small.

"Sorry, I guess I'm out of the loop on this one."

The response was a dead giveaway to the Director. He knew that the General would never admit to such a thing, his ego was far too big, he was a man who thought he knew everything. Something was definitely going on and the Director was going to get to the bottom of it, but clearly not with the General's help.

"Well, thank you General. I hope you have a pleasant weekend and I'll see you again next week. Perhaps next time I'll visit your office, see what kind of accommodations you are working in."

Though the General didn't want him anywhere near his office, he couldn't refuse. It would be socially unacceptable and would set off red flags. He had to appear as if he had nothing to hide.

"That's too kind of you Mr. Houng. I am happy to come to you; but, of course, you are always welcome in my office." The General thought he might get lucky and persuade him to keep the appointment as it had always been. In either location, he was sure the man would be late. The General could never figure out why people who were consistently late couldn't be consistently on time. It was a character flaw in his mind, one that said something important about a person.

"Well, General, you've always been so accommodating and I am always tardy to our meetings, I feel I owe you something so next week I'll come to your place."

"That's very generous Director, I also wish you a pleasant weekend," the General replied as he gathered his papers and left this musty, dark, and dismal world for the heat and pollution that awaited him outside. Guozhi was waiting patiently to return him to his office, but the General was so rattled by the questioning that he decided not to return. He instructed Guozhi to take him to his house, only blocks away from the MND compound. After some rice wine and little time in his hammock, he'd figure out what to do next. Between a possible leak and the troubling updates he'd received in the report, he was starting to get a headache.

CHAPTER EIGHT

Back at the lab in Panzau, Amelia and Justin were analyzing water samples and, like the General, they were also starting to get headaches. But there would be no rice wine and naps for them, time was limited and they had to get to the bottom of this potentially dangerous situation. They took environmental hazards very seriously. For the past three hours they had undertaken a series of tests on water samples gathered by the staff from various points around the island, but still that hadn't learned anything definitive.

"We need a break," Justin said.

"No, we have to keep working. I want to find out the contents of the water samples, I need to figure out the different chemicals involved. Perhaps the combination of several substances is masking their true identity."

"Exactly, that's what I've been frustrated with now for the past month. But I've waited this long for an answer, another hour won't make much difference. Let's go to Pete's and get some lunch," Justin replied.

"Is it lunch time already?" Amelia was amazed at the time.

"Actually it's the middle of the afternoon. Lunchtime was over hours ago, but with your jet lag time doesn't mean much."

"I am fine, I can keep working," she offered but he was having none of it.

"Well, good for you but I certainly can't wait any longer. I'm a growing boy and I can't be missing meals."

"Oh well, in that case, we must go. I don't want to stunt your growth," Amelia joked.

Justin grabbed his keys to lock up, since the staff was out doing field work. They walked to nearby Pete's restaurant, a place Amelia assumed, wrongly, to be named for its owner. When she asked who Pete was, Justin got quite a laugh out of it. Amelia wasn't the first to ask this question, most visitors had the same expectation, after all, it was a logical assumption. Over burgers and fries, pretty tasty ones at that, Justin explained "the Pete story." Many of the islanders believe in a type of voodoo. While most were not true believers, they'd rather not take any chances. Better to be a little superstitious than to risk getting on the wrong side of a ghost. Justin was sure it was a scam by the voodoo priest and priestesses to make money. In a place like Panzau, with a bad economy, people had to cash in on whatever was available and fear was a pretty big money maker.

As the story goes, there was a famous ghost named Pete, who allegedly wandered the island eating food wherever he could find it. The stories were legend of chicken legs and jerked beef disappearing off the kitchen table, half-eaten cakes left on window sills, and fruit disappearing from bowls. These events were more likely the work of mischievous children eager to add to the folklore or one of the voodoo artists trying to increase their income. An expat, named Rick, looking for a new life on a remote island — code for running from the IRS — came to Panzau, liked it well enough to stay, and opened the restaurant. Rick decided to capitalize on this well-known tale and named the place after Pete, the hungry man ghost. The way he figured it, if Pete was looking for a place to eat he might as well have his own place to call home. And it was just good marketing. Word quickly got around, attracting locals and tourists alike who came to hear the story and find out about the latest Pete "sighting." Rick did nothing to dissuade the visitors. To the contrary, he made the rounds at the tables with tales of how Pete had been in recently and helped himself to a pie or some french fries, occasionally a steak. Perpetuating the Pete scam only added to the folklore and thus the number of customers at Rick's. It was clearly good for business. The place had a huge following, serving three meals a day, and open as a bar until 2 a.m. every night.

There were only three restaurants on this island so one couldn't be afford to be picky; although, some locals who took voodoo seriously refused to set foot in the place. They believed in, and were afraid of, Pete. Amelia wasn't sure what there was to be afraid of if the worst he did was roam about eating other people's food. But if you have a fear of ghosts, even a friendly, hungry one was to be avoided. Pete's food certainly was an obvious improvement over the Jesus Saves diner. Now Amelia was looking forward to completing the trilogy with a visit to Panzau's third fine dining option. But perhaps the bar had been raised too high and rather than progressive improvement, she might be disappointed by the remaining restaurant. Amelia wasn't going to bother to ask the name of the third restaurant, she was saving that intrigue for later.

"How about some mango ice cream?" Justin asked. "Pete's has the best on the island."

"And clearly the competition is fierce," she replied with a smirk.

Laughing at this remark, Justin agreed, "Well that aside, it is worth a try. Shall we have some? A little sugar high to pump us up for a few more hours of work."

"Sure, why not? I don't eat enough ice cream. I need more ice cream in my life," she said, sounding like a corny 1930s movie. This island was starting to affect her or was it that demon jetlag. Whatever it was, she felt more relaxed and was starting to think life in a place like this wouldn't be so bad, especially with Justin around. He was easy to talk to, had a great sense of humor, and didn't take himself too seriously. Although he was very serious, committed and passionate, about his work and about protecting the environment. She liked that, people should feel that way about their work. We'd all do a better job if we did.

Rick himself delivered the ice cream, clearly with an agenda to find out who the "new girl" on the island was. "So, Gibbs, whose your doll here?" wheedling his way into the booth next to her, clearly a sensitive modern man.

"Watch out Rick, she's a professional, smart woman and she may take your head off. This is Amelia and she's an environmental engineer from the EPA," Justin replied.

"Ahhhh, geez another G-man—excuse me, G-woman." She assumed he had bad memories from encounters with the IRS. "Why am I not surprised? Gibbs here has been complaining for weeks about these freaky things that keep washing up on shore. I'm sure Pete is involved," Rick opined.

"Nice to meet you Rick. Good food here, I am sure I'll be back. Who knows, maybe Justin is on to something, we're checking it out," Amelia replied

"Nah, probably nothing serious. But if there is, no doubt it's a government conspiracy." He laughed, but she wasn't sure he was truly joking.

"Do you think Pete could really be involved? Have you seen him recently?" Amelia asked as a bit of a jab, but Rick only seized the opening to add intrigue to the Pete story. Apparently, the latest sighting occurred last week and involved some fried chicken. She listened intently, or pretended to, knowing you don't want to make any enemies on an island this small, especially of someone who operates one of the three options for a meal.

Justin cut the encounter short on the premise that they needed to get back to the lab, which was true, but she suspected it was to protect her from Rick. They paid the bill, thanked Rick for the update on Pete, and headed out into the mid-day sun, which was taking its toll. Normally the temperature didn't go above eighty-five degrees, but today the thermometer was bumping close to that one hundred mark and people were feeling the sting of it. Plenty of kids had headed to the ocean and were enjoying some relief in the water; although, the water near the shoreline wasn't much cooler than the air temperature at this time of year. Cool or not, she was wishing for some beach time herself. But this wasn't a vacation, there was work to done and Justin was anxious to move on with it.

Back in the lab they decided to move on to examining the dead creatures that had washed up in the past few days including mollusks, eels, and jellyfish. Each had some unique deformities they'd never seen before, nor hoped to see again. Some appeared scorched, others had growths, still others had malformed limbs. Whatever was maiming and killing these poor creatures was highly toxic. One or two of these could be an anomaly, but given the consistent number washing up in the past weeks, humans or the result of their actions had to be the cause.

The two of them dissected portions of the jellyfish first, carefully examining the growths under the microscope and running tests on the flesh to determine what kind of chemicals could have caused this damage. They spent the next three hours on test after test before getting some results. There was a positive test for Phosgene oxime, then another positive for Chloropicrin, both highly toxic. But several others tests were not definitive. They suspected a mix of chemicals, or perhaps it was too diluted at this point. They were starting to have a little hope, though both were tired, especially Amelia. It was getting late.

With jetlag nipping at her heels, Amelia almost fell off the stool and Justin insisted that she go back to the hotel and get some rest. They'd made some progress, tomorrow would hopefully bring more results. Amelia urged Justin to head home as well, but he wanted to clean up the lab and look at a few more samples. But first he locked up and drove her back to the hotel.

"I hope you get some rest and feel better tomorrow, we've got a full day ahead of us," he said as he patted her on the arm.

She was about to nod off, but his touch gave her a chill. Somehow it felt kind and when she looked into his face, Amelia felt that his blue eyes were peering into her soul. Now she was sure she had lost her mind. She shrugged it off, getting out of the truck quickly.

"Thanks, I'll be fine tomorrow and don't you worry, I'll be up to the task. I came to work and we are going to solve this mystery. We have to save those creatures, and perhaps ourselves, for that matter." She had no clue how true that would soon become.

CHAPTER NINE

Amelia was happy to see that no unwanted visitors had been in her room while she was away, or at least as far as she could tell. There were the geckos, of course, who had taken up permanent residence along the ceiling, but as far as they were concerned, the humans were the intruders. Amelia wanted to fall face first on the bed, but headed for a shower first. The water felt good on her face, slightly warm and falling down like raindrops, she was starting to like this sunshower. Mostly she was happy to get rid of that sticky feeling left by the humidity. Despite the jet lag clouding her mind, she couldn't stop thinking about the deformed marine animals. She'd never seen anything quite like it. Amelia liked a challenge. She'd never been one to back down, so she was determined to find the cause. From what she had seen today, it was imperative they find the answer and soon. This type of toxicity in the water was going to harm a lot of lives and not just those in the ocean.

She heard the telephone ringing and was tempted to ignore it, but out of habit, if nothing else, she jumped out of the shower and grabbed the receiver. Amelia's mother had taught her never to ignore a ringing phone. It could always be an emergency and even though that was seldom ever the case, she couldn't let it go unanswered.

"Hello," she said in a breathy voice after the quick dash from the shower.

"What are you doing over there? You sound completely out of breath." It was her mother.

"Mom, what's wrong? Why are you calling?" Amelia's heart pounded with fear.

"Why nothing is wrong, I just miss my baby and wanted to see if you were having a great time."

"Mother, I'm not here on vacation. It's work."

"Well yes, but you are on a remote tropical island, surely you must be having some fun."

"I just got here yesterday and we've been working all day today so I haven't really seen very much yet. But it is very lush and green and beautiful."

"Who is we?" her mother inquired, rather nosily.

"We? What are you talking about?" Amelia knew exactly what she was talking about. She wanted to know if the other half of that "we" was a he. Her mother was notorious for trying to fix her up, she didn't want an old maid for a daughter.

"We—the we you were working with today. Who is he? What does he look like?"

"How do you know it is a he?"

"Well, just a guess but I thought you told me it was a man, a marine biologist I believe, who asked you for help." Her mother had a memory like an elephant, which sometimes remembered things it shouldn't.

"Justin is very nice and professional."

"Oh, Justin is it? Glad to see you are on a first name basis already. Do tell, what does he look like?" Her mother needed fodder for gossip in the small town in Louisiana where she lived. Amelia could only imagine the stories her mother must be telling, vivid details of Amelia's job, who she dated and probably how much money she made. No doubt she sufficiently inflated it all.

"He has blond hair, blue eyes. Very cute, but like I told you I am here to work." Amelia quickly noted.

"Plenty of people find the love of their life at work. Don't be all work and no play; otherwise, you'll end up an old lady with a house full of cats for companions." Her mother was so encouraging.

"Ok mother, I'll try to have a little fun while I'm here but don't start checking the mail for a wedding invitation anytime soon. Besides, I'm only here for two weeks and that's not long enough for a proper courtship, now is it?" Amelia knew that would get her attention because her mother was nothing if not proper — and a bit of a prude — she would never say the "S" word. Sex was only for marriage in her mother's world.

"Amelia, you act like the lady you are. Don't think just because you are on an island where no one knows who you are, that you can behave any old way you choose."

"Yes, mother, I'll be sure to behave myself." Amelia wondered sometimes if her mother knew how old she was.

"I know you will dear, I just want you to enjoy yourself and find a special man to marry, soon. Now get some rest and I'll call again in a few days for another report. Your Dad and I are headed to the grocery store now. Love you bunches, sweetie."

"Love you, too, Mom. Bye." Poor Dad, Amelia thought. She couldn't figure out why he kept going to the grocery store with her mother after all these years, as if they couldn't buy groceries without being together. But then they were always together, had been for almost 40 years now. Amelia couldn't imagine spending 40 years with anyone and if she didn't move quickly, she would never have that chance to see if she could.

Amelia decided the shower was just too nice not to finish so she jumped back in and three minutes later the phone was ringing again. She wondered what her mother had forgotten to ask.

"Yes mother, what did you forget to tell me about catching a man?"

"Excuse me, is this Amelia's room?" Justin asked.

Amelia was mortified and needed a quick save but in her jetlagged and almost brain dead state, she couldn't manage a believable story.

"Sorry, I thought it was my mother."

"Do you always say things like to your mother? Is she a sales rep for e-harmony or match.com?" Justin always seemed to have a quick retort.

"Very funny. What's up?" Amelia wanted to change the subject as quickly as possible.

"Just wanted to let you know that I'll be there at 8:30 a.m. to pick you up and we can grab some breakfast as Jesus Saves or maybe Starbucks."

"There's a Starbucks?" Amelia was getting her hopes up.

"Maybe in fifty years. Are you OK, you sound rattled?" Justin laughed, realizing she didn't get his sense of humor.

"Sorry, I guess it was wishful thinking. I'll be ready and hopefully, rested by then. Thanks for calling."

"No problem. Sweet dreams. Maybe you'll catch a man in your dreams."

"Goodbye Mr. Gibbs." Amelia slammed down the receiver and got ready for bed. Pretty quickly she was sound asleep and dreaming; although, not about her prince charming. Quite the opposite actually, she was having one of her "frustration dreams." Tonight's dream took her to a shopping mall, a vaguely familiar place, but not one that she could pinpoint in her memory. She was lost inside with no clue how she ended up there, the place was a maze with no way out. She saw some familiar faces but no one seemed to recognize her. She felt very confused. Wandering from place to place she encountered bright lights, signs and displays, mannequins that came to life. The names of the stores were not familiar. There was a waterfall where children splashed and played, she tried to join them but a security guard stopped her while a crowd gathered, laughing and pointing as if she were a crazy person. She managed to get away from the guard and ran to another part of the mall where she climbed atop a pink pony on a large carousel. As she rode up and down, round and round, she could feel herself growing dizzy. When she managed to climb off the pony, she walked into every inlet and outlet but couldn't find an exit. Finally, she saw a telephone booth, where she tried to call for help, but she couldn't dial the correct number. Despite starting over again and again, she could never get the sequence right. She was interrupted by someone knocking on the telephone booth. When she turned to see who it was, she woke up. Amelia, in her sleepy, jetlagged haze, realized the knocking was actually at the door of her room and growing louder by the minute. When she finally managed to grab her robe and open the door, she found Justin standing there.

"Rise and shine, sleepy head. Are you ready to go?" he asked.

Amelia couldn't believe, not only was it morning, but that she had overslept, again. How could she feel so tired, as if she had only been in bed for an hour? But now it was 8:30 a.m. and there she stood with morning breath, bed head, and dressed in her PJs. Had she not been so confused, she would have been completely embarrassed, Miss Sleepy-head indeed.

"So sorry Justin, I guess I overslept. I had no clue it was morning already. Just give me fifteen minutes and I'll make myself presentable, Amelia offered.

"Fifteen minutes?" he asked.

"I am sure I should be offended. What, do you think I look that bad? Do you think I can't be decent in fifteen minutes?"

"I didn't mean it like that at all. I just meant there's no need to rush, I can come back in thirty minutes, an hour. Besides, I think you look just fine." He really was a charmer or perhaps, just full of crap. Either way, she kind of liked it. Truth or not, compliments can be nice.

"Sure, right," Amelia couldn't act as if she thought he was serious. "Come back in thirty minutes and I'll be good to go. I'm sorry, really, it's the jetlag. I'm usually always on time." She felt the need to defend herself for some strange reason, to give an explanation for her unusual behavior, which was completely reasonable given that she was twelve hours off her normal time zone.

"See you at nine," he replied without turning to walk away. He just gave her a funny grin as she shut the door in his face. She seldom met a man that held any real interest for her, especially after knowing him for only two days. She tried to pretend it was the heat, or perhaps the humidity, making her crazy. People always say "it's not the heat—it's the humidity," turns out there were plenty of both in Panzau and not just with the weather.

When he came back at 9:00, Amelia was ready to go. Freshly showered and dressed in comfortable linen, the best fabric for this climate, she was game for some breakfast, even a Jesus Saves breakfast. Justin was relieved to see her thinking clearly now, especially since they were getting a late start. They had a lot of ground to cover and he wasn't a patient man when it came to his work. Amelia apologized repeatedly, but Justin completely understood. Jetlag after a long trip from the States can take quite a toll, it's hard to adjust with a twelve hour time difference. That was a large part of the reason he seldom made it back to see his family, what family he had left. Since his Mom passed away he found it hard to go back and he'd lost touch with a lot of his old pals. They lived in different worlds now and it was hard to relate. At first Justin's friends found his life intriguing and exciting, living vicariously through his exotic existence on a tropical island. But they quickly lost interest and their conversations inevitably turned to things that Justin had no experience with, like kids and soccer tournaments. Not that he didn't one day hope to have that life as well, but for now his children were in the ocean.

Jesus Saves was really hopping this morning, but it wasn't the gourmet cooking that drew them in. It was decent enough fare, especially for breakfast, but it didn't explain the large crowd. What did explain it was the upcoming annual festival, known as Walawala day. The planning committee was holding its final meeting to iron out the details for the parade, vendor booths, speaker agendas, and entertainment options. Next to Christmas, this was the biggest celebration of the year with pretty much every islander and ex-pat in attendance. It was a State holiday so it brought out a crowd. It was one of the few times when folks could show off their talents, meager as they might be. From the conversation and the chaos, Amelia wondered whether there was any hope for it all coming together in the next ten days, but perhaps there was a method to their madness, time would tell. The islanders had been hosting this event for more than fifty years, so chances of success were high, despite all appearances to the contrary.

Following some runny eggs, greasy bacon, and white bread toast, Justin and Amelia were off to the lab again for more tests and hopefully some answers today. The staff were there when they arrived, had been for more than two hours, but they'd be gone by mid-afternoon. The work ethic in Panzau was not what Amelia was accustomed to, but she chalked it up to the heat and the laid back culture. She definitely wanted to take a little of that attitude with her back to the states.

Most Americans work far too many hours, still a lot of the ole Puritan work ethic lodged in their DNA, high productivity but at what cost. Americans were ridden with stress and heart disease, a little more time for smelling the roses was definitely in order. Most people were caught up in the ladder climbing, the competitiveness was fierce, and if you didn't play along it would cost you — promotions and money. Amelia promised herself that when she got back to the States, she'd make a concerted effort to get out of the office by 5:30 p.m. at least two days a week. It didn't sound like much, but it was a start.

Amelia and Justin headed out to the pier to collect some samples for comparison with yesterday, hoping against hope that they would reveal much needed answers. But when they got to the water they made a disappointing discovery, more jelly fish floating dead, even more deformed than the previous ones. Justin ran back to the lab, grabbing a bucket to collect the jellyfish, while Amelia filled up five vials with sea water. She couldn't imagine what could be killing the marine animals in this bizarre way, it didn't make sense to her but she knew they had to find the answer, and soon.

Back in the lab, the entire staff got busy with testing but around three o'clock they were getting antsy, clearly wondering how long Justin expected them to stay. They liked Justin and respected him, especially his work. But their priorities were different, nothing was urgent. If they appreciated any danger to the ocean or eventually to themselves they didn't show it. In fact, they had what Amelia felt was a very flip attitude. She didn't understand their view that it was all about destiny, seemingly having no control over how their lives turned out. They didn't create this problem and they didn't see why they should, or perhaps even could, solve it.

Justin was so engrossed in the work that he hadn't even noticed the time. In fact, they'd skipped lunch. Amelia had noticed that fact, or at least her stomach had. She suggested they take a break, hoping that Justin would realize the time and let the staff go home. "I'm not hungry." he said at first, a bit bluntly. But Amelia insisted they needed a break; regardless, they weren't getting anywhere with the tests. When Justin looked up and saw the time, he apologized and told everyone to knock off for the day. While he, too, felt they were a bit lazy by American standards, he long ago realized it was pointless to try and change them. Island culture was different, no better or worse, but just different. One had to accept it to live and work here, unless they wanted to go crazy, in which case they might be asked to leave, or worse, run off the island.

Once he got his mind off the tests for a few minutes, Justin realized that he, too, was hungry. Today Amelia would get the pleasure of trying out the third, and final, dining option on the island, the Golden Manatee. It was an interesting choice of names considering there were no manatees in this part of the world, nor were manatees golden. But there in the middle of the restaurant was a gold, well golden colored, manatee fountain. The poor creature was about four feet tall, standing on its tail, looking immensely troubled as water shot from its mouth in a steady free fall into the shell shaped font below it. Apparently the owner had found it on E-bay, while shopping for kitchenware for the restaurant. Jema, the owner was hooked on E-bay. She loved the competition of bidding, monitoring her offers daily, sometimes hourly, often raising her bid well beyond the actual worth of an item when she got caught up in the frenzy.

The manatee had apparently been an easy purchase, given she was the only bidder and bought it for a song; although, shipping wasn't cheap. A novice sculptor in Los Angeles designed and carved it, coating it with a shiny gold veneer. It had been on display, and for sale, in the sculptor's art supply store for several years. When he needed more room for supplies, he decided to list it on E-bay and take whatever he could get to free up some space. Amelia felt sure he was lucky not to have to pay someone to take it off his hands; although, it was an interesting conversation piece.

While the food wasn't as good as Pete's, it was certainly an improvement over the Jesus Saves Diner. Amelia ate a club sandwich, Justin had a burger with breadfruit fries, they both drank more of the tasty fresh lime juice. Even over lunch, neither could let go of their work, continuing to discuss why the testing hadn't revealed any known substances. Of course, they didn't know every chemical in the world, but between them they knew most of the commercially available products, particularly those containing toxins.

"Did your Mom call again?" Justin asked, suddenly changing the subject.

"What?" Amelia was surprised and didn't really understand what he was talking about.

"Your mother, remember her or did you make up that story about her calling the hotel?" he said with a chuckle.

"Oh, yes. My dear mother. In fact, she hasn't called. Perhaps I should be concerned. She might still be at the grocery store or maybe my Dad finally got tired of going and left her there. It's funny how people behave after being together for so many years. My Dad never hears my mother the first time she says anything, unless it is preceded by the word food."

The memory of his mother caused a pain in his chest. He missed her so much and wondered what she would think about what he was doing now. He knew she would be proud, no matter what he did, that was just the kind of mother she was.

Amelia noticed the hesitation and didn't explore it further. Trying to return the moment to a lighter note, she said, "She'll probably call tonight for an update, she needs gossip to spread around at the church socials."

"Well, I am sure the church ladies would be particularly interested in the Jesus Saves Cafe. Although, they may be disappointed to find out that it's not in the mission business," Justin offered.

"I'll be sure to fill her in on the Cafe, as well as about the 'foaming at the mouth' manatee. I'm sure she'll be disappointed that I don't have any seedy details about people's lives here."

"Make it up," Justin suggested, apparently quite serious.

"What? You think I should make up stories to tell her?"

"Why not? She won't know the difference and it's all quite harmless. Sounds like the church ladies need to shake things up a bit anyway. Maybe they'll even want to visit if you make it sound good enough. You'd be doing the local tourism industry a huge favor."

"That's what I am afraid of and then I'll be caught! Never lie to your mother, she'll always catch you. Mothers have mind reading skills the rest of us can only dream of." Amelia was afraid the mother references were upsetting Justin so she quickly suggested that they head get back to the lab. That suited Justin fine. He really didn't want to get emotional in front of her, he barely knew her, and, more importantly, he couldn't lose that tough guy image.

When they arrived at the lab, it was immediately apparent they'd had guests, unwelcome ones. The lock was broken, beakers knocked over, the day's work pretty much destroyed; although, it wasn't a great loss since nothing had been discovered. The greater concern, at least for Amelia, was the reason someone had broken in. What were they after? Where they out to hurt her and Justin? Given what happened the first night at the hotel, she was starting to wonder what she'd gotten herself into. So much for paradise. Justin didn't seem all that disturbed, but he was angry at the loss of the work and the time it would take to clean up. He tried to convince himself, and Amelia, that it was some young thugs looking for something they could sell. While the island was generally pretty safe, theft was a problem, especially with young unemployed men. It wasn't just the lack of jobs, it was about have and have nots. There was a general attitude that it's ok to steal from "the rich." They have the means to replace whatever was taken. It was an attitude that Justin really despised. He could deal with the lack of a strong work ethic, but stealing—it was too much for him. Oddly enough nothing seemed to be missing.

After more than an hour of picking up, throwing out, and mopping, the place was in shape to start over, which was exactly what they'd have to do—first thing tomorrow. It was after five o'clock and Justin didn't have the heart to start again tonight. This set-back had really ruined his mood. He was angry at the loss of critical time. Amelia was only there for two weeks and he needed to make the most of her expertise to solve this dilemma and, besides, he didn't want her to spend the entire trip working. Justin wanted her to see the island, maybe do some hiking, at least get in a little beach time. Despite its limitations, he was proud to call this place home, if only temporarily, and wanted to "show her the town" — such as it was. Justin was determined for her to have a little fun and suggested a boat ride later, they could check on some traps and knock out two birds with one stone.

Amelia agreed. She was past the jetlag and ready for another distraction, besides Justin. Her imagination was running wild — someone, someone with resources, didn't want them to find out the sources of the contamination. Amelia told herself to stop thinking this way. This was a small island, with plenty of poverty, and plenty of excuses for someone to break into the lab. Besides, nothing was gone, at least nothing they knew about.

Justin dropped Amelia off at the hotel with just enough time for her to catch a quick nap before their boat trip. "I'll be back for you at 8:00. I hope you'll be awake this time," he said with a laugh.

"Don't you worry, I'll be ready at 7:59," Amelia quickly replied as she jumped out of the truck. As she reached her door she heard the telephone ringing and rushed in to grab it. As she suspected, it was her mother — who else would be calling her here? There goes the nap, she thought. But her mother kept it short, she'd probably figured out how much this was costing her. There was nothing new in her world, but she hoped something was in Amelia's.

"Did you solve the big mystery yet, find out what's killing all those jellyfish?" her mother asked.

"No, not yet." She almost told her about the break-in at the lab, but thought better of it. Amelia knew that would scare her mother and she would demand that she leave immediately.

"What about that man, how's the relationship going?"

"What relationship, I only met him three days ago and this is work, not a Carnival cruise." Sometimes her mother was too much. What did she think was going to happen in two days?

"Better get moving, you haven't got long. He sounds like a catch, better get a hook in him."

"The only think I might get a hook in here is a fish. And given how unsuccessful we've been so far with the research, that's not looking very likely. No time for play." Amelia felt the need to explain for some reason. She was always defending herself against her mother's matchmaking advances.

"Hmm, well you know what they say about all work and no play. Try to enjoy yourself, you never have any fun."

"That's not true and you know it and in any case we are having some fun tonight. He'll be back in an hour to pick me up for a boat ride," Amelia responded.

"Oo la la, a romantic evening cruise. Now that's got potential." Her mother was very pleased with this development.

"It's not a romantic cruise at all. He just wants me to see a bit of the island. In fact, I wonder if you've been talking to him — making suggestions about what to do for fun." Amelia was joking, but if her mother had Justin's number she probably would call.

"Well, whatever it is, have a good time. I have to go. Meeting the girls for lunch at Magnolias. Bye sweetie, I love you."

"Love you, too, Mom." Amelia knew her mother meant well and she didn't want to be alone. It hadn't been a conscious choice but the right man just hadn't come along. Granted she wasn't doing much looking, but after college where there is a ready and unending supply of beaus, the pool seemed to shrivel quickly. She knew she should make a concerted effort to put herself out there, at events and in places where she might actually meet someone. But Amelia couldn't think about that now, she needed a quick nap and she was determined not to embarrass herself again. She would definitely be ready on time.

And ready she was at 7:55 p.m., sitting in one of the bamboo chairs located in the open air, thatched roof reception area that served as the hotel lobby. Amelia wasn't going to keep him waiting or have him beating on her door again. She was ready to depart when he drove into the roundabout in front of the hotel in his lovely red, or rusty depending on perspective, "limousine." Amelia half expected another wisecrack about this morning, but Justin seemed a distracted and didn't mention it. He barely spoke as they drove to the marina, if you could call it a marina. It was little more than a long pier with six boats. Justin's landlord had a fishing boat docked there that he let Justin use whenever he needed it.

It was dark already. The sun always sets around 6 p.m. this near the equator, where daytime is always twelve hours of sunlight, give or take thirty minutes. It's basically sunrise at 6 a.m. and sunset at 6 p.m. year round. But tonight there was a full moon, ninety percent full, and its reflection on the water left a glistening shade of gray, the color of cold steel on a fishmonger's table. The tide was low and light ripples broke silently along the water's edge, the gentle swish of the waves occasionally interrupted by a fish or dolphin playing in the moonlight. It was as if they knew they were being watched and felt obliged to put on a show.

Amelia was sure that the dolphins were gossiping. She listened intently to the squeaky sounds they eked out, imagining their conversation: *Hey, Fred*—now why couldn't a dolphin be named Fred?—*look at those crazy gringos in the boat, what do you think they are doing? Probably wondering what we are saying to each other Betty,* yes Betty—it's a very good dolphin name. *Nah, they aren't smart enough to know we can talk. Maybe they came out here to go skinny dipping, never realizing we'd be laughing our dorsal fins off at them. Let's mess with them if they jump in. Can you put on the music from Jaws, give them a real scare. You are a naughty dolphin Fred, let's get out of here and have our own skinny dipping party. Now you're talking and who's the naughty one now.*

Justin untied the boat and pushed it slowly away from the dock, jumping inside just in the nick of time — another thirty seconds and he would've been going for a swim. Amelia loved being on the water at night, especially with a full moon, the light dancing on the water like raindrops on tin foil. The water here was shallow and they had to get some depth before letting down the small outboard motor. At least it had a motor, she'd expected a row boat; however, there was no evidence that the motor worked or that it wouldn't conk out on them in the middle of the ocean. Amelia wasn't convinced of the seaworthiness of this little "cruise" vessel. After a little flooding, Justin managed to crank the motor and get them headed into the gentle night breeze. It really was a perfect night, weather wise, at least.

With no one in sight they cruised slowly along guided only by the moonlight and the sounds of the dolphin. Amelia was sure she heard the dolphins telling her to be careful, things are never as they appear. She was brought back to reality when she heard Justin say, "Did you see that shark over there?"

"Shark, what shark?" Amelia asked, trying to stand up and almost falling out of the boat.

"Careful, sit down and don't worry, it's just a reef shark.

"Just a reef shark?" she asked.

"Yes, they're harmless. Really, he, or she, isn't going to bother us," Justin reassured her, which was perfectly true. The shark wasn't what they needed to be concerned about. They'd have other visitors, with more sinister plans, before the night was over.

CHAPTER TEN

The Lieutenant was out at 6:00 a.m. for a run around the neighborhood, stopping for a quick pet of Mrs. Heverstein's Corgi, and back for breakfast with Amy before heading off to another day at the Pentagon. Today, breakfast was blueberry French toast and sausage links, one of his favorites. It was fast and easy for Amy, who had a full day ahead of her at the downtown fair. She'd been up since four, in fact, baking cookies and cakes, roasting pork for her Cuban sandwiches. The Cuban was always a big seller. Everyone loved her "secret" recipe and people were still talking about the sandwiches from last summer's fair. She'd never tell of course, but the secret ingredients were nothing more than cumin and honey. Most cooks used only brown sugar, but she found that the honey added an extra twang.

Amy made two of the sandwiches for the Lieutenant, threw in a pack of kettle chips and a couple of the chocolate chip cookies for today's lunch. He was a lucky man, and he knew it. How many other guys at the Pentagon would have a Cuban pork sandwich for lunch, or a wife who even made their lunch? He'd be lucky if he could last until noon without breaking into his fancy new lunch bag for a snack. Amy loved to buy the latest gadgets and when she found the insulated lunch bag, she just had to get one for the Lieutenant. It was made from recycled plastic, and fortunately, Amy bought the black one instead of one of the tie-dye or fru fru colors that were also available. He had enough qualms about carrying the bag, it was too metro sexual for him, but at least the black one was a little more manly. He would have been just as happy, actually much happier, with a brown paper bag.

It was one of those hot humid days that seem to be so prevalent in the D.C. area during summertime. The summers seemed to be getting hotter with each passing year. The winter had been one of the worst in recent history, now summer was following suit. By the time he got to the metro station his arms and face were already sticky with humidity. He hoped the air conditioning on the train would be working today, one could never know for sure. It was almost unbearable to be underground in such tight quarters with hundreds of other people and no air.

Fortunately, the air conditioning on the train was working, which was indeed a blessing when they ended up stuck in a tunnel for ten minutes because of a disabled car ahead of them on the tracks. Thank goodness the Lieutenant wasn't claustrophobic. It was a crowded car and plenty of people were getting antsy before they were finally able to move. There was plenty of air conditioning at the Pentagon, too much of it most of the time, particularly if you were sitting all day. Occasionally he'd get up and pace around the halls to warm up and take a break from his superhero daydreaming. Today was going to be a busy day so he wouldn't have much time to travel the world and save damsels in distress or deactivate bombs in their final seconds. The Lieutenant had serious work to do today.

But before he could focus on this new project, he had to deliver today's reports. The reports, if there were any, usually came to his desk around 9:30 or 10:00 a.m., and unless there was another priority, which there seldom was, he delivered them immediately. The Lieutenant didn't even speculate about the contents of today's reports, nor did he engage in daydreams of shooting communists along the Mekong. He had been assigned to work on a new policy report for Afghanistan, a task that interested him very much. His adventures would have to wait, this assignment was serious and he wanted to give it his best.

Afghanistan was one of the world's current hot spots and things weren't going all that well, for the Afghans or the U.S. military. Every month the number of dead grew, casualties became common place, and the Taliban seemed to be increasing in number and strength. But the Lieutenant knew that in the end no one could stand up to the U.S. military, it was the best in the world. It seemed he had a selective memory. In his mind, it was just a matter of time and a few tweaks in the strategy before they would prevail over the rag tag band of bandits that were the Taliban. Never mind, that the Lieutenant had not been there and had little knowledge of the long, tumultuous history of the Afghans. They were well known for their brutal reprisals, with many an invader finding their head impelled on a stick or shipped back to their native country as a warning to others.

Down the hall, behind those locked doors, the analysts knew plenty about their subjects and what to do with the information they received, most of the time. But this one had them scratching their heads. Things were definitely not getting better; in fact, there had been yet another explosion, providing an additional set-back to finalizing this operation, now almost five years in the making. Even more disconcerting, was the fact that some yahoo ex-pat in the Pacific was raising questions about anomalies in the marine life. Were the two connected in some way? They were dealing with chemicals after all, chemicals that had never been tested before so anything was possible. Whatever was going on, they had to keep a lid on it. They'd put off the inevitable long enough, it was time to run this up the ladder, let someone else make some decisions about how to proceed. Even with their top level secret security clearances, they didn't have the authority to make this kind of decision. These guys didn't even know the real name — Jungle Juice — of this operation or its ultimate goal, they didn't really want to. Too much information was a bad thing, it could get you killed.

They both agreed to flag it for further investigation at a higher level—to send it to the General in charge for a decision on next steps. It would go directly to a General since it was listed as TOP SECRET, actually it was SPECAT, special category above top secret that severely restricts access to the information. The analysts were surprised, even with their high-level clearances, that they had been privy to some of this information. But someone with their specialized background had to review the technical aspects to fully understand what was, and more unfortunately, at least from their perspective, wasn't happening.

Little did they know that when the General realized what was going on, their involvement would come to an abrupt end, making them all the more suspicious about this operation. There were at least twenty operations at the SPECAT level, but none seemed to have the kind of secrecy and limited access that this one did. They were left to wonder whether this one was a decoy, a tin can inside a tin can. From their limited access, they could only imagine how deep this ran, but they hoped to never find out. They hoped the world never found out.

The Lieutenant was busily reviewing a two foot stack of reports—background information on Afghanistan, current troop levels, intel on the Taliban. It was fascinating reading, especially about the Taliban. They were much more organized than he expected and the size of their organization was certainly bigger than he imagined, or that anyone in the military could be comfortable with. The bad part, the Taliban ranks were growing, too many disenfranchised young men with no jobs, fed up with the lack of services offered by their government. Enough is enough and many had chosen the self-help remedy of providing a "government" that would at least meet some of their needs while also getting rid of the foreign crusaders. From what the Lieutenant could discern the President of

Afghanistan was, in reality, the mayor of Kabul. He had no control outside of the city.

Had the Lieutenant paid much attention to the news, he would've known the vast majority of what he read in those reports. It wasn't classified information. He'd hoped for more interesting details, but assumed that this was just the tip of the iceberg. The "good stuff" would come later. He wanted to believe he was always in the loop and that titillating news about U.S. plans to put the Taliban out of business, once and for all, would be forthcoming. If anybody could do it, he knew the U.S. military could—and he was sure they would.

The General, on the other hand, wasn't sure he could put the genie known as Operation Jungle Juice back in the bottle. It's one thing to relocate troops, even undercover spies, but if this thing had made its way into the ocean that would take resources even he didn't have. Both to clean up and also to keep hidden, which at the moment was a higher priority for him. He'd been in the military for thirty-seven years, he had a clean record. He didn't want to be the scapegoat on this one, especially when he had plans to retire in three years. Over the years, General Foley had come to be one of the military's preeminent specialists on chemical weapons, making a name for himself during the Gulf War. He knew pretty much every chemical substance in existence and its effects on humans and the environment. His goal was to avoid wars, but when they came, to win them at any cost.

What General Foley read in the reports troubled him, but he was sure it could be kept under control, it had to be. But he needed a plan, a plan involving the fewest people. If this operation got out of hand, it could seriously damage international relations. But his real concern was for himself. He needed time to think, to gather more details, and develop a strategy for putting this right. At first, he had doubted that this operation could succeed, had even argued against it given the high risks. The General knew that the cost of failure would be devastating. But in the end the choice was not his, he was told that failure was not an option, the word came from the highest levels. So Operation Jungle Juice went forward and had been moving, though not always forward, for the past five years. The original plan had anticipated a timeline of two to three years, but its' implementation had left the General hamstrung. The Pentagon was in no position to insist on completion according to a specific timeline. There was no incentive for the "contractor" to finish the work — in fact, quite the contrary. Keeping the U.S. government on a string certainly had its advantages.

The U.S. government also had the Lieutenant on a string, but he didn't mind. He knew his day would come, they would need him and he'd be there. There for his country, there for his government, there to make a difference. He knew he could be a hero, if called upon, and not just in his daydreams. But for now, he'd wait and do whatever he was asked. That was why the Lieutenant said yes when asked to take his current position. Sure it was beneath him, but he had nowhere to go but up, and he was assured he would.

In his past, General Foley had been a hero, had his day in the sun, several days in fact. But he wasn't looking for another one now. He needed to keep this situation under control, which meant figuring out a realistic plan. So he decided to take a break, clear his mind with some fresh air and see if he would get inspired. Besides, it was almost lunch time and unlike the Lieutenant, his wife didn't make him a Cuban pork sandwich, or any sandwich for that matter. He needed to grab something to eat, an easy excuse for a quick departure.

The General didn't mind eating alone, but preferred not to sit by himself in a crowded restaurant. So he picked up a burger and some fries at Five Guys and headed for Arlington Cemetery. Although, not a typical lunch location, the cemetery always inspired him. The mandatory "silence and respect" signposts throughout the place assured him of a little peace and quiet. Maybe it was the reminder of all those who'd gone on before in the name of freedom, those who made the ultimate sacrifice for our country, that buoyed his belief in doing whatever was necessary to protect the American way of life. He knew he was rationalizing, but some risks were worth taking—worth hurting people, even dying for—if it meant protecting the cherished freedoms his forefathers had fought and died for.

The General wondered what it was like at Gettysburg, Antietam, Vicksburg. Those battles were a different type of war than any he'd experienced in his lifetime, wars like Vietnam, Iraq. In Iraq they'd had the latest equipment, using computers and highly specialized weapons. Even in Vietnam there were cutting edge, at that time, helicopters and machinery. He couldn't imagine fighting ones' "own," especially in hand to hand combat. Some of those very "own" were buried there—in Arlington; union men and confederates laid out in the same cemetery. The General suspected that some of both would want to turn over in the grave if they knew. There was a special section for Confederates soldiers that he had visited often enough to remember the names—Henry M. Shaw, Wilson Taylor, James Scales—all from Alabama. He took a special interest in those Alabama soldiers because he'd been stationed at the Anniston Army Depot in Alabama for several years. During those years, he'd grown to appreciate the congenial and rather colorful southern characters he'd met. Southerners were a different breed. They knew how to tell a good yarn, how to fry anything, and most of all how to make you feel welcome. As long as you were welcome. Getting on their wrong side was another story; a fact well proven by the long and brutal battle they'd managed to wage with far fewer men and resources, while nonetheless holding strong for the four long and bloody years of that Civil War.

General Foley envisioned himself perched atop a smoky black stallion, riding saddle to saddle with General Lee in the final days at Gettysburg, the two of them discussing battle strategy and planning a game changing victory for the south. One has to wonder "what if" — what if the South had prevailed in that battle, gone on to take the Capitol and won the war. The General had often wondered, given all of the history he knew of the Civil War — he'd pretty much read every book written on the subject — whether General Lee wanted to win anymore, whether losing was, in the end, winning. How could the nation have survived, divided by loyalties, battered and bruised in body and pride? It would never have worked. General Lee was a good soldier and more importantly a good man, one who had seen enough of dying and was ready for some living.

In the quiet and serenity of the cemetery with only the occasional hum of a lawn mower, General Foley imagined his conversation with General Lee at Gettysburg. He felt sure that together they could have changed the game plan, met the union head on and taken Cemetery Ridge, instead of losing so many lives and retreating back into the South. Three days of combat, 50,000 plus lives lost, a fierce battle that was a turning point in the war — perhaps the beginning of the end.

With the gift of hindsight it's hard to believe that President Lincoln thought, as he so eloquently elaborated in his Gettysburg address, that the world would not long remember what he said that day, when in fact few words have hardly been more remembered. Lincoln was right when he admonished the crowd not to forget what happened there, fortunately no one did. It's a part of the nation, a place in history, a battle never to be waged in quite the same way again. So many gave so much, that the U.S. could be the nation it is today. That was one of the many reasons, General Foley did this work — how he justified the means to his end — an end that would ensure peace and security for his nation. It was worth it, whatever it took — well, almost.

The rows and rows of small, somber, white marble tombstones gazed back at him like blank slates. The conversation was one sided, he could say whatever he wished, but no answers would come. Today, of all days, he wanted them to talk back, to tell him what he should do, what decision would be the right one, for everyone. But maybe there was no right decision. The words of Abraham Lincoln's second inaugural address rang in his head. Both sides prayed to the same God, invoking his aid, but, "the prayers of both could not be answered. That of neither has been answered fully." Mind you, he knew he was no Abraham Lincoln and this wasn't a Civil War, but he hoped his "enemy" in this dilemma wasn't praying for assistance. Somehow he felt sure they weren't, at least not to the same "god."

He watched a family with two young children standing silent in front of a fallen President, at the tomb of John F. Kennedy. Nearby were his brothers, Robert and Teddy, who gave so much in the service of their country—not the type of service the General had given, continued to give—but a service more public and memorable. He felt a twinge of jealousy. For all he had achieved, few knew him or how much he had done to protect the U.S. He doubted they ever would. Now he feared he might be left with a legacy he hadn't hoped for, one that would smear all those years of devotion. If this situation got out of hand, he'd be remembered for all the wrong reasons.

One of the character flaws that plagued General Foley was a misplaced sense of pride. He knew a lot about chemical weapons, he knew a lot about many things, but he wasn't good at recognizing what he didn't know. And even worse at admitting it, forget asking for assistance. He thought he knew better than others, thought he could figure his way out—he had so many times in the past. But in those desperate moments when common sense and luck failed him, he tended to make serious mistakes. Even when he emerged from the flawed situation with the facts laid bare, he would refuse to take the blame. He didn't like to be wrong, no one does, but he was especially bad at it.

He ran through the history of this operation in his mind, remembering all of the mishaps, misinformation, and misgivings about its feasibility. Over five long years, there had been a series of ups and downs, highs and lows, a belief that success was near only to have it fail once again. This partner couldn't be trusted, they knew that from the start, but it was the only way he could keep this under the radar. There were too many leaks, too many big mouths, too much media inside the United States to keep anything a secret. Those days were gone. Leaking information anonymously on the internet was the future and it was here to stay. People can easily be bribed, threatened, or just want their fifteen minutes of fame. No, the truth about this one could never see the light of day. He'd make sure of that.

Yet, the question still remained — how was he going to resolve this situation? His friends in the cemetery hadn't been of any assistance today. He was working without a net on this one. But he was the General, with thirty-seven years of service under his belt, well trained and well thought of. He'd suck it up and make a decision. Life was hard at times, but somebody had to make the tough decisions. Today that was him.

The General took one more, long look around the thousands of tombstones. A different family now stood at the grave of JFK, a group of students were headed up the hill to the Custiss-Lee house, and the hum of the lawnmower grew louder. And then it hit him, he knew his next move. The devil was indeed in the details, but he thought he could make it work. He bid his silent friends goodbye and headed back to the Pentagon. For now, this was just between him and his fellow soldiers at Arlington, they could be trusted to keep quiet and no one else needed to know, at least not yet — maybe not ever.

CHAPTER ELEVEN

The sun was starting to peak over the top of the mountain with beams of yellow light sparkling on the dewy grass like diamonds, a jewel Lin knew she would never have. That was a rich woman's dream. But the diamond sparkles of the morning sun were enough for her. She was very happy this morning, her son had brought home excellent marks from school yesterday. Seems he was doing particularly well in science, which buoyed Lin's hope that he might one day be a doctor. If she could only contain his rambunctious nature and channel that energy into his studies, imagine how well he could really do. As usual, her husband took little notice; he said, "Good work son," but offered no further encouragement. Lin knew she would have to wage this battle alone. Her husband had no ambition, he didn't see the need. What good was ambition in this tiny town where he could barely find work? He wasn't going anywhere, wasn't moving away, didn't want to for that matter. He was happy with mediocrity in his life. They had food to eat, a place to live, a lovely child. What more could anyone want? And these mountains, who could resist their beauty and serenity? Gang could spend half the day just looking at them. Sometimes he did, much to Lin's chagrin.

The conversation on the walk to the factory that morning was mostly about the school marks, a little bragging was in order for some of the women. Others were disappointed, but they masked it with hope that the next semester their children would show improvement. There were always excuses, sometimes blame for the teachers, no one wants to accept that their child isn't the best. Inevitably talk turned to Mr. Kao and the events of yesterday. They mocked him, running and screaming from the building and then demanding so vehemently that they clean the place up. He was so self-important. Did he really think he was going to get promoted to a big job in the city? Talk about a little fish in a big ocean. He'd be lost and he'd drown, quickly. Besides what they were doing in the lab apparently wasn't producing any income, or so they assumed, since there was no apparent commercial production. That was one of the mysterious things about the whole affair. Was it strictly research and development? Were they going to actually produce something once they found the ultimate formula — one that didn't blow up their lab? The workers, all twenty of them, were never told and they knew better than to ask. But if this venture couldn't turn a profit, Mr. Kao wasn't going anywhere, except maybe to the hospital the next time they suffered another mishap.

Nothing was going to spoil Lin's good mood today, not even the nasty Mr. Kao. Let him rant and rave and try to berate them into productivity. If he wasn't smart enough to see just how counter-productive that actually was, then let him waste his time and energy. The man was full of bad karma. Perhaps she should light a candle for him, or better yet, hire an exorcist. Maybe a course on how to win friends and influence people would be in order for Mr. Kao, but no doubt he'd think he should be the one teaching it.

Lin knew that today would be difficult. Mr. Kao was sure to be in a bad mood, the evil spirits would not have deserted him yet. Lin imagined how unhappy his life must be, filled with venom and anger toward others. She was sure he was shortening his stay on this earth with that kind of attitude. Lin couldn't imagine harboring such vengeance; hers was a life filled with peace. Hating others only brings harm to yourself. We all have a choice in this life — to live in peace and harmony with man and nature or to be filled with hate and vengeance. She had chosen the former, too bad Mr. Kao had not done the same.

Some would say that the mentality Lin possessed was not possible. How can one live in peace when others around you bring trouble and hardship to your life? You can't live in a bubble, but Lin knew that it wasn't really important how others behaved toward you, but rather how you behaved towards them. She worked hard to block out the evil spirits, dismiss bad behavior, and rise above the pettiness of others. It was a Zen skill her mother had tried to teach her and for the most part she had tried to follow. Meditation had brought her many advantages and provided transcendence from the daily annoyances of life that, left to fester, could turn into a boil.

When Lin was only seven her mother took her to a rice paddy filled with the biggest lotus flowers she had ever seen. Hardly a sound could be heard, except the occasional noise of frogs. The memory of this place was burned in Lin's memory along with the words her mother said—"if a moment of anger should come, imagine this place, become the flower and grow beyond the bad feelings. Never give in to evil or your soul will die." Ever since, when faced with life's difficult moments, Lin would close her eyes and look for that peace. The image of the flowers, and more important her mother's words, had served her well. She was seldom a victim of stress. Lin would never need the anti-anxiety drugs that were common place in so many developed countries.

When Lin and her co-workers arrived at the lab they could sense that something was afoot. Beyond the obvious three Chinese men in gray suits, there was a somber and serious mood that permeated the building. Everyone went silently to their work stations and pretended to look busy, very busy. They all knew the situation was precarious; jobs were hard to come by in this village. Many were afraid, very afraid, that the lab would be closed and their source of income might be lost forever, at least any steady source of income. The fear kept them all quiet and focused as the suits passed through each department with hardly a word spoken. The suits listened intently as Mr. Kao explained the operations and lauded their achievements, few as they were, in an obvious attempt to ingratiate himself to his superiors.

The suits seemed underwhelmed, but in polite Chinese tradition they listened intently and nodded, thanking Mr. Kao for his service. As they passed through Lin's department she overheard part of the conversation. Clearly, pressure was being put on Mr. Kao and this little operation to produce — whatever it was that they were supposed to be producing. She also overhead them thank Mr. Kao for his "continued discretion." Discretion about what she wondered. What is the big secret here? If only she knew the answer, that enviable sense of peace she had might, at last, be shaken.

It was obvious the group of suits was upset over the recent explosion at the lab. They spent considerable time observing what was left of the remains, but Lin and her co-workers had done a pretty decent job of cleaning the place up so there wasn't much to see. They argued, but quietly, so that the staff couldn't hear. There appeared to be a disagreement among themselves; hopefully, over whether to fire Mr. Kao. Losing him as a boss would be a dream come true.

After the tour, the suits went to Mr. Kao's office where they inspected the records, looked at numerous lab reports, requested samples of recent experiments, and also checked the financial records. Kao was smart enough to keep two sets of books, just for such occasions. In any case, these guys weren't the auditors. The financial check was just for show, perhaps to put a little fear into Mr. Kao, but certainly not a serious attempt at identifying any impropriety. They seemed far more interested in the various concoctions that had been tried and found wanting, and particularly interested in their storage and disposal. At one point Lin was called into the office and asked to explain the process for maintaining inventory and questioned as to whether any materials had ever gone missing. This line of questioning made her somewhat apprehensive, fearing that she might be accused of stealing. But she knew she hadn't done anything wrong. What would she possibly want with any of these chemicals? Lin managed to remain calm, in stark contrast to Mr. Kao's obvious nervousness and profuse sweating. Kao could have never explained the process himself. But for her help, he'd been in a pickle. He knew nothing about the way things operated here, he spent most of his day sitting in his office sipping tea and reading newspapers.

After thirty minutes of grilling, Lin had sufficiently satisfied the suits about the lab's inventory procedures. Thankfully, she was a very organized person and had kept meticulous records, documenting every substance that came and went. Never mind, whether the gold digging Mr. Kao had his own set of financial books, she wasn't going to get caught in a scandal, and no way was she going to take the fall for the likes of him. Lin's peaceful character served her well in these situations. She was not flustered nor was she arrogant. Her demeanor gave others confidence in her truthfulness and allowed her, particularly in this situation, to remain in control and pass muster with her superiors. Not that she saw them as somehow superior. In fact, she didn't. She didn't see them as better or worse than herself; although, she was well aware that they had power over her. Lin knew better than to cross them, but she was not afraid. The suits realized she'd done nothing wrong and had no reason to suspect her of any complicity, so she was allowed to return to her work station without further interrogation. She wondered if they felt as confident that Mr. Kao was being honest with them, but then she didn't really care. Better for everyone if they found him a thief and replaced him, except for the old adage "better the devil you know." It was entirely possible they could end up with a worse boss.

For today at least, it didn't appear there would be any repercussions for Mr. Kao. He had apparently been successful in convincing everyone that the explosion was unavoidable, a normal hazard in this line of work. How he managed to explain the lack of results after this significant length of time was another matter altogether. Maybe he was smarter then they realized, or maybe these men weren't really interested in success. The truth of what the lab was doing remained a secret to the staff; they were all suspicious, but ignorance was bliss. Things had changed in Taiwan, significantly in the last ten years, but knowing too much was still a liability. They preferred to remain in the dark and instead keep their jobs.

When Mr. Kao finally emerged from his office, looking haggard and a few years older, no one dared to speak, not to each other and certainly not to him. As he peered over the top of his round, gold-rimmed glasses, he looked like a character in one of those Chinese comedies — a waiter or perhaps, the manager of laundry who, try as he might, just can't seem to have any success in life. And success was exactly what was on Mr. Kao's mind this afternoon, it looked like they'd all be staying late. In his usual style, he berated the staff for what he considered their stupidity and lack of ability to finish the task at hand, blaming them for the explosion. He made clear to everyone that time was of the essence and there could be no more delays. But they'd all heard that one before, usually at least once every six months or so, and given that lack of any consequences in the past, none were expected now. Threats, especially idle ones, had little effect on people's motivation.

It was clear, if not from his words, at least from the distraught look, the hand wringing, the pacing, that Mr. Kao was a man under serious pressure. Lin was glad she didn't have his job, except maybe for the paycheck. Mr. Kao began to yell and stomp and snort — about everything and yet nothing in particular. He wasn't making much sense, but everyone decided to look busy, and try to ignore him. They were afraid if any eye contact was made, they'd be in for some serious ridiculing or even worse, they might be fired. Mr. Kao's face began to turn red, his nostrils flaring like a mad bull and his eyes seemed to grow smaller by the minute. They half expected smoke to start coming out of his ears.

If Mr. Kao blamed Lin directly as the root of his problems, he didn't show it. Though she knew she had done nothing wrong, Lin also knew that wouldn't stop Mr. Kao from somehow making it her fault. He had a way of never taking responsibility, an interesting trait for top management. In his current situation he wasn't sure who to blame, so he was mad at the world. But he knew that some positive results must be forthcoming soon or he might be departing forthwith, hat in hand so to speak.

Everyone busied themselves, organizing beakers and jars, cleaning their work stations, to give the appearance of efficiency and purpose, almost as if they knew what their mission was. One wonders whether it would have been better or worse if the staff knew what they were doing. Would anyone have quit? Would they be afforded such a luxury? Or would they bother to even care? Perhaps some would be so morally offended they might leave or take more drastic measures to put a stop to it. Not likely in a place where dissent was naturally unwelcome. Nor did anyone much care what the rest of the world was up to when they were more worried about where their next meal was coming from. No, it wasn't their place to judge or even to have an opinion. It was their job to work and most of all, to get paid. And get paid they would on Friday afternoon, assuming they weren't closed down before then. Getting paid on Friday was a blessing for some but a curse for others. It was always nice to have that feeling of wealth before the weekend, assuming you are able to control your spending. Those prone to compulsive behavior and drinking in particular, tended to lose it all by Monday morning and suffer for the remainder of the week. It was actually their families who were doing most of the suffering, finding creative ways to make ends meet, to put food on the table until the next payday came along, only to repeat the cycle.

One of Lin's colleagues, Changpu, was just such a fellow, heading straight to the nearest bar every Friday afternoon and barely sobering up in time to make it to work on Monday. Alcoholism wasn't a common problem in Taiwan, but it was very sad for those afflicted by it, even more so for their families. Lin had often seen Changpu's wife rambling in garbage heaps looking for scraps decent enough to make a meal for their daughter. She had often wondered if Changpu felt less than a man because his only child was a daughter or whether he, like many other Chinese men, believed that daughters were a burden. It seemed he couldn't be burdened with making sure she was taken care of. Lin had seen the girl a few times with her mother, playing on the side of the road with old tin cans and plastic bottles, probably the only toys she had. She was a beautiful child with a perfect nose and rosy cheeks that reminded you of crab apples. It was such a shame that a father couldn't appreciate such a sweet and precious child. Changpu didn't seem particularly skilled in the parent department or in his work for that matter. He'd been the source of injury at the lab on more than one occasion when he misread the formulas or didn't pay attention to the labels on the chemicals. Lin was amazed he hadn't been fired, but even in Taiwan there was a good ole boy's network and he was apparently part of it. Mr. Kao let Changpu do things no one else would ever get away with. It wasn't as if he was a creative genius or even relatively smart for that matter; in fact, his name meant forever simple in Chinese. At first glance, his parents obviously had good intuition about the future of their new baby boy. Lin wondered about the connection between names and lives—whether the name sets the course for the future or whether people tried to live up to the name they were given. Either way, Changpu had been successful in living up to his—forever simple, indeed.

It had been a trying day for everyone at the lab. In need of relief, Mr. Kao decided to strike off early knowing the suits were now long gone, and take his pal Changpu for a round of libations at what passed for a pub. He didn't really care who saw them head off together or whether the rest of the employees would sit down on their fists and lean back on their thumbs. There was only an hour left in the work day, but Mr. Kao was too disturbed, nerves frayed to the end, to be concerned about these things today. He'd get moving Monday to set things right and make sure the lab lived up to the expectations laid out for him this morning by the suits. Besides he needed to get creative to figure out his future plans and the rice wine had a way of getting the creative juices flowing.

As soon as Changpu and Kao were out of site, the rest of the employees did exactly as expected. They all sat down outside the building for a cup of tea and to wait out the remainder of the day. They couldn't simply leave. This town was too small and Mr. Kao would see them meandering back down the hill, assuming he hadn't already imbibed too much of the creative juice, as it were. No, they would put in their time if not their effort. Life had a way of evening things out in the end and they knew that tomorrow Mr. Kao would pay for his bad behavior, at the very least with an unwelcome headache. In the long run, they knew he would truly get what was coming to him It wasn't their place to extract revenge, revenge had a way of helping itself.

The visit of the suits had sparked the rumor mill about what was really going on at the lab. What was so important that these men would come all the way from Taipei, assuming they were from Taipei, to see firsthand what was happening? The workers had debated this question so many times before, never reaching any conclusions, but rather speculating about experimental drugs or a global conspiracy. They never wanted to know for sure, but it didn't stop them from enjoying an opportunity to let their imaginations run wild. In the end it didn't really matter, they would never figure it out on their own, nor did they care to because it could only make life more complicated. They were thankful to have their jobs and preferred keeping them to knowing the ugly truth about their role in a scheme concocted by devious and calculating people — people they would never meet.

Though there was one oddity that stuck out, at least in Lin's mind. If these men were so important, they could fire Mr. Kao and surely would given his, their, lack of success in producing any — at least to her knowledge — positive results. Were they actually looking for any outcome, product, solution here? Could this operation be some type of decoy? Who were these suits? Who did they work for? Her mind was racing so fast it gave her a headache. There was definitely something strange going on here. Clearly this wasn't a profit-making enterprise, but someone was investing a lot of resources and pinning a lot of hopes on some results that might never materialize.

"What time is it?"

"What time is it, Lin?" the voice asked again, "Hello Lin, what's going on in that head of yours?"

Lin realized she had drifted away, mentally, from her co-workers. She also realized she was the only one wearing a watch. It was a gift from her father, given to her when she graduated from high school. It was a frivolous and expensive gift, at least by local standards, but on occasion he liked to splurge. He was so proud of Lin and had high hopes for her becoming an important doctor or scientist. And even though she had married and not pursued his dreams, he realized that you have to let your children go their own way. He was unusual in that respect, at least for a Taiwanese man. But Lin was his only daughter, his only child, and he loved her dearly. He never wished she had been a boy. He couldn't understand why a parent wouldn't love their child more than anything—regardless of their sex or their abilities. Children were life's most precious gift and Lin was more precious than most, at least to him.

"Oh sorry," Lin responded as she looked down at the beautiful watch that was her most cherished tangible possession. "It's 4:30. We have only thirty more minutes to waste—I mean enjoy—the absence of our dictator," she said with a chuckle. Lin recalled the night her father had given her the silver watch with its large face. She remembered well the words he told her—"there will never be enough time, use it wisely." Lin had tried hard to remember that adage over the years, especially when it came to her own precious son. She lavished her time on him knowing that one day he'd grow tired of being a momma's baby, anyone's baby. Before she knew it, he'd be a grown man with his own priorities and limited time. Lin understood what her father meant. It wasn't about wasting time daydreaming or doing things others might find useless. It was about making the moments count, about spending your time wisely with those who mean the most in your life. Time was not a luxury to be wasted on pursuits that had no value or brought no joy to your life. Time was a gift, but one that could easily be repossessed, usually with no warning at all.

More tea was poured all around, although it had grown tepid. No one seemed to care, the joy of a few hours in peace and quiet, without Mr. Kao breathing down their necks, more than made up for the warmth of the tea. They grew tired of the speculation about the lab and moved on to a more important discussion about the proper preparation of suncakes. There was considerable debate, disagreement actually, about whether to use molasses or honey. Lin had always loved suncakes. The fragrant smell of them baking was as a familiar childhood memory that brought her great comfort—even now, especially now when she was feeling sad or lonely. Lin's mother made suncakes with the most flakey layers, rising to a perfectly rounded puff. She used honey and so did Lin. Lin didn't understand the strong opinions on opposite sides of this argument. It was a pastry desert, how could one or the other be correct, shouldn't you just make it to suit your own taste buds?

The suncake debate served to fill the remaining thirty minutes left in this troubling day. Nerves were frayed, some had headaches, others didn't really care, but couldn't deal with conflict. The Taiwanese, at least in this tranquil part of the country, preferred to remain non-confrontational. Mr. Kao being the exception, of course. They preferred not to let stress, especially from their work, creep into their daily existence. It was just more than most could handle. They preferred the simple life, but don't most people, given a choice.

At 5:00 p.m. the group was on their way down the mountain, half expecting to run into Mr. Kao stumbling drunk in the streets. They hoped they wouldn't see him, lest he start accusing them of all manner of insubordination in his inebriated state. He didn't mind embarrassing them in front of the entire village if necessary. Mr. Kao never understood how improper that kind of behavior was, that it made him look even more like the tyrant he was. Fortunately, he was nowhere to be seen. Though Lin could've sworn she'd seen one of the suits, sans the suit, headed back up the hill towards the lab. She dismissed the thought, convincing herself that she wouldn't recognize him out of context and wearing different clothes. She'd only seen him briefly this morning and couldn't be sure of his features. Why would he be going back to the lab after hours?

Lin resisted the urge to let her mind run amuck. There'd been enough of that for one day. She must have been mistaken; although, it was pretty easy to spot strangers in this small village. Whoever this guy was, he looked out of place. She didn't have time to think about this, let alone to follow him and figure out what was going on. She had dinner to cook, homework to do and clothes to mend. If he was up to mischief, fine. It wasn't her place to stop him. But she'd be sure to have a look around at the lab first thing in the morning to see if anything was out of place or missing, if only for self-preservation. She didn't need any accusations of stealing.

Lin's husband was in a chatty mood that evening. He'd actually had a productive and financially lucrative day, after picking up some construction work for a new bicycle shop. They were renovating an old building downtown that needed considerable repairs. New walls were to be erected inside, a ceiling lowered, the roof repaired, and plenty of painting. Gang was handy with this type of work and the project would keep him busy for at least six weeks, assuming he'd stick with it. He had a short attention span.

Gang—his name meant strength, which was probably his best asset—was able to carry twice the weight of most men in this town. His strength was purely physical; emotionally he was child, always would be. But perhaps his childish traits served him well in the end, at least as a baby sitter and companion to their son. While it didn't make him a good parent, at least he had a good relationship with Bingwen. They had happy times together, but when it came to discipline or nurturing, the responsibility fell to Lin. He should have used his physical strength more wisely to support the family on a consistent basis. Fortunately, he'd decided to for a few weeks, which would take some worry off Lin. With the winter coming soon, work would be hard for Gang to find.

Gang seemed unusually interested in the new design planned for the bicycle shop, but Lin wondered how interesting it could be. It was a bicycle shop after all, not a museum. But Lin was loath to discourage his interests since he had so few. Despite plenty of chores to be done, she listened to him ramble on for almost an hour about their plans to use tires and spare parts as decorative art throughout the store. Lin had to admit it did sound inventive, particularly for this little mountain village. It was about time somebody started thinking outside the box. This whole country was a box. But boxes were easier to keep people in, which was exactly the way the government wanted it.

His animated description made Lin wonder if Gang might actually have some design talent. But even if he did have the talent, he didn't have the desire to stick with it, to stick with anything. She'd heard about attention deficit disorder in children, she was pretty convinced he had the adult version. Gang had a habit of getting overly enthused at the beginning of a new opportunity only to have it quickly fizzle out when he bored of it. Work somehow became, well, too much work for him and he couldn't be bothered to actually persevere through the good and the bad. Lin had accepted many excuses for his behavior, had even made them herself during the early years of their marriage. She knew his family life had been less than perfect with a father who wandered in and out of his life. Lin was convinced that his early life was, in large part, the source of his problem, but she had grown tired of propping up their family day in and day out. She loved Gang, in some ways—in most of the ways that mattered to making their marriage work. But she knew she couldn't change him, or anyone for that matter, so she had wisely learned to accept him as he was and to carve out a world for herself that didn't require his input or support. That way, she wouldn't be disappointed when he failed her.

Too many times she had allowed herself to believe that he would change, that he was going to be more dedicated and supportive. He'd promised to repeatedly. But each time she had been disappointed and learned, for her own sanity, not to believe his empty promises. Lin knew he wanted to be better, that he was well intentioned, that most likely he was also disappointed with himself and that the fear of failure was what kept him from following through. But it was just too hard emotionally, to pretend he was more than he was or could ever be. We all have our limitations, Lin included.

Gang was so motivated tonight that he even offered to give Bingwen his bath and get him to bed; something that hadn't happened in months, perhaps a year or more. Gang only wanted to play with his son, not actually take care of him. Bingwen laughed until he almost cried, thrilled to have the attention of his father. A boy needs his father.

Lin welcomed the help, for a change, and was actually able to get to bed before midnight for the first time in a very long time. Her nightly routine included not only cooking dinner and washing up, but also washing clothes — by hand, helping with homework, and doing her meditations. Meditations were a priority, not to be performed before other tasks, but to be done regardless of the hour. She had to remove the cares of the day from her mind so that she could find peaceful rest, precious little of it that she got. Lin was always up by 6 a.m., often earlier. Mornings were another busy routine of preparing breakfast, getting Bingwen ready for school, making sure he actually got there; and of course, getting herself ready and to work on time. Even though Mr. Kao was often late, she couldn't take that chance herself. Besides, she had great pride in her work, holding herself to a higher standard than others. Being late was akin to cheating in her world. Not that Mr. Kao and whoever actually was profiting from their work deserved that kind of devotion; regardless, to her it was the principle and an example she hoped to set for her young son. In the end she knew cheaters never won, or so she kept telling herself. There had been plenty of times when she wasn't convinced, but she had to believe that what goes around comes around, that one day, maybe not even in this life but in a life to come, everyone gets their due, even the slippery Mr. Kao.

Later that night in bed, Gang was still talking about his day, the bike shop, the other guys he was working with. All Lin could do was hope that he was this excited in a week, two weeks, a month. She didn't really care if he was excited just as long as he was still employed. He rattled on for almost an hour while Lin pretended to listen and tried not to fall asleep, though she desperately needed the sleep. She couldn't get the events of the day out of her mind, despite her meditations. Something wasn't right about the inspectors who came to the lab today. For that matter, something wasn't right about the entire operation. Lin knew she wasn't going to figure it out tonight, maybe not ever, but she had a hunch that things were not as they seemed. But then, they seldom are.

CHAPTER TWELVE

The Lieutenant and Amy had a very different life than Lin and Gang, and not just in material terms, though no doubt there was a significant gap in that department as well. As they awoke that morning on the other side of the world there was a dishwasher, a microwave, a washing machine — modern conveniences that made life an easy one by comparison, and which provided more time for fun and entertainment. But it wasn't just the conveniences that made them different. Amy believed in the Lieutenant, trusted that as sure as the sun came up in the mornings that he would always take care of her. She never had to wonder whether he would get up and go to work every day, doubt his ambition, or live a life of quiet desperation that she was powerless to control, or, more importantly, change. Amy was lucky, she had a charmed life and she knew it.

But no life is perfect and who's to say what is a "better life" — all things are relative, that judgment depends on one's perspective. Lin's life was physically harder, she had a lot of family pressures, but she lived in a place that she believed was the most beautiful place on earth. But her basis for comparison was extremely limited. No matter, she felt that she had everything she needed, who could ask for more. It's a gift to be satisfied with what you have.

Amy, on the other hand, had a life of convenience and choice, a stable home where, so she believed, jobs and money would always be available. An idyllic small town life in the middle of a metropolitan area with all the benefits of a big city, who could ask for more? Who indeed? In her mind, like Lin, she had everything. Had she met Lin she would have felt sorry for her, seen her world as one of poverty —

not just financial poverty, but a quality of life poverty that she couldn't imagine anyone being satisfied with. But Amy had never heard of the village where Lin lived, she knew very little of Taiwan and it was doubtful that she would be able to find it on a map.

Amy didn't need to know anything about Taiwan, her life was in Alexandria, D.C. and Virginia. Beyond that she wasn't too concerned. Her biggest worry today was whether she'd made enough Cuban pork sandwiches. It wasn't even noon yet and she was down to only six, they'd gone like hotcakes. She only wished her jewelry would sell as well, but there were lots of jewelry exhibitors, even if their quality didn't match hers. No one else had those sandwiches. There were regular sandwiches, but not any that compared to Amy's famous Cuban pork. She had a bit of a following, a group of faithfuls who could always be counted on the show up early and buy several. Amy liked that feeling of being known for something, she could understand how easy it was for actors and rock stars to get hooked on attention. We all have egos and they like being fed.

It had turned out to be a lovely morning — the weather not too hot, at a time of year when hot is the norm, hot and humid. She'd always heard people say "it's not the heat, it's the humidity" but she'd never really understood that concept as both seemed pretty unpleasant to her — it was hard to distinguish which was worse. Today there wasn't so much of either and more importantly, no rain. Nothing would ruin a street festival faster than rain. You couldn't blame folks for not wanting to get drenched just to look at some crafts and eat food they probably didn't need anyway.

"Hello, Amy. Do you have any more of those tuba sandwiches?" asked Mrs. Heverstein. Amy had been daydreaming and didn't even see her walk up with her little Corgi, Gepetto.

"I saved one just for you Mrs. Heverstein," replied Amy, trying not to laugh at her mistakenly calling it a tuba sandwich. Amy was far too polite to correct her, what did it matter anyway. "Are you and Gepetto enjoying this fine day?" she asked.

"Indeed, we are. Gepetto likes to come to town. He's such a well behaved dog I can take him anywhere and I do take him just about everywhere. We're best friends these days it seems," Mrs. Heverstein said, never noticing that Gepetto was trying to chew the leg off of Amy's exhibit table.

"How much dear?" asked Mrs. Heverstein.

"One dollar," replied Amy. She actually sold them for five dollars but she knew Mrs. Heverstein was on a fixed income. Amy knew if she simply tried to give her one, she wouldn't take it and would probably be embarrassed.

"Well dear, the price is surely right but you're not going to make much money at that price," Mrs. Heverstein mused.

"I do it mostly for the fun of it anyway. It's the jewelry I make a little money on, though it doesn't seem to be selling very well today," Amy replied.

"It's early, I'm sure it'll pick up later on. You make such lovely pieces, you've got a real talent," mused Mrs. Heverstein.

"Thank you, ma'am. I enjoy it. It's a real creative outlet for me, especially during the summer when I'm not teaching."

"What grade are you teaching?" Mrs. Heverstein asked.

"Fourth grade. Next year I'll have thirty students in my class. It's a lot of kids, but with budget cuts we all have to take on bigger class loads. At least it's not thirty first graders, they're a real handful," Amy said, laughing, in fear, at the thought of that many tiny ones in one classroom.

"Right you are dear. I can't imagine dealing with that many children at once. It was all I could do to handle the two I had at home. Lord knows, I loved them dearly but they tried my patience on many occasions," said Mrs. Heverstein.

"Well, I think it's different when you're their mother. Most of them mind me better than they mind their parents. At least they know they'll get in trouble at school. Seems not many parents believe in consequences these days, "Amy replied as she glanced downward just in time to see Gepetto chewing on her jewelry boxes. She did her best to draw his attention to something else and away from her boxes. Apparently Mrs. Heverstein's eyesight wasn't up to par; she never noticed what the little guy was up to. It took her a couple of minutes to realize Amy had disappeared beneath the table to wrestle her jewelry boxes from the mouth of the hungry little canine, who was now salivating profusely as he chomped into the wood like it was a choice cut of beef.

Amy didn't want to offend Mrs. Heverstein but she'd invested a lot in these boxes and teeth marks weren't going to make them shabby chic. Gepetto wasn't giving up easily. Amy had to grab the box out of his mouth, putting it out of harm's way onto the exhibit table. Only then did the elderly woman realize what her precious little Gepetto was doing, apologizing profusely for his bad manners and the damage to Amy's pretty boxes.

"Oh my, I don't know what's come over him. I guess I better get him home for a snack." Mrs. Heverstein began to exam the jewelry box to see how much damage was done, but with her eyesight Amy doubted she'd pick up on the series of teeth marks now left on three corners. "I'm so sorry dear, please let me replace it for you."

"No, that's not necessary Mrs. Heverstein," Amy grudgingly replied. "It's still usable. I'll just touch it up a bit with some Old English when I get home. No harm done." But there was plenty of harm done. Nevertheless, she couldn't put this guilt on Mrs. Heverstein. She was just a sweet old lady with a chew happy companion.

"Well, you let me know if that doesn't work. I won't have my Gepetto destroying other people's property," Mrs. Heverstein boldly proclaimed. Despite her assurances, Amy had a sneaking suspicion that this wasn't his first infraction. But he was such a cute little dog it was hard to be angry with him, especially when he stood there, all ten inches high, head cocked sideways with a "please forgive me" smile. Amy suspected Gepetto had perfected that look to get himself out of trouble and it worked, she was taken in.

"I'm sure it'll be fine, don't worry about it. Just head on home and get him a snack." Amy was trying to save the other exhibitors, since it was unlikely Gepetto would suddenly give up his propensity for munching on other people's property. "And enjoy your sandwich, you'll have to let me know how it was."

"I will. I'm a great food critic," she said, laughing as she tugged on Gepetto's leash. "Good luck with you jewelry and I'll let you know about that sandwich."

"I'll be looking forward to it. Be careful getting home." Amy cautioned and with that Mrs. Heverstein made a hearty stroll up the sidewalk to the shuttle bus, as hearty as a woman her age could.

As Amy watched Mrs. Heverstein grow smaller and smaller, strolling slowly but surely up the sidewalk, a man she hadn't notice before was suddenly very interested in her jewelry. He was short with olive skin and almond eyes, maybe Asian, but she couldn't be sure. She wasn't well traveled and found it difficult to determine ethnicity. Not that she cared, she was no racist — it was just an observation. But he was the one who seemed to be making all the observations, not only of the jewelry, but of her. When he refused her offer of assistance, she grew a bit concerned, letting her imagination run away with her. Was he going to grab some of the jewelry and run? She realized how ridiculous that sounded and turned her attention to another customer, one who was actually interested in buying something.

And buy something she did, several somethings — three necklaces, a bracelet, six rings, and a Cuban sandwich to top it off; early Christmas shopping she said. Amy was thrilled to make this much money on one sale, especially this early in the day. She couldn't wait to tell the Lieutenant about her good luck and maybe she'd also tell him about the Asian-looking man who was hanging around her booth, but that would probably just worry him. What could the Lieutenant do about him anyway, she didn't know who he was and she'd probably never see this man again. Amy hoped she didn't see him again, something about him gave her the creeps. When she finished putting the money away from the sale he was gone and without buying a Cuban sandwich. Obviously he wasn't from around here.

Over at the Pentagon, the Lieutenant was thoroughly enjoying his sandwich. Never mind his colleagues ribbing him about that cute little lunch box his wife had bought for him or how she spoiled him with all these treats. He didn't mind, he was man enough to take it. Anyway, he knew they were just jealous.

"Where'd you get that purse, Lt. Ansley?" barked one of the Sergeants at the table.

"Yeah, very stylish, matches your shoes," cried another one. "Is it available in navy?"

"Pretty soon they'll start making it in camouflage and it will be standard issue for everyone. Then you'll see I was ahead of the pack on this one," the Lieutenant retorted. "In fact, maybe I'll just start making them myself, get a big contract selling them to DOD and make myself rich. Isn't that what all these 'beltway bandits' at the contracting firms do anyway?"

"Bright idea Forrest Gump, let me know how that works out for you. If you were such a talented businessman you wouldn't be pushing paper in this place." This from a new guy who was barely out of diapers. What did he know about the business world? Nonetheless, it stung a bit. The Lieutenant was tough, but he still had an ego. True, he did push a lot of paper, but they were important papers and he knew it was only a matter of time until a top secret assignment came his way. Then they would realize how important he really was around here, or would they? If it was actually a top secret assignment he couldn't tell these guys about it anyway.

"Don't knock Forrest Gump, seems he did pretty well with the Bubba Gump Shrimp Company." They all laughed and moved on to other topics while the Lieutenant moved on to his day dreaming, imagining that great assignment that was sure to come his way. He knew he'd be rewarded for doing the little things, the dirty work, and not complaining about it.

The Lieutenant tuned out his buddies and the chatter of the lunchroom as his mind wandered away again on one of his superhero adventures. This time he was off to the back streets of Belgrade chasing Mafioso's who were formerly part of Arkan's gang of thugs. The Balkans had seen their share of troubles in recent years, in their entire history to hear the Serbians tell it. Trouble seemed to find them. There was no end to the shady characters that managed to hold power, officially or otherwise. Many had profited from the war. There's always someone ready to take advantage of the misery of others.

Though Arkan was long gone, gunned down in very dramatic fashion in the lobby of the Intercontinental Hotel, his cronies had regrouped, if for no other reason than a lack of gainful employment. Well, gainful employment of a legal nature. Not that there was any desire to redeem themselves and go straight, but rather that times were tough, even for the underworld.

In the Lieutenant's little scenario they were back in business, moving arms and even worse, plutonium. While they thought no one was looking, they'd gained access to small amounts of weapons grade plutonium and were trying to market it, as covertly as one could, to some of the less friendly nations of the world, including Iran. They arranged for a meeting in Belgrade, at Kalemegdan Park where the Danube and Sava rivers converge, and where the old war heroes gathered to play checkers. Sure it was a big open space, but where better to hide than in plain view. Children played, women sold their handmade wares, budding artists painted the local attractions, and life went on as if all was well with the world. People knew better, but they chose to ignore it. What good did looking for trouble or even acknowledging it do for them? Life was hard, better to be oblivious and make it all a little easier to swallow.

In his superhero world the Lieutenant was, of course, aware of this covert meeting—more than aware. He had strategically located himself near the Stefan Tower where he could watch the show. He wasn't sure who might show up, but he'd know them when he saw them. He'd memorized the pictures of every known member of the former Tigers. They wouldn't send a new recruit to handle something this sensitive, so he was sure to see a familiar face. For the Iranian side, he was at a loss. The intelligence on that side of the fence was slim to none and all the more reason for him to ferret out the identity of their agents. If he could blow this deal out of the water, he'd be renowned in intelligence circles, not to mention potentially saving the world from imminent disaster. The Lieutenant knew how to be dramatic, but if you are making it up, you might as well make it big.

Two bearded guys with a healthy swath of black hair appeared in the distance, dawdling along the outer path of the park, stopping to watch the ships passing by and munching on a cone of french fries. The Lieutenant wished he had some of those tasty fries, he loved eating them, even in his imagination. Not far behind the thugs were a group of young women in some of the tightest, shortest skirts he'd ever seen. Times had changed in the former Yugoslavia, sex and the city now included the city of Belgrade. He couldn't help but wonder if the girls were somehow part of the operation, designed to draw attention away from the two guys. Unfortunately, they had drawn the Lieutenant's attention and now he'd lost his target. Panic set in quickly as he scanned the perimeter, catching site of a group performing a traditional Serbian dance, dressed in full regalia to achieve maximum effect.

How could these two guys just disappear? The Lieutenant finally realized they had sat down on a bench near the wall overlooking the Danube. A close call. If he lost them, he'd be in big trouble. He took a deep breath and his heart started beating again. He found a decent field of vision just in time to catch the contact move in and join the thugs on the bench, a motley crew for sure. The Lieutenant couldn't understand how people like this lived with themselves. Did they have an utter disregard for the value of human life or the suffering of others? Or, was it pure greed?

The Lieutenant was well poised to get decent pictures of the meeting with his superspy camera, the latest high-tech gadget available, hidden within his sunglasses and operated by a voice activated system. Say the magic word and voila. Click one, two—a couple of steps to the right and a few more snaps. He was very pleased with his photography work, but he'd love to hear their conversation. However, that was someone else's job, another super spy with another high tech gadget, picking up whispers from more than a hundred yards away. He'd hear the tapes later, right now it was his job to keep an eye on the meeting and get as many pictures as possible. Hopefully, these thugs would find themselves on a rendition trip to an undisclosed location, compliments of the U.S. government. Plenty of folks were complaining about the use of renditions, but he understood it, agreed with it, felt sure it was making us all a little safer. These were the bad guys, they were hurting people. The Lieutenant was on the side of right and usually, the side of might as well. Of course, it was easy to be the tough guy wielding brute force when it was only in one's imagination.

It was a bit of force that brought him back to the cafeteria, when one of his buddies gave him a walloping slap on the back. "Where are you Lieutenant? We've asked you three times what time the soccer game is this Saturday."

"Oh, sorry. I was just thinking about..." fortunately he stopped in time. They wouldn't understand. He didn't even understand, but he always had a good time on these little excursions. "...about the report I'm working on, pretty serious stuff, has me a bit distracted. The game is at two in the afternoon, should be a good one against those marines. They think they're the toughest guys around."

"Speaking of reports, it's time we all got back to work. Need to earn our keep around here," said one of his sergeants. They cleared away their table, adding to the recycling bins, what few were available. It made no sense that an operation the size of the Pentagon couldn't manage a better recycling program. But that required private companies willing to collect and process the stuff and apparently there wasn't a big market for that in Virginia. Even with all these progressive, tree hugging democrats around D.C., they couldn't seem to make a dent in moving the green revolution forward.

The Lieutenant knew he needed to get back to his desk, but who would notice if he was gone for a few more minutes. He couldn't resist venturing back to Belgrade to see if the Iranians had shown up. They hadn't, but a couple of even more sexy Serbian girls in very short skirts had and they were getting plenty of attention, and not just from him. The bad guys were checking out the merchandise, the female merchandise, and appeared to be paying little attention to anything else. Those long legs barely disappeared beneath their three-inch skirts and their well-rounded cheeks threatened to fall out the back side. A man could hardly be blamed for losing his focus, even one on a covert mission involving highly dangerous chemicals that could destroy the world. Women rule the world, even without trying. These women had no clue what was going down just a few yards away. Or did they? Were they actually part of the plan, a distraction from the meeting? The Lieutenant doubted their involvement, they were too young and there were too many of them.

Out of the corner of his eye he noticed a couple of guys approaching, eating bags of popcorn, and carrying a copy of Blic, a local newspaper. Maybe they were Iranians, he couldn't be sure, he didn't really know what an Iranian was supposed to look like. And even if he did, wouldn't they try to disguise themselves, they couldn't afford to stand out. Serbian prison wasn't high on their list of tourist destinations. The Iranians were there to make the introduction, see if these Serbs were for real and get the hell out of town. Nothing serious was going to happen today, no matter what the Serbs or the Lieutenant thought. They were sure they were being watched and they were right. Silently they were laughing, between bites of popcorn and occasional glances at the newspaper — as if they could read Serbian — at the apparent inability of CIA agents to remain anonymous.

When the Lieutenant took a closer look he saw the Iranians stroll past the Serbian contacts, walk to the observation point and double back around, finally sitting down on a bench, away — far away, from the sexy group of girls. Not that they weren't interested. Women in Iran would never wear so little, but they knew better than to be distracted, they were serious about this job, even if today was just a decoy. They had plenty to learn on this trip.

And the Lieutenant had plenty to learn as well. He wanted to make a name for himself in the spy world, as a man who could be trusted and more importantly, who could deliver the merchandise. He wanted to nail these guys and be the big shot that broke up the Iranian nuclear mafia. Besides that, he'd be saving the world from annihilation, no doubt promoted to a five star general — skipping past the first four handily. They'd probably make a movie about him and not least of all, he'd be seen as the ultimate stud by his dear Amy. Not that she wasn't duly impressed already, or so he assumed.

Just as the Serbians approached the park bench with the Iranians, the Lieutenant heard someone call his name. Oh crap, his cover was blown. He'd be caught, perhaps killed, at the very least thrown out of the CIA. When he felt the tap on his shoulder he was swiftly transported back to reality — a quick ride from Belgrade to Virginia. The Lieutenant looked up to find his boss standing over him with a sullen look that didn't bode well for him.

"Lieutenant, do you have something more important to do than finish that report?" his boss asked.

"No sir," and in a moment of quick reaction the Lieutenant bounced back with, "in fact I was just contemplating the next section — the final section — so I could finish it this afternoon. I find that it helps to think away from my desk." Though his boss gave a suspicious look, he let it pass and suggested he try to think from his desk for the rest of the day, finalizing that report before going home. The Lieutenant wasted no time in packing up his man purse and heading back to this post. Belgrade would have to wait.

Back at his desk, the Lieutenant chided himself, not only for getting caught, but for his insufferable daydreaming. But he couldn't waste time, he had to finish this report and he was nowhere as close as he'd insinuated to his boss. Now he'd be working until at least 7:00 p.m., if he was lucky. He better call Amy and let her know he'd be late. She was easy enough to convince that he had truly important work to do — that his government needed him more than she did.

The Lieutenant left a message for Amy at home. She wasn't back from the street fair apparently and didn't answer her cell. Maybe she was selling loads of her jewelry or perhaps she had run off with one of those Serbian thugs. Neither one was very likely. She had invested a lot of time, and no small amount of money, in her jewelry business, with precious little in return. But he knew how much she enjoyed it, so he couldn't begrudge her this hobby. He wasn't actually worried about whether she made any money, but he wished she'd invest a little less.

But now it was time for him to invest some serious thought and time into this policy report. Otherwise, he'd be here all night. He'd have to do some more research, get into some classified files—as far as his security clearance would allow—and come up with some reasonable recommendations. The situation in Afghanistan seemed to deteriorate by the moment with continued revelations of corruption, bank fraud, general mismanagement—it seemed there was no end to the disappearance of U.S. tax dollars. No one had ever been able to control that part of the world. The U.S. was up against a formidable foe in the "great game"— the struggle for empire. The Lieutenant hoped there were no Afghans in the park back in Belgrade. Iranians he might have a shot against, the Afghans—not likely.

Three hours later, still struggling to finish the report, the Lieutenant made his way to the cafeteria for a little caffeine boost—a Dr. Pepper, his favorite but a rare treat. He considered a snickers bar but decided he'd have to run two extra miles to burn off that many calories. Refusing to linger long around the cafeteria for fear of being confronted again by a superior officer, even at this late hour, he decided to take a stroll along one of the corridors. At this time of the night, at any hour actually, there were people at work here. It was quieter at night, but there was still plenty of activity. What he didn't expect to see was two four-star generals heading into a secure area where he, of course, had never been. He only recognized them because he'd seen them on television occasionally. This was odd, something was up.

The Lieutenant retreated quickly to the cafeteria, turning on the television to see if he'd missed some major world event, but there were only the usual beltway squabbles and politics. He felt a twinge of pride that he might well be ahead of the game, with inside knowledge of a major event that would break by morning, when he could brag to Amy and perhaps his colleagues that he had seen it coming. Now he wanted to stay as late as possible, feigning continued work duties, to see if he might catch a glimpse of them again, or others who might join. But then he realized his imagination was running amuck again. Even if he did see them, so what? He wasn't going to learn anything, perhaps there wasn't anything to learn.

Down that long sterile corridor behind the secure area, serious conversations were underway, fingers were being pointed, plans debated, but no solutions reached. Who knew what, when did they know, how many — hopefully few — knew? Oh to be a fly on the wall, to see how, if, they could wiggle their way out of this one. They'd be lucky not to go to jail, perhaps to escape being tarred and feathered. But their hubris left them with a misplaced sense of being able to, yet again avoid blame. They assumed they were smarter than the rest of the world, or at least smarter than the people they needed to outsmart. Containment was the key, but what would it take to contain this situation. They couldn't be sure about who was involved and the extent of their knowledge. Too many people in too many locations had become part of this quickly unraveling scenario.

It became clear that no resolution was going to be reached tonight and the arrogance, or blind hope, that the U.S. could always find a resolution — one in its best interest — led them to abandon the discussion. With clearer heads tomorrow, perhaps they could find some innovative and realistic solutions. The group began to disband and leave the building individually, avoiding attention that could raise eyebrows or worse a reporter's microphone.

The Lieutenant was putting the finishing touches on his report when he saw General Foley, one of the best known and most disliked generals, stroll past and head, presumably, for the nearest exit. He waited intentionally for another fifteen minutes or so to see who else might emerge, only to be disappointed when no one, other than the night watchman, passed his way. He was already an hour past the time he promised Amy he'd be home, so he put aside his imagination, and his unproductive surveillance, and headed for the exit himself.

He didn't see General Foley, or any other generals for that matter, on his way out and certainly not on the metro when he was headed home. Generals didn't take the metro, or so he thought. But he did see that same guy he'd notice a couple of times around the house and on his way to and from work. Before he had chalked it up to coincidence, figured this guy took the same route to work or lived in the neighborhood, but at this late hour he found it a bit suspicious. It even made him a bit nervous and not many things made him nervous. With so few people on the metro, he grew concerned this guy might be planning to rob him, especially given how dark some of the stations were. Metro wasn't good at replacing light bulbs.

Trying to appear confident, the Lieutenant took stock of who was in his train car, realizing there was only one teenage couple at the back. He considered whether he needed to get off at the next stop and grab a cab, but decided it was safer to wait until they were at an above ground station. There would be better light and he could make a quick exit to the street. Maybe the Lieutenant was letting his imagination run away with him again, but the guy appeared to be keeping an eye on him at every stop, ready to jump off and follow him if necessary. He grew even more concerned when the couple got off at the next stop and he was left alone in the car with this creep. To calm his nerves and not make himself look suspicious, the Lieutenant pulled out a paperback he kept in his backpack and began to read, glancing nonchalantly, every few minutes, over the top to see what this guy was up to.

The Alexandria station couldn't come soon enough. Even though the Lieutenant kept telling himself this was just another Joe on his way home, he wasn't convinced. Sure enough, the guy followed him out of the train, keeping a respectable distance. The Lieutenant, with a brisk gait, headed to the turnstile and got into the street light as quickly as possible. The next time he managed a look, he couldn't see the guy anywhere. But just because he didn't see him, didn't mean he wasn't there.

CHAPTER THIRTEEN

Out on the ocean Justin and Amelia were taking in the beauty of the full moon, round and golden, so low in the sky it felt as if you could reach out and grab it. There was a stillness on the ocean, hardly a sound beyond the occasional fish jumping from the water. The dolphins had departed for their own private party. Small ripples of water caressed the side of the boat making a rhythmic rocking that could easily put one to sleep. But, how could anyone sleep under a moon so bright. Amelia wondered if it always looked this way so near the equator or whether this was just her lucky night.

"I ordered it especially for you," Justin said.

"What?" Amelia asked, not catching on to what he was saying.

"The moon, of course, or didn't you notice?"

"How could I NOT notice? It's amazing, but forgive me for not believing you had a hand in that," she said pointing skyward.

"Oh you of little faith," he laughed, "you really give me no credit."

"Yeah, right—but at least I give you credit for getting me out here at the perfect moment to see just how amazing it is." She was sure that was no accident, he'd been here long enough to know the peak viewing time. What was he up to?

"Not to disappoint, but the bright light makes it easier for me to find the traps and collect my specimens." Amelia's heart sank a little at Justin's proclamation, but she chose not to believe him, at least not completely. Justin, on the other hand, was pleased with how cool he'd played this moment. He normally picked up the specimens in the daytime but she didn't need to know that, at least not at this particular moment.

Justin pulled the boat alongside a small island, if such a small piece of land qualified as an island, and put down anchor very gently to avoid hitting any coral — which reminded him of why he really should do this in the daytime. Although, he'd done this so many times he practically had these spots memorized. The last thing he wanted to do was destroy the already imperiled coral, nor did he want to step on it and get cut. That stuff was vicious, especially the fire coral which was so beautiful, but so very painful if you touched it.

Justin waded into the water, wearing his aqua socks for protection, large flashlight in hand. Before he even reached the trap he could see the door was open and he knew he wouldn't find anything inside. The lock was cut, clearly intentional.

Amelia could see the disappointment on Justin's face, even in this pale moonlight. He'd been working so hard trying to figure out what was going on. They desperately needed the specimens to figure out what was maiming and killing the sea life he so wanted to protect. Amelia was disappointed, too. She was vested in this now and wanted to know the source of the contamination. She wondered why someone would deliberately cut the locks.

"Hand me that tool box, please," Justin requested. "I think I've got a new lock in there to replace this one." Amelia stumbled around the boat trying to find the tool box, almost falling overboard when her foot found it first.

Once he got a new lock on and put the trap back in place, they moved on to another location, hoping for better luck. Amelia thought she heard something in the water, but figured she was just spooked and didn't bother to mention it to Justin. This spot was even more remote than the last one, tucked away on the back side of a bigger island in a small inlet that would be easy to miss even in daylight. But at least better fortune awaited them, the trap held an octopus, but in this dim light they couldn't see whether it had deformities.

Justin, happy to find a specimen to work with, quickly grabbed the octopus and threw it into the tub of sea water inside the boat. He checked the trap again and found a couple of large prawns that he also threw in the tub before replacing the lock and jumping back into the boat, just in time to hear the sound Amelia had heard earlier. Though neither of them could see it, a boat was approaching, the whine of the motor low but clearly audible and growing louder. Their location in the island made it difficult to see who might be approaching and besides, it happened so fast there wasn't much time to focus on details. When the shots rang out they knew they were in trouble. It was a rapid fire succession, pop-pop-pop. Was it one gun or more? They couldn't tell. It was all so surreal that all they could do was react. Fortunately Justin reacted quickly.

"Get down," Justin yelled as he physically threw himself on top of Amelia. He grabbed the flare gun from the emergency kit, getting off a shot with lightning speed. He hoped it might scare them off, a flare was no match for the bullets that had pierced the side of their boat, but he had to do something. Besides, they might get lucky, someone else — someone not wanting to shoot them — might be in the area and come to their rescue. Pop-pop-pop, there it was again, another round of fire as they sped away in what appeared to be a long black speed boat. Although, it was still difficult to see in the low light. It was impossible to see the face or faces of those onboard.

"Are you ok? Were you hit?" he asked Amelia, who was literally shaking with fear.

"I'm fine," she managed, putting on a bold face but he knew she was scared. He was scared. "What the hell was that all about?" He wished he knew, but for now he was just glad they neither of them had been hit. With flashlight once again in hand, Justin surveyed the boat to see what kind of damage it had sustained. Other than a couple of small bullet holes in the fiberglass they seemed to be in good shape. Fortunately the holes were well above water level, and while they would definitely need to be repaired, they'd be able to get back to shore without taking on water. At least he hoped they'd be able to get back without the shooter coming back for more target practice.

"Let's get out of here, fast," Justin said as he fired up the engine and pointed the boat's nose toward the island's shoreline. He was trying hard to hide his trepidation, knowing full well the other boat could be lurking behind one of the many small islands, ready to pick them off as they passed by. So much for his plans of turning this into a romantic evening. Surviving this incident would no doubt create a bond between them, but it definitely wasn't what he had in mind. Getting to play the savior is a great role for a man, but you want the danger to be more perceived than real.

On the ride back to shore, a million possibilities went through Amelia's mind, none of which made any sense to her. Why was someone shooting at them? She bounced around some bizarre theories, everything from a local mafia to an international gang of thugs. Could it be someone from the island?

Thoughts were racing through Justin's head as well, but he didn't think it was anyone from the island. He feared they'd stumbled onto a much bigger situation than a few dead fish and he certainly didn't want to be swimming with them. A sinister side was developing to this situation, one he wasn't happy about, but one that made it all the more intriguing and, unfortunately, dangerous. There must be a bigger story and they needed to find out what it was, preferably without anybody getting shot. Was it just the panic of the moment, was his mind running amuck, or was there a real secret here, something dark and dangerous, something the world didn't need to know about? Were they really on to something or were they just in the wrong place at the wrong time?

Under the lights of the pier, they got a better look at the damage to the boat and realized how lucky they were not to have been hit. "We have to go to the police," Amelia noted and Justin nodded in agreement, seemingly lost in a trance as he stared at the bullet holes. Amelia had to wonder if he was more shaken than her or if was just trying to make some sense of it all.

Justin naturally knew the police chief personally and, in fact, had his phone number on his cell. This was part of the reason Justin was so startled by it all. He knew everyone here and as far as he could tell, they liked him. Why would someone try to kill him? But he had to consider that it wasn't necessarily someone who lived on the island. In fact, it was highly unlikely. There wasn't much crime in Panzau but when it did happen, it wasn't too hard to solve. The local culture required people to apologize to their victims and make reparations; likewise, the victim should accept the apology. Though it was a system that some found odd, it worked for this small family oriented community. Otherwise, living peacefully all these years would have remained elusive.

The police chief wasted no time getting to the dock. He liked Justin a lot, and he liked peace and quiet in his community. He was going to get to the bottom of this. The chief paced the pier, rubbing his chin, trying to imagine a motive, without any success. He called his investigators, taking them away from their families at this late hour, to make pictures and get statements from Justin and Amelia. But they didn't really mind, they had so few opportunities to investigate a crime, this actually excited them. Not that they hoped for more crime, but it was a reprieve from the day to day boredom they usually felt.

"Bullet holes indicate a .22," said one of the young investigators after getting a close up look. Fairly typical ammunition you could buy almost anywhere, but not in Panzau. The island didn't have any gun or ammunition shops. If you wanted them you had to buy off island. There was little need for weapons, no hunting, nothing to protect oneself from — usually.

"Not much else we can do here tonight," noted the other investigator, "We've got their statements, the pictures, and we've roped off the slip here as a crime scene. Probably won't make Mr. Signo happy to lose the use of his boat, not to mention the damage. Last time he loans it to you Justin," the investigator said with a chuckle, adding, "and he may raise your rent."

Rent was the last thing on Justin's mind, though he did appreciate an attempt at some humor — he needed a laugh. While he tried hard to convince himself that this was all a mistake, that these shots were meant for someone else, he couldn't shake the feeling that he was, in fact, the real target. What he had to find out now, was why.

At this moment, he was more concerned with Amelia's well-being and getting her back to the hotel. She'd held up amazingly well, but he was afraid that tough exterior she so proudly displayed was just that and inside she might be about to collapse. When he said he'd take her back to the hotel, she suggested they go to Pete's instead, for a drink. That suited him, he could use a stiff one after what happened tonight. But, first they needed to stash the latest specimens, all of which were dead, in a secure place. Normally that would be his lab tank, but after all that had happened in the past few days, he knew that would be a huge risk. Amelia's quick thinking suggested they hide them in one of the, currently empty, sea water fish tanks at the restaurant. Luckily there was no health inspector to worry about, unlike in the U.S., and besides they'd retrieve them first thing in the morning before the catch of the day arrived and someone mistakenly cooked them for lunch.

A couple of gin and tonics later, Amelia and Justin had analyzed every possible scenario for tonight's attack, not the least of which was mistaken identity. That was wishful thinking on their part. Rogue fisherman, foreign military, rival islanders, Thai cross dressers — they'd come up with them all, and the more they drank the more colorful the options became. Luckily they were within walking distance of the hotel and Justin's apartment as well, so no driving under the influence. They could stumble home in safety, earlier events notwithstanding, and hopefully get a decent night's sleep. Tomorrow would bring a lot of work and clearer heads needed to prevail, both to figure out what happened tonight and to solve this mystery.

Justin walked Amelia to her bungalow, even though she told him it wasn't necessary. He could have left her at the front entrance but given what happened before at her room coupled with tonight's event, he wasn't taking any chances. Besides, he wanted more time with her, especially now that his inhibitions were relaxed by the gin and tonic. As she rumbled through her purse for the keys, he began to rub his hand across her back. At first she froze, wondering how she should respond. She turned to face him anticipating what she might say, but there was no time. He kissed her, in a brief, too brief, moment, before backing off and apologizing. He was clearly embarrassed though not regretful. Before she could say anything he took the key, opened her door and was gone.

Amelia, despite all that had happened, maybe because of it, couldn't seem to get to sleep, which turned out to be convenient when her mother called again in the middle of the night. Fortunately, Amelia thought better of telling her mother what had happened tonight; otherwise, she'd demand that she get on the next plane out of there.

"How's it going with Mr. Right?" she asked.

"What are you talking about?" Amelia replied.

"You know what I'm talking about — that Jared, or Jake or whatever his name is — Mr. Marine Biologist." Oh dear, her mother really was too much, but she wasn't about to tell her what had just occurred between them.

"Do you know what time it is?" Amelia asked.

"Of course I do, I've been telling time since I was 4 years old. It's 2 p.m. and I thought I could catch you before you went to bed and not wake you up again."

"Mother, it's 2 p.m. where you are — it's 2 a.m. here, there's a twelve hour time difference!" Amelia said, emphasizing the here.

"Oh dear, I'm so sorry. I just can't seem to adjust to this time difference. I'll do better next time, but since I have you awake now, has he asked you to marry him yet?"

Amelia didn't know why she bothered to get into these conversations with her mother, there was no winning. The next time she called, Amelia would tell her mother the wedding invitation was in the mail and that she'd better rush out and buy a yellow mother-of-the-bride gown. Or better yet, Amelia would tell her mother they had married on the island and ask her to plan a reception for their return to the U.S. next week. That would get her wound up. Except, then her mother would accuse Amelia of being facetious and having no concern for her.

Amelia managed to cut the conversation short by saying she had only a couple of hours left for sleep and, more importantly, that she had to meet Mr. Marine Biologist first thing in the morning. That encouraged her mother to hang up so that Amelia could get some "beauty sleep" and look her best for Justin. But, once off the phone, sleep didn't come easily, perhaps because she was still so tense from being shot at — imagine — or perhaps because she thought she heard someone outside her window. Although, she suspected that was truly her imagination.

That 6:30 a.m. wakeup call came very early, especially after that 2:00 a.m. call from her mother. But, Amelia, eager to have some answers today, managed to get out of bed and get ready in short order. She'd promised to meet Justin back at the restaurant at 7:00 a.m., both for breakfast and to collect their specimens. This time he was the one running late, apologizing profusely when he showed up at 7:20 a.m., clearly with bed head and looking generally disheveled.

"Sorry for being late. Given this was my first time to be shot at, I couldn't seem to get to sleep." He seemed to be avoiding the obvious elephant in the room, but Amelia wasn't going to bring up the kiss. Besides, she wouldn't know what to say.

"Well, I got another call from my mother in the middle of the night," Amelia said.

"Sorry about that, she can't seem to get the hang of the time difference, huh?"

"Apparently not, "Amelia said with a laugh.

After a short stack of pancakes and two cups of coffee they were ready to take on the world, even though they didn't realize that was pretty much what they were up against. Hiding the specimens at the restaurant had been a good call, no one had noticed them and they grabbed the bag and were on their way to the lab. Although neither one dared to say it aloud, they both hoped the lab was still there when they arrived. Given the previous attack on the lab and the shooting incident last night, it appeared they were getting a little too close to the truth and someone wanted to shut them down.

Fortunately, the lab was still standing and there was no evidence anything had been tampered with. Word had spread quickly, as it always did in Panzau, about the shooting last night. Although the staff wasn't in yet, they had all called to see if Justin and Amelia were ok. They were flabbergasted as to why someone would want to attack the lab or Justin. The folks of Panzau were generally a peaceful lot, it was hard for them to imagine this violent attack, especially against someone they cared about. They preferred to live and let live, but now their own quiet and peaceful existence had been pierced.

Justin got to work immediately, examining the severely deformed octopus. Not only did it have extra limbs, there was an unusual fluorescent yellow tint on its tentacles. Under the microscope it appeared to be a skin rash with a series of bumps producing the yellow color. When Amelia took a look, it sparked her memory of a case with similar deformities to ducks found in a contaminated pond. Run-off from a local chemical plant made its way into nearby ponds, killing off all the ducks and most of the fish in the area. While Justin did further examinations, Amelia began her research about this previous incident, trying to determine what chemicals were involved and whether it could possibly do the same to marine life.

About mid-morning, the start of the day for most employees on this island, the Police Chief wandered in to discuss last night's events and see how the two of them were holding up. There wasn't any news to report, the bullets found in the boat were being analyzed but with their meager lab the most information they were likely to get was the type of gun. If they were lucky they might be able to trace the ammunition to the point of purchase, but only if they got some help from a bigger law enforcement agency.

Justin was more concerned with what he was seeing under the microscope than what the chief had to say. He'd never seen anything like it and every time he found a new specimen the deformities seemed to be worse. This couldn't be a natural phenomenon, which made it even scarier. What was the source—some government experiment gone awry, the unfortunate results of commercial testing, or worse, intentional poisoning? But who would do that and why? Justin was afraid of the answers to those questions.

Amelia, on the other hand, wanted to know who was trying to kill her and, more importantly, why; two questions the chief didn't have any answers for, at least not yet. He pressed Amelia for more information — did she see anyone, what did the boat look like, how could someone have gotten close enough to shoot without her and Justin noticing? She freely admitted she'd heard something, a hum similar to a motor, perhaps some voices. But there were lots of noises — the water lapping against the shore, owls, tree frogs, she wasn't expecting guns shots. What she did fail to mention was the distraction of being out in the moonlight with Justin, but that was information the chief didn't need to know, and which Justin, certainly didn't need to know.

The Chief said he'd be in touch when he had more information and asked if they wanted protection, said he could spare a couple of deputies to keep an eye on the lab. Amelia wanted to take him up on the offer, but Justin quickly declined. Amelia didn't know whether these guys were trained in protection, but from her perspective their presence might bring some peace of mind. Nonetheless, Justin seemed adamant that it wasn't necessary. He thanked the chief but said he "didn't want to take his men, who were plenty busy" — now that was a stretch — "away from their regular work protecting the good citizens of Panzau." The Chief didn't push the issue, he figured Justin was a big boy and capable of taking care of himself; and as for Amelia, he knew Justin would take care of her — it was clear he had his eye on her.

Amelia stayed busy most of the morning with her research, but she was distracted, and not just by Justin. Every sound made her jump, even the benign ones like the scraggly dogs scavenging in the garbage cans and the chatter of the local birds. Given last night's scare, not to mention the surprise of the kiss, it was hard to focus. She had checked out several reports about toxic substances harming animals and tried to recreate some of her previous research.

Justin asked her to pull together a list of toxic substances and the companies producing them. It was a shot in the dark but they had to start somewhere. Amelia gave up her research and starting looking for the information Justin wanted. Finding companies in the U.S. and Europe wasn't too difficult, but for Asia and most of the developing world, it was another matter. The material needed serious organization if it was going to have any practical use, so Amelia developed a spreadsheet identifying the company, where its labs where, and the various toxins being produced. Most of this information wasn't necessarily reliable or up to date, but she listed everything she could find, they'd sort it out later. Better to have too much information rather than not enough; although, it would take some time to wade through it all. They got so caught up in the work that the entire morning slipped away and it was only when Justin's stomach began to growl that they realized it was 1:30 p.m. The two of them decided to head over to Pete's for a quick burger.

All the talk at Pete's, of course, was about the shooting last night. Everyone was shocked, concerned, and wanted to get the story first hand. The rumor mill had been rampant all morning and not entirely accurate. The stories ran the gamut from the boat being sunk to Amelia taking a hit in the leg. There was plenty of speculation about Justin and Amelia, out on the ocean under the "honey" moon — the romantics were looking for a love story.

Justin was clearly distracted and more than a little baffled by the whole situation, so much so that he didn't even hear Amelia when she excused herself for the ladies room. When he looked across the table and found her missing, Justin had a moment of panic. The likelihood that someone would kidnap her at Pete's was pretty slim, but yesterday at this time he would have sworn their chances of being shot at on the ocean were nonexistent.

Amelia reappeared looking a bit startled. "Who's the cook here?" she asked.

"Manny Rikati. Why?" Justin replied, curious as to what this was all about.

"Well, the ladies room has a window next to the kitchen and I heard him talking about how several of the squid that came in this morning 'looked funny'. Apparently he thinks they are some kind of delicacy and plans to serve them. I don't think that's a good idea, someone could get sick, seriously sick. Should we talk to him?"

Justin didn't bother to answer her question. He barreled through the kitchen door and started screaming loud enough for everyone in Pete's to hear him. Poor Manny didn't know what he'd gotten himself into, with the squid or with Justin. Justin demanded that he hand over all of the deformed seafood or he would go straight to the health inspector — who, as he well knew, probably wouldn't do anything about it. But Manny didn't want any trouble with Justin and he certainly didn't want to risk anyone getting sick. Even though he could take the opportunity to blame it on "Pete," sick customers wouldn't be good for business. Justin bagged up the squid and a couple of grouper from Manny's stock, threw some money on the table and grabbed Amelia by the hand. They were getting out of there, Justin was livid and needed to cool off, somewhere else.

Back at the lab Justin felt bad about his overreaction with Manny, but his nerves were on edge, understandably so. After examining the squid and grouper he saw similarities with the octopus and shrimp he found last night. There were extra tentacles, the same rash, and the unnatural fluorescent color. He wanted to find out where Manny got this catch, but decided it could wait until tomorrow when the tension died down.

Meanwhile, Amelia was compiling the list of companies producing toxins, which continued to grow steadily. As she compiled the list, she was surprised at the amount of information readily available; although, she wondered whether any of it would prove useful for their situation. Whoever was involved — a corporation, a government, a rogue person — wasn't likely to leave a trail, at least not one they could easily find. This kind of toxicity, if left unchecked, could threaten a lot of lives, including hers and Justin's. Amelia was starting to comprehend why someone was shooting at them.

CHAPTER FOURTEEN

A staff meeting, a rarity at the Taiwan facility, had been called for noon. No doubt, it would cut into their already short lunch break. Lin wondered what could be so important that Mr. Kao would actually call a meeting. Imaginations were running wild in the lab this morning — would they be shut down, were some people being fired, was their pay going to be cut? Who knew what might happen with that moron at the helm. Everyone was very nervous, especially after the most recent accident and the visit of the suits. Lin didn't even want to consider the possibility of the lab closing. There had to be a better life for her son, and for the moment, working here was the only way she could make that happen.

Lin imagined a world where young Bingwen didn't have to walk up the hill every morning, beautiful as it was, to be belittled and yelled out by the likes of a Mr. Kao. Many a night she had laid awake in bed with visions of him as a doctor, inventing a cure for some terrible disease or caring for sick children. Perhaps he'd become an engineer designing spaceships or building robots, real world-changing work. She had no concept of how complicated that work might be and as unfortunate, or perhaps fortunate, as it was, she had no clue what her work was doing to change, or possibly harm, the world. For her, it didn't really matter anymore, she knew that door was closed. But, she was looking out the window to another world, a better world where Bingwen had not just the talent, but the opportunity to be all that Lin had never had the chance to be.

But now was not the time for day dreaming, Lin had work to do and if she didn't hurry up she'd be staying late.

If her son was to have a better life, she had to get home at a decent hour to tutor him. If only Gang would put in as much effort as she did with this child, no doubt he'd be a genius. Instead he only wanted to play with him and only when it suited his schedule. Gang had long ago lost any ambition, if he ever had any to start with. Providing the basic necessities for Bingwen was ambitious enough for him and even that he failed at most of the time.

At noon, in his perversely magnanimous way, Mr. Kao allowed the staff to eat their lunch outside while he held his precious meeting. Apparently, this was his idea of multi-tasking, multi-tasking on his employee's time. He wasn't inclined to lose a productive moment, or so he believed. Mr. Kao had no clue they would take the time back in their own way. Management skills were just one of the many challenges this country faced. With many more just like Mr. Kao, no doubt they were doomed to subordination by China or some other world power.

The meeting began on a benign enough note with Mr. Kao thanking them for their efforts, a rarity from him, but an obviously insincere attempt to garner loyalty and buffer what was to follow. He made it clear the lab was in trouble. Of course, they'd figured that out for themselves even before the suits showed up. They had to produce, had to develop a reliable product without blowing the place up. The pressure was on, they had a month to get it right or their jobs were in jeopardy. To drive that point home, he informed them that an investigation was underway regarding the most recent explosion. Whoever was found responsible would be fired. What a happy end to the meeting, Mr. Kao thought fear would inspire them to greatness. That might work on some people — not many — but certainly not on Lin, she was smarter than most.

With their lunchtime wasted on the meeting, there was no time to discuss what it all meant. The gossip would have to wait for the walk home. Some folks were agitated, scared perhaps, but most went on as always. They'd heard this song before, though today there was a more serious tone.

There was a new formula, one that came with enhanced safety precautions. Typically they were advised to wear gloves, masks, sometimes other protective gear — when in reality, it should have always been mandatory. Their safety wasn't the concern to whoever was funding this mysterious enterprise, but now the instructions required full hazmat suits. Lin was often left to wonder what kind of chemicals they were actually dealing with, what happened when they were combined, and whether there were long-term health consequences. Knowing she wouldn't get any answers to these questions, she tried to ignore the obvious hazards to herself and her co-workers — sometimes ignorance is bliss. In the end, did it really matter? What difference would it make to any of them? They really had no options. Her expectations were low, she just hoped there wouldn't be another explosion.

By the middle of the afternoon they'd manage to mix up a small portion of the new formula. Mr. Kao had, wisely for once, advised that they try it on a small scale. If there was an explosion; hopefully, it wouldn't be so severe. The lab looked as if it had been invaded by aliens with everyone suited up in the pale green hazmat jumpsuits and oversized goggles.

When the first batch panned out without incident, other than melting some plastic equipment, they decided to expand the quantity and hope for the best. Lin carefully followed the instructions, not only for the quantity, but the order in which the chemicals were combined. Once the chemicals were combined she sent them to the centrifuge room for her colleagues to do their magic. Despite the initial success — at least there was no explosion — she was relieved to have it out of her section, not because she feared being fired if something went wrong, but because she was concerned about harm to her and her co-workers. Lin's normal Zen-like mood had an ominous feeling today and she wasn't sure why. She hoped it was her imagination, but more likely it was the result of Mr. Kao's bad karma spilling over into her life.

Whatever it was, her intuition was right on target. She smelled the burning and felt her eyes begin to sting at least a minute or two before the explosion rang out, blowing a hole in the tin roof over the centrifuge room. The lab fell into utter chaos and everyone was running for the door. Lin froze, but someone grabbed her, pulling her out of the building and back into reality.

That reality included something akin to a small mushroom cloud forming over the top of the building. Everyone in town would be able to see it shortly. The fire department was already on their way. The sirens could easily be heard heading up the hill, the strained shriek of their tired old water wagons wafting across the valley. She heard Mr. Kao whining as he was pulled to safety through his office window, cautioning them not to damage his suit. A fine time to think about appearances. He was lucky anyone bothered to rescue him, especially after that staff meeting. It was quite a sight to see him being pulled from his office window, his short legs unable to reach the ground without assistance. Lin wasn't sure whether his door was blocked or whether he was just so scared he panicked and went for the window. But, he was flailing about like a fish, arms and legs in all directions, glasses pushed up on his forehead and his precious suit all askew.

By the time the local fire brigade laboriously made its way up the mountainside to the lab, the damage was pretty much done. Having escaped his office, Mr. Kao was sitting under a divine tree, coughing and yelling for someone to bring him some water. Lucky for him, at least physically, his exposure was limited to smoke inhalation. But he might not be so lucky with the suits, they were not going to be happy.

A few of the workers were pretty badly burned and had to be transported to the local hospital. Most were suffering from the exposure to the fumes, eyes burning and skin itching severely. The fire chief ordered the lab closed for the rest of the day and sent everyone home with a word of caution that he would be talking to them later as part of his investigation. Mr. Kao headed straight to the nearest bar for some soothing libations. Lin and her coworkers headed home, glad to have an early furlough; although, not under these circumstances. It was a miracle the injuries weren't more serious given the size of the explosion. But perhaps it was the long-term effects that would prove to be the real danger, only time would tell.

"I'm doomed, my career is over," Mr. Kao repeated over and over, noticeably slurring his words as the rice wine kicked in. "Why me, why me? Those idiot employees of mine, they were out to get me." He seemed to have forgotten they were only doing as they were told, by him, and that someone else altogether developed the formula. Not to mention that people were injured, some sent to the hospital. No one paid much attention to him, undaunted by his selfishness and lack of concern for others. His reputation was widely known. He wasn't well liked.

Mrs. Kao, well aware of her husband's tendency to imbibe heavily when under stress, decided to take the situation in hand when she heard what happened at the lab. She knew he was under scrutiny. Although, he didn't talk much about it at home his irritability and continued sniping at her told her what he wasn't saying. Rather than let him embarrass himself further and possibly kill himself in a drunken stupor, she began perusing the local hangouts to rescue him, from himself. It didn't take long, there weren't many places he could be. When she found him, Mr. Kao was laid out on a wooden bench, moaning, occasionally throwing out another "why me?" and in danger of falling to the floor — a concrete floor, that while it probably wouldn't kill him, might result in some broken bones. She had enough trouble taking care of him, she didn't need an invalid on her hands.

It was no small task to talk him out of the bar. If she'd been a bigger, heartier woman, no doubt she would've just yanked him up by the hair of the head and drug him the entire two miles home. With a little man handling of her own, which thoroughly embarrassed him, she managed to get him into a car and back home before something even more embarrassing happened. How could men be such dim wits? They couldn't handle life's little challenges without falling apart. If women were like that, the world would've gone to hell in a hand basket a long time ago.

All the way home Mr. Kao continued to repeat his mantra of doom—"I'm ruined, ruined I tell you. I'll be fired by morning for sure." Though Mrs. Kao didn't know the details, she seriously doubted he was in that much jeopardy. It was likely to require some proverbial ass-kissing, but if her husband had any talent, that was at the top of the list. He'd survive, he always did.

Perhaps that was wishful thinking on her part. If he was indeed fired, not only would he have lost a decent job but he'd be hard pressed to find another one with that black mark on his record. That would mean she'd have to find work and that wasn't a happy prospect for her. Being married to him was hard enough, but at least he provided for the family. If she had to be the breadwinner and take care of the whiner as well, she wasn't sure she could handle it.

She figured she could worry about that later. Right now she just wanted to get him shut up and in bed. That was no easy task given his continued ranting and his inebriated state. All of his common sense had apparently been left at the office. Mrs. Kao pleaded with him not to worry about the situation and hope for the best in the morning, but he wasn't to be consoled. He searched the house, looking in every nook and cranny, for the rice wine he had left under the sink. He had in fact left it under the sink, but Mrs. Kao being the bigger thinker had sold it to one of the town drunks for a little spare change for herself. She assured him he was confused, that he drank all of it weeks ago and that, in any case, he'd had enough—quite enough.

Eventually he gave up the hunt and passed out on the couch, much to Mrs. Kao's delight; although, at this point she wished she'd kept the wine for herself, she needed it—desperately. Her nerves were frayed, dealing with this hopeless creature and worrying about the fallout from this latest explosion. She knew he was under serious pressure to perform at work, even though she had no clue what he actually did. Surely nothing going on in this remote and lonesome village could be important enough to cause this level of consternation. If she only knew. But, for her sake, it was probably better she didn't.

Morning came soon enough and Mrs. Kao awakened to the sound of rattling pans in the kitchen. Her first thought was an intruder, but why would they steal her pans. Outside her window the morning dew glistened on the hillside, its flawless lush green blades presenting a view that was hard to ignore, but for the noise from the kitchen. She was surprised to find that Mr. Kao did indeed know where the coffee was. A headache was fast approaching and he was eager to stave off the pending hangover symptoms. Convinced that he was going to face possible firing today, he couldn't be off his game. He had to find some answers, answers that would satisfy the suits and give him a stay of execution.

"Making me breakfast?" Mrs. Kao asked and without skipping a beat added, "I'll have two eggs, over easy and a bowl of miso soup."

"Are you dreaming, woman? I'm not the cook around here," Mr. Kao scowled. "I'm glad to see you're up at last. Are you accustomed to sleeping all day?" An interesting comment at six thirty in the morning. "It's you who'll take the orders—make me a cup of coffee and some soup. Important work awaits me today."

"Last night, you were sure of being fired. Do you think you still have a job after yesterday's explosion?" Mrs. Kao asked inquisitively, with a hint of fawned concern.

Mr. Kao didn't answer, but his look said it all. She took the pot from him and started the coffee. She didn't want to be his slave, but she'd rather him stay out of her kitchen. It would be easier in the long run.

Despite his confident remarks, inside he was scared to death. There was a possibility, a very strong one, that this could be his last day at the lab. He'd been warned, given repeated chances to succeed, and yet—explosion after explosion—no results. Amid the thundering noise in his head and the aches in his muscles, he tried his best to formulate a reasonable explanation. Could he blame someone else, did they get bad chemicals, was he given the wrong formula? Surely it couldn't be his fault. He'd convinced himself it wasn't his fault, but the fact remained that he was the manager and the failure to produce fell on his shoulders. The question was how to put it on someone else, satisfy the suits that it was all beyond his control, beg— if necessary, for one last chance; although, he'd had three last chances already.

He was holding his head in his hands, pressing on his temples, rocking back and forth when Mrs. Kao sat the cup of steaming coffee in front of him. It was a strong cup, he could tell from the color, pitch black, and the fragrant burnt bean smell coursing through the kitchen.

Mr. Kao held the cup up and said, "Perhaps you could add a little hair of the dog to get me going?"

With a look of amazement and scorn, Mrs. Kao reminded him that they'd been through this last night. There was no rice wine, nor any alcohol for that matter, left in the house. Now she was truly glad she had sold it. Let him suffer for his sinning. The answer to his question, and his coffee cup, was an emphatic no.

Dejected and aching, he hastily laid waste to the cup of coffee and asked for another one; a request she was willing to fulfill. He was still drunk, only now he was a wide awake drunk. His pickled brain worked hard to find a solution, one that would be believable, one that could spare the lab a shut down. While he didn't really care about all those peons who worked for him, he realized he'd be ostracized by the town for losing this vital source of income. He had to find a way to survive.

When he arrived, late, at the office he expected to see a padlock on the door but instead he saw his employees, the fire investigator, and his secretary patiently waiting for him. He wasn't sure why they even bothered to show up. Perhaps they were just mocking him, more likely they came for their money — what a bunch of sheep, they could never make it in his position.

His phone was ringing when he got to his desk and as feared, it was one of the suits. In true fashion, he immediately launched into a long and convoluted story of how it wasn't his fault, but he was cut short. "Mr. Kao, we don't want to hear another one of your verbose and useless explanations. The formula was wrong, we've fired another scientist and we'll be delivering updated instructions. It should be available first thing in the morning. I trust you'll have the place cleaned up and ready to go or this will, in fact, be your last opportunity."

Man, had he dodged a bullet. The revelation that someone else was indeed at fault only fueled his already oversized ego. Of course, he couldn't just appreciate his luck and keep his mouth shut, he immediately started spreading the word that some dimwit scientist had nearly killed them all and thanks to his quick thinking they — lab and life — had been saved. His version of the truth seldom bore much resemblance to reality.

Mr. Kao had less success with the fire investigator who was growing weary of spending 90% of his resources responding to fires at the lab. This time he was playing hardball and threatening to shut the lab down until the cause was fully investigated and determined. He, unlike Mr. Kao, was concerned about human life and the danger the lab might be posing. He had a job to do and he tried to do it well.

That dimwit, Mr. Kao thought, he can't shut me down. I won't stand for it. Pacing his office like a caged lion, his head continuing to pound louder by the minute. He was reviewing his options. He could plead, but he'd sooner lose his job than cow tow to this lowly public servant. Perhaps a little pay supplement might grease the wheels. Local government employees, being poorly paid, were notorious for taking bribes, but he couldn't be sure if this guy was on the take or not. That could easily backfire. He considered having Mrs. Kao wrestle the chief — she'd done a pretty efficient job with him last night. That gave him a bit of a chuckle in a day that needed some levity. His best hope was to get someone else to deal with the chief, a person with some charm, a talent he was short on. Lin was his best hope. Mr. Kao recognized her skills — smart, even tempered with enough common sense and diplomacy to win over the fire investigator.

"Lin, in my office now," Mr. Kao shouted from this doorway, always the uncouth soul, not bothering to even have his secretary summon her. But then why bother. Things were so dismal for him today, polite behavior wouldn't make any difference. He needed help and he needed it fast.

Everyone in range stared at Lin, fearful of the fate that awaited her in the confines of Mr. Kao's office. They all knew she was a model employee and, more importantly, that she didn't have anything to do with the explosion. They were perplexed as to why her head was presumably on the chopping block.

Mr. Kao, not knowing how to grovel to an employee, got right to the point rather than offering the olive branch. "I need your help."

Lin's first thought was why should I help him? But fortunately she engaged her brain before her mouth and didn't say it aloud. She waited to hear what possible plan he was going to ensnare her with.

"This fire chief is a most unreasonable man. He wants to close the place and cause us all to lose our jobs. I know you don't want to see your colleagues penniless and hungry. I need you to reason with him, convince him it was an accident—beyond my control." It was always about him. "Tell him we aren't doing anything dangerous."

Lin wasn't sure how she could convince anyone of those facts. History was against her—she'd lost count of the number of explosions—and she really didn't know whether they were doing anything dangerous or not. With no other employment options at the moment, she chose not to find out for sure.

"And just exactly how am I supposed to do that?" she asked, with all good reason.

"That's for you to figure out. Why do I hire you people, to sit around all day and collect wages? Now go and don't come back until you've convinced the man to leave the lab open."

A tall order had been placed upon Lin's shoulders, but for once Mr. Kao had made the right choice. He had chosen someone who could succeed where he had failed. Lin knew the fire chief well, he played cards with her husband and, more importantly, he did understand the importance of the jobs to this community. He just wasn't inclined to make an easy go of it with Mr. Kao.

Mr. Kao watched from his window as the two of them talked in what appeared to be a heated conversation, but that was only for appearance sake. They were actually talking about their sons, while throwing in a few loud words and arm gestures occasionally to make it look real. They kept the "argument" going for as long as seemed reasonable to agitate Mr. Kao even further. They so seldom got an opportunity to harass a more deserving person. If Lin were a deceptive person, she could have really milked the situation, made Mr. Kao sweat. But, she didn't want to be responsible for a heart attack and she feared he was on the verge of one.

The Fire Chief loaded up his equipment, as primitive and worn out as it was, and headed back down the mountain. Mr. Kao continued to pace in his office, stopping with each lap to peer out the window in an attempt to assess Lin's progress. He met her at the door when she returned and pulled her into his office demanding a report, hopeful for good news, but still fearful he was ruined. When Lin explained that he'd been given, yet another, reprieve, he practically danced with joy, quickly forgetting that she'd saved him. Lin knew there would be no thanks, no appreciation of what she'd done for him, nor any recognition that she was a dedicated and competent employee.

Next time, maybe Kao would let Lin handle "the suits." Perhaps her charm, or whatever it was, could convince them to leave him alone. But he knew he was kidding himself. There was a hierarchy, one which would never allow an employee, especially a female one, to interact with executives at that level. If he didn't make a success of this lab very quickly there'd be no need for anyone to talk to "the suits" — the place would be closed. Time had run out; it was now or never.

CHAPTER FIFTEEN

Time was truly something Justin and Amelia needed more of. They'd been working night and day, or so it seemed. Sleep had certainly been in scarce supply. Fortunately, no one else had tried to shoot them. Amelia was glad she didn't tell her mother about the shooting incident. She didn't want her to worry, Amelia was worried enough for the both of them.

The list of companies and toxins was taking shape, much to Amelia's surprise. They could match the list to the chemicals they'd identified in the marine life and perhaps pinpoint the source. But still they would have to figure out how they were delivered. Was it intentional, was there a leak, could it be illegal dumping? She wondered out loud, about a possible nuclear leak. There were plenty of facilities in Japan and China.

Justin didn't think it was nuclear related. He knew what that would look like and this was different, a very bad kind of different, one he had no experience with. He loved the ocean, this was his life and he feared for the devastation this could cause if it continued. He had to find out what was causing it and put a stop to it.

The police chief stopped by again, but with no real news, not that they expected any. His guys had been back out at the island snooping around for more evidence but they hadn't found anything. No one had seen any suspicious boats or new visitors to Panzau. While he didn't know a lot about what Justin's work, he couldn't imagine why anyone would want to shoot him. The chief was more than a little curious as to why this happened shortly after Amelia showed up.

The chief obviously had more time than work. He continued to hang around the lab and was really starting to get on Justin's nerves, but he couldn't afford to piss off the local law enforcement, especially since he might need them to keep himself alive. The chief didn't mean any harm, it was just the local culture. People didn't have a lot to do in Panzau and even if they did, relations with people were more important. It was the lifestyle here, Justin understood, after some painful lessons learned, that nothing could be rushed. Life was just not that urgent.

The chief wanted to talk about fishing, canoeing on the mangroves, the latest gossip. There seemed to be no end to this pointless conversation. Justin was beginning to suspect that he just wanted to hang around Amelia. The chief had never been this friendly before. Justin did his best to appear busy, since he was in fact extremely busy. He answered the chief's questions politely while trying to make it clear he had urgent work to do. Finally the chief's radio went off, some kind of domestic disturbance, and he had to go check it out. He promised to return soon, this time with better information about the shooting. Justin thanked him profusely, knowing it was unlikely to happen, and not feeling any safer whatsoever.

Justin decided they needed more specimens for further testing, so he and Amelia headed out to the other side of the island where he had some additional traps. Amelia was thankful to get out of the lab for a while. Her brain was starting to fry from all that research. The paved road ended about fifteen minutes into the trip and turned into a set of dirt ruts with plenty of potholes, but Amelia hardly noticed. What she did notice was the bright fuchsia of the bougainvillea, the yellow, red, orange hibiscus, and varieties of palms she never knew existed.

Justin and Amelia took a small canoe through the mangroves, the heat of the day burrowing into their skin when they passed into the open water. Amelia let her hand drag alongside the canoe to get some relief, occasionally splashing her face and legs with the cool water. She'd forgotten her sunblock today, she had other things on her mind. When she splashed Justin, it only made him realize how hot it was. He couldn't believe he forgot to bring bottled water, but he'd been caught up in his thoughts rather than possible dehydration. The birds, tree frogs, and a world of other critters chirped in harmony, a rainforest choir, making it difficult to imagine danger lurking here.

When they reached the first set of traps, they were both disappointed to find them empty, but relieved to find they were only empty, not tampered with. Justin had trouble finding the next set, everything looked so similar in the mangroves. An eel swam perilously close to the canoe, and when Amelia mistook it for a snake, she screamed. She hated snakes.

"Do you have something against eels?" Justin asked in response to Amelia's shriek.

"No, not at all, it just surprised me." She was glad to have the confirmation that it was in fact an eel. Why they seemed less daunting than snakes, she wasn't sure, probably that venom thing.

"I could catch it for you, we could cook it for dinner," Justin chuckled.

"Very funny. You leave that poor eel alone. Let's stick to finding these traps and getting out of here. It's hot as hades on this water," Amelia replied.

"You're not kidding. You think I'd have better sense than to come out here in the heat of the day. I'm not thinking straight these days and I'm sure it's all your fault."

"My fault?" Amelia retorted. "Don't blame this on me."

"Well, before you arrived, no one was shooting at me." His attempt at humor fell flat. It wasn't that he found any of this amusing, but better to laugh than cry.

The canoe bumped into the next set of traps but unfortunately they were also empty, open and empty. The locks were gone and it was clear they'd been tampered with. Justin's brow wrinkled, his eyes squinted and finally he just put his hands over his face in utter frustration. Amelia tried to console him but her heart wasn't in it. She was also disappointed—disappointed and apprehensive. At least it was daylight, but she wanted to get out of the canoe and back to the lab. While Justin sat shaking his head, she scanned the horizon afraid that shots were going to ring out at any minute.

"Let's get out of here, now!" Amelia demanded. At first Justin didn't move, but then he realized what she was afraid of. They didn't waste any time getting the canoe back to shore and hitting the road to town. He wasn't sure whether he was more worried about the lack of specimens or the fact that someone was sabotaging his work. Both were making his life difficult and dangerous.

On the drive back to town, Justin realized how serious this had turned. How could he have gotten Amelia into this, he had to send her back to the U.S. and soon. Whatever was going on he wasn't willing to put her in any danger to find out.

"You have to leave, tonight," Justin declared.

"What? No way, why would I leave? Besides there's no plane, you know that," Amelia quickly retorted.

He did know that, but wasn't thinking that far ahead. Justin just knew that he wanted to get Amelia to safety and then figure out why someone was trying to put a stop to his research. Commercial flights only operated every other day and a flight left earlier that afternoon. There was no way she could leave before day after tomorrow and only if he could get a ticket. He had to get her one. He just hoped it wouldn't be too late, for her. At this point it couldn't be soon enough.

"Amelia, I'm sorry, I don't know what I've gotten you into. You have to go back to the U.S., back to safety. I have no clue why someone is sabotaging the research, or if they even are. But someone has bad intentions, clearly, and I can't let you stay here and be in danger."

"I came here to help and I'm going to do just that. I'm in this until we find out what's going on. My life hasn't had this much excitement in years," Amelia said, surprising even herself.

"Excitement is one thing, but this is something different. You could get hurt. No good can come from you staying. I won't have it." His obvious feelings for her beginning to show.

"You 'won't have it' huh? I don't think you have any say in it. I'm staying, end of conversation." Amelia was getting her feathers ruffled now. Apparently Justin thought she was a scaredy-cat and as a matter of fact, she was a little scared but not enough to run. No one was going to get the better of her. Besides, she had to find out what was going on here. She was intensely intrigued—professionally and otherwise. As a scientist she needed to know the cause of these deformities, but as a human being she wanted to know why someone was trying to kill them.

CHAPTER SIXTEEN

Mr. Kao was on the mind of more people than just his employees. While most of them loathed him, they had no control over him. But not so at the defense headquarters in China, where his antics and, most importantly, his lack of success were being vividly discussed. It had become painfully obvious to all but those with their head in the proverbial sand, that he was not the man for the job, at least not if they expected to finish this project in their lifetime.

The problem was finding anyone who could do better, but more critically someone who could be trusted. To his credit, there'd been no leaks — at least not the informational kind — about what was really going on there. Despite his lack of business acumen, they were sure he was loyal, that his allegiance to the nation was sound. Apparently Mr. Kao was a better actor than anyone could have imagined. Everyone has a price, for some it's much higher than others, but the element of greed always rears its ugly head at some point. For a man like Kao, the bar wasn't set very high.

It was no wonder he was always brown nosing the suits or anyone else they sent out to the village of Zhushan. They'd paid him a small fortune, by local standards, and all they had gotten for it was delays and excuses. Maybe it was time to give up, at least on Kao. Some of the suits wanted to find another place, another man, to finish the job, but others argued that too many people knew already. Too much had been invested to fail. Besides, failure was not an option in their position. If Kao went down, they'd go with him.

But Mr. Kao would have to take a backseat, a more pressing dilemma was high on the agenda today. Seems some marine biologist in the Pacific had discovered deformities in the marine life and was a little too diligent in trying to figure out why. Efforts to scare him off hadn't worked so far. This could get messy. The most recent report from their security services indicated that now a woman, employee of the EPA, was involved in the search. The two of them were a formidable team, bent on getting to the bottom of this issue, more for passions sake than for scientific research. But, never mind the reason, they were a pair of hungry dogs on a bone. The security services felt sure the pair had no clue as to the source of the contamination. The question of the day was how to keep it that way.

The suits were disappointed at the lack of skill exhibited by their local thugs in Panzau. They didn't want to kill Justin and Amelia, at least not yet, but apparently their scare tactics hadn't dissuaded these two from continuing their work. They couldn't understand why the woman hadn't left already. Why would she would risk her life, especially for this man she hardly knew and some remote place she'd probably never see again? They couldn't figure out her motivations for continuing, severely underestimating the strength, not to mention, the intelligence, of American women.

Killing someone had not been in their plans. Well, not in the research and development phase at least. But if necessary they would to do whatever it took to keep the lid on their experiment. The suits, too, had felt justified, sure that right and might was on their side. They were pressured by both their superiors and a desire to be superior, knowing, and mostly ignoring, the possible consequences of what they considered a necessary evil to protect and promote the welfare of the nation and take their country to where it should've always been — the top of the world.

Thank goodness the group was small, they were only three, but they had at least four different opinions. It was clear that a consensus could not be reached today. They hoped, falsely, that they wouldn't need to make the difficult decision with which they were currently seized. They hoped that the theory of "ignore it—it will go away" would work for them, when, in reality, it seldom worked for anyone. On the one hand, perhaps Justin and Amelia would never figure out what was going on. Although, given their scientific background it was highly likely they could determine the nature, maybe even track the origin, of the culprit harming their precious little marine friends. On the other hand it was fairly unlikely they'd be able to track it back to the true instigator. They were scientists, they knew chemicals—they weren't spies. Their undercover abilities were, at best, limited. Somehow those, seemingly reasonable, conclusions gave them some peace, misplaced as it was.

Before they parted ways, one of them asked, "Shall we advise our security services to continue surveillance on the island? And authorize them to 'contain the situation' if necessary?"

"Yes," was the short and, perhaps not so, sweet answer.

"Yes to which? Both?"

"Yes and yes."

Was this guy practicing to be a dry-witted comedian? Better keep his day job. After a further, albeit brief, discussion it was decided to go with the status quo. Without even knowing it, they were taking an enormous leap of faith that could impact the eventual outcome of, perhaps the most important task they'd ever had. Something about hindsight being 20/20. A hard lesson to learn.

"And what of Mr. Kao—status quo for him as well?"

"Seems it's always status quo with him; regardless, of what we do. Nothing ever changes."

The suits agreed there was no acceptable replacement available, no person—no man, who could be trusted. There was no one who could make this project move any faster, or assure the success they demanded. And, in any case, this was not the time to change horses in the middle of the stream. They had been very favorably impressed by Lin, but she was a woman, after all. That would never do, women couldn't be trusted. Talk about hindsight, time would truly tell.

It was a lucky day for Mr. Kao, even though he'd never know it. By all rights they should've just had him killed and been done with him. But Zhushan was too small a village and there would be too many questions. This was a place and time where suspicions were to be avoided at all costs, where bigger priorities and bigger fish dictated the decisions. Kao was a small fish, one that had just avoided biting into a big hook. A hook that could yank him from the precious and cushy life he was living and thrust him flailing and thirsty onto to the deck of a boat bound for the nearest fish market, where he'd no doubt be chopped up and sold to old ladies bargaining away a few Yuan on supper for their families.

For Mr. Kao, it was definitely die another day. Despite being filled with evil, he somehow managed to have great luck. But luck is a fickle friend and one that can, and most often does, abandon you in your hour of greatest need. Kao had better hope that luck stayed with him longer than with most folks, he'd certainly tried its patience. Perhaps he didn't appreciate the situation he was in, had grown comfortable with the life he'd been able to build with the extra money. He'd forgotten who he was, like the small town boy who moves to the city and, in effort to be accepted, denies his former self, forgets his roots and pretends to be the sophisticated and brilliant gentleman that he is not. But this approach usually has a limited existence before the culprit is called out and sent packing, tail between his legs, hoping against hope that the folks back home don't know what happened. But they do, they always do. Yet, in their kindness or perhaps because of their own life experience, they are somehow willing to forgive, if not forget, and take you back into the fold.

If the good folks in Zhushan knew what Kao was up to, despite their gentle and kind spirit, it was pretty unlikely they'd be so forgiving. This small and fairly close knit community generally stuck together, helping one another in their hour of need and acting as an extended family to all but the vilest of characters. They knew Kao was a nasty man; they just didn't yet know the extent of his depravity. But Kao didn't care whether the village folks liked him, when you have money, who needs friends. Perhaps the day would come when he'd find out just how desperately he did in fact need friends. But most likely he'd be left wanting, wishing and hoping, that he'd been a different sort of fellow and learning the hard lesson that no amount of money can buy friends, true friends. Sometimes, there's not enough money in the world to save a soul from the unfortunate fate they've created.

The suits weren't really interested in Kao's friends or his soul, they had more control over his fate than he did. In his hubris he failed to appreciate how fast the winds of fate could send him tumbling down the hill, head over heel, of this scenic mountain village, straight to the bottom of the South China Sea. If he had any appreciation for the dangerous situation he'd placed himself in, his demeanor certainly defied it. He remained a man disrespectful of others, living large in the face of those with a meager existence. He blatantly exerted his feeling of superiority in a community where pretention was considered in very poor taste—the poorest of taste, even among the poor, especially among the poor.

Poverty characterized the majority of Zhushan's inhabitants, even though they didn't really see themselves as poor. They didn't know anything different. Most of this village's inhabitants were in the same boat—a sailboat, certainly not a yacht—drifting somewhat aimlessly on misty blue water, pushed to and fro by a cool and calm breeze, enjoying the scenic ride rather than bemoaning the meagerness of their assets. This village, lush and lively, gave its inhabitants everything one could want. It wasn't the kind of prosperity most of the world expected, but rather the kind of wealth that is priceless—a sense of peace, the love of family, a simple and stress free life, lived in a place of infinite beauty. There was a lot to be thankful for here.

The suits didn't mind selling Kao down the river to their superiors, except for the fact that they would, most likely, be equally blamed for his failures. They had every incentive to skew the facts in their favor and hope for better days ahead. All that really mattered in the end, was in fact, the end result. As they prepared the bi-weekly report for General Peng, they felt justified in presenting the progress of Operation Red Panda in its best light. All of these operations were fraught with difficulty, sometimes impossibility; few actually succeeded, at least to the degree expected by Chinese officials. So what if they didn't tell the truth, the whole truth—truth was in the eye of the beholder anyway.

The report, like most others, would elaborate on only the necessary facts, suggesting a breakthrough was near, that testing was going well and should soon be concluded. But, most importantly, they lauded the fact that there were no leaks, no missing documents, no Wikipedia reports that could rat them out. The latest explosion at the lab warranted only two lines, explained as an equipment failure rather than a lack of chemical compatibility. No discussion of the damage, or the fire chief, or Lin's very eloquent explanation of the processes at the facility. Even talking with her could be seen as a sign of weakness. No, General Peng didn't need all the unfortunate details—if he got them, he might be the one exploding. Not that this most recent event was very serious, given the many blow-ups they'd had; but, it might be one explosion too many. The General would likely fire Mr. Kao, and perhaps the suits. They couldn't risk that possibility.

The report was short and that alone would likely raise the ire of General Peng, but it was preferable to what might happen otherwise. They had to account for Justin and Amelia, too; although, they weren't known to the General by those names. The General was aware of the situation, so the suits couldn't avoid providing an update, especially since security services were keeping an eye on the two of them. This part was a tougher sale, they knew what the General would be thinking: How could they have not scared off these two already? Why not just get rid of them?

The suits somehow managed to make it sound as if Justin and Amelia were harmless amateurs on an eco-vacation, roaming about the island, hiking through lush green forests, fishing in cobalt blue waters, and enjoying lunch at the few, and disputably appetizing, restaurants to be found. They even considered embellishing on the story with a budding romance. It wouldn't be unlikely, given they were two single, relatively young, and attractive people with mutual interests—as odd as the notion of romance seemed to the suits. What did love have to do with it? Arranged marriages were considered the norm in their world, a norm that worked well for most and they could see no reason to change. Love only led to trouble, look at how many Americans were divorced. But as Americans were want to do, at least in the movies the suits had seen, they reveled in falling in love on beaches, the cool breeze wafting through their long curly hair, the sun setting at their back, as they stared dreamily into the eyes of this person they thought would love them forever. But who, in reality, would most likely be on another beach with someone else in under five years, or in some cases the next day.

They decided against the budding romance theory. The General wasn't interested in intrigue. Better to stick to the facts, their version of the facts, of course, rather than creating their own reality. If they were caught providing false information to the General—well, they didn't really want to think about their prospects for continued employment. No, better stick with the rosy, but at least somewhat realistic picture they had agreed to paint.

They led the General to believe that Justin and Amelia were in fact very scared—not so far from the truth—and were likely to give up soon. The report even suggested that Justin was likely to leave the island when Amelia returned to the U.S., rather than continuing the mostly benign work he was doing before the deformities started materializing. He'd been there about as long as any foreigner ever stayed on that island, unless they were in the witness protection program. They'd checked to be sure he wasn't in the program.

They made sure to report how often the police chief had been seen at the lab, not realizing he was mostly dropping in to get a look at Amelia, rather than conveying any substantive information about his investigation. He didn't have anything to report and he never would. The chief wasn't really interested in solving a crime where no one had actually been physically injured and besides, he'd never find out who took those shots at Justin and Amelia. These folks were way out of his league.

The suits finished off their report with the assertion that Justin and Amelia were not a serious threat—an exercise in wishful thinking—but recommending that security services maintain surveillance just in case anything changed. They weren't out of the woods yet on this one. Short and sweet, enough facts to keep them out of trouble with the General, but not enough to raise suspicions, causing undue questions they couldn't answer, at least not truthfully. It was the truth, as they hoped it would be.

One of them always hand delivered the report to the General, realizing the need to maintain the integrity of this top secret operation. Actually, it was beyond top secret. Officially, it didn't even exist. Even fairly benign information, like that contained in the report, could easily fall into the wrong hands, ending not only the operation itself, but the careers of those involved. Not to mention the risk to national security and the fact that international diplomacy would be irreparably harmed. Instinctively, they all knew those facts. Yet, they still couldn't, perhaps didn't really want to, appreciate the seriousness of what they were involved in, the lives that could be affected, how the world could be changed. But how could they? They weren't the only ones bending the truth. Why is that when people lie, they don't expect the same in return? A house of cards. If only, this was a far more dangerous game than cards.

"Is that for me?" the General barked.

"Yes, sir. It's the weekly report on Operation Red Panda."

"Quiet, you know there's no such operation. Besides, I'm well aware of what it is. Otherwise, why would I be seeing you? Go now, back to your cage, tiger cub."

The suit, about faced and headed back to this own world, one where he was more comfortable, where he didn't have to take this type of treatment from his co-workers. He knew better than to respond to the General. He'd tried it once, never again.

Back in his office, the General read with eagerness the scant and slanted information contained in the report. He was well aware of the suits proclivity to tell him what they thought he wanted to know. Of course, the General hoped for more details on a possible romance between these two biologists. Details of liaisons, particularly with sordid details of sexual encounters, hopefully taped for his viewing pleasure, made him very happy. He so seldom got such juicy information, but well rewarded those who provided it. If the suits had any sense, any ambition for promotion, they would embellish, not downplay, the sleazier facts of these covert operations. Well, he'd have to get his jollies somewhere else today. For a man such as himself, there were plenty of places to do so and no one would dare speak of it. Rank has its privileges.

The report's suggestion that these two biologists weren't capable of sniffing out the truth was highly unlikely in his mind. Determined people usually found a way. They would have to be stopped. Maybe not today, but at some point—unless they were smart enough, or scared enough to give up. He'd keep his eye on these two. He couldn't afford to have this operation blown and besides no one would miss a couple of odd ball Americans hanging out on some remote Pacific island.

CHAPTER SEVENTEEN

Generals read a lot of reports, no matter whose military they work for. Back at the Pentagon, General Foley was in the same position as General Peng, wondering whether what he saw on paper was any reflection of the truth or just the wishful thinking of a group of dimwits not worthy of the position they held. Sure, there were a lot of sharp, sophisticated people among their ranks, but they were more the exception than the rule. In his experience, truth was relative. People saw what they wanted to see and more often than not, they provided unreliable facts, either for dramatic effect or for their own personal gain.

What he read made his head hurt. It wasn't supposed to happen this way, though he always knew they ran the risk of being discovered. He just didn't think it would be by some hapless biologists in the middle of nowhere. Did they know what they had found? Would they figure out where it came from? Was it a chance he was willing to take? It wasn't as if he could run this one up the ladder and let someone else make the decision. It was him, all him, who had to make the call.

General Foley couldn't be sure how much, or how little, these two knew about what they'd stumbled onto. Perhaps he'd get lucky and they would just go away, but it wasn't a chance he could, or was willing, to take. He hated hurting people, but he'd hate getting fired even more. Maybe it was time to retire; although, he wouldn't know what to do with himself and besides, he had to see this one through. It was his duty.

Moonlight was starting to creep between the standard issue metal blinds—at least they weren't *army* green—that flanked the two windows behind the large but utilitarian desk he called home at least five, and more often than not, seven days per week. It was the only light in the room, save the small green—but not *army* green—shaded lamp which served as one of the few decorations in his office. The lamp stood tall and svelte like a soldier itself, providing a dim but defined radiance, the product of these new-fangled, never-say-die, light bulbs that economy and the government required him to use. He didn't mind the darkness, he'd spent many a night lurking in fox holes or creeping through jungles. Often, guided only by glimmers of moonlight that were able to intrude through the thick cover of trees, the smell of fear real, but somehow palatable because this was the life he'd chosen, the only one he knew. He was a man who thrived on danger, but sometimes even he could be overwhelmed. He wasn't going to let this be one of those times.

The plan he had developed, with inspiration from his fallen colleagues in the Arlington Cemetery, had promise. But, it's greatest failing was his lack of ability to share it with others. He recalled, with a bit of chagrin, the suggestion that no man is an island, that burdens are better shared; however, those fanciful and eternally hopeful expressions weren't meant for men like him or situations like this. No, this was a once in a lifetime situation, opportunity, challenge—he wasn't sure how he to define it.

The General had to get to Panzau and quick, without anyone knowing it, or at least knowing why. As he leaned against the filing cabinet, the moonbeams casting a shadow of the blinds on the wall across from him, he pondered how to approach them, how to get these two so-called scientists to cooperate. Were they patriotic sorts who could be convinced of the need to support their nation? Or were they Americans who hated America, didn't support the military, and thought the government was filled with conspiracies? Normally, it would be easy enough to get their background information, at least a quick analysis of what kind of lives they'd led so far, whether they were democrats or republicans—not that he really cared how they voted, but it might reveal their leanings. But the need for absolute secrecy meant he had to be careful with his personal investigations.

He'd already Googled them to see what was in the public domain and found a few articles Amelia had written, but they were strictly scientific and didn't reveal any personal opinions. There was even less about Justin; although, he did learn that he'd been awarded grants from the Department of the Interior and NOAA, the National Oceanic and Atmospheric Administration, to fund his little lab in Panzau. Neither had a criminal record or any bad debts, credit scores proved good. There was the usual professional profile information, both had gone to state schools—he could be thankful for that—no sense of privilege, little likelihood they were tree hugging liberals. The General wasn't very open-minded. His way was the right way, if you didn't think like him, you were simply wrong. He had always lived in a very regimented and methodical way, with discipline and consistency at the heart of his existence, never straying far from a set of beliefs and behaviors that he considered part of his duty.

If these two were true Americans, his appeal to their sense of duty should prove sufficient to resolve the situation. He could understand if they initially proved reluctant or needed convincing of the merits of what he had in mind, but he was quite capable of being convincing. Just ask his wife. But this was more complicated, required a greater leap of faith than they might be prepared to make, at first. But once they appreciated their options, or lack thereof, he was sure they'd choose the right decision—his decision.

But first he had to get to them and there was no time to waste. In just a few hours the moonlight would bloom into daylight, filling the Potomac with glimmers of yellow, washing away the night as another day dawned on this city of power and might. He felt lucky to be a part of it, he wanted to remain a part of it. He grabbed his briefcase, threw in a few files, closed the blinds and locked the door. The green lamp, the soldier, stood at attention, keeping watch over his kingdom while he ventured to a destination unknown to most and home to few.

In less than thirty hours, the General had made his way to Panzau, landing amid the flowing green palms and cascading blue water. The landscape was more spectacular than he could have imagined; although, the country itself, architecturally speaking, was nothing to write home about. He'd imagined it like the jungles of Vietnam, haunting memories peppering his brain with visions of underbrush so thick you had to machete your way through. The smell of death real and sickening. But here, here the smell of life was all about food and flowers, smoke and seasonings, garbage and gardenias, giving the place a festive atmosphere.

It wasn't too hard to find these two, Amelia and Justin. In a town with less than 10,000 people, a man with the General's background could easily ferret out the foreigners, especially attractive female ones, but so could a one-eyed man with a ten year old map. Given the dearth of suitable accommodations in this place, it was inevitable that the General would wind up at the Venus and Mars in a room a few doors down from Amelia. The name made him scoff, Venus and Mars, right. All of this talk about the differences in men and women was just a ploy to sell more books to the hapless fools who couldn't find a mate. He knew what women wanted—a real man, a man who knew how to protect them and provide for them, not any of this metrosexual, I'm in touch with my feelings crap.

He didn't know whether it was the sound of the waves, rhythmic and sure, or the lack of sleep, but the General could barely keep his eyes open. But, it was too early for bedtime and he wanted to get his circadian rhythms inline and decided he had to find a way to keep himself awake, at least for a few more hours. His way was exercise. The General threw on his running gear and hit the beach. He was a great runner with the grace of a gazelle, sailing along with an almost perfectly smooth stride, posture always erect. His speed wasn't what it used to be, but not bad for a guy his age. But this wasn't a marathon, unlike the task he was up against, which could well turn out to be the race of his lifetime.

And what a lifetime it had been, the places and things he'd seen, many of them he'd rather forget, some he had. This night, a night filled with luscious light from a low rising moon, reminded him of another night, some twenty odd years before. Another beach, another moon, another woman. He could still see her clearly, long silky hair, blacker than the night, eyes as brown as dark chocolate and a voice so subtle and sweet you had to strain to hear it. But you did, because you so wanted to hear it.

"Robert, dear Robert." She always seemed to be repeating his name — or at least the name he was using at that time. She touched his arm with her fragile fingers, gentle and soft like the ocean breeze. Even now it sent shivers up his spine. And when they kissed...words could not describe the tender, luscious lips, soft but pressed hard against his. He knew it was wrong the moment it happened, a betrayal not just of his marriage but of his loyalty to his country. Thankfully, he'd had the sense to walk away. He probably should've walked away sooner, but in that telling moment where there was a point of no return, he'd made the right decision.

She was a spy for the Viet Cong. He had no proof, barring a gut feeling, but it was a chance he couldn't take. He ran, quite literally, as he was doing now, back to camp that night and made sure they were never alone again. Not that she didn't try, but he was pretty good at avoiding things he didn't want to face. He never told his wife or Uncle Sam, nothing good could've come from either one knowing.

Many times he'd wondered, as he did tonight, whether she was really a spy or just a young woman looking for a way out of a war that seemed as if it would never end. And even when it did end, would leave years of poverty and despair, horrors that no-one should have to face. Yes, maybe she wanted to find a better world, maybe she only wanted comfort, to lose herself in the moment and forget for a little while the world she was forced to live in. Either way he couldn't chance what he had, couldn't risk losing his job or his family. He'd seen weaker men go down this path, caught up in the moment, blinded by the circumstance they found themselves in and unwisely believing they could walk away unscathed. Some did, most did not.

Still, he'd thought of her often, debated whether he should have found out if she really was a spy and exploited the relationship for the sake of the mission. If she was a spy, she would have been looking for information from him. It wasn't likely he would have gotten any actionable intelligence from her. Besides he knew he was trying to rationalize an excuse to do something that was wrong, no matter how you spun it. Most of all he knew the guilt would consume him, eating away at his conscience, bit by bit, coming in fits and starts that could be managed at first but would eventually become an albatross around his neck. He couldn't handle the guild and on that occasion, even as a younger and much more foolish man, he realized that fact and made the right choice. Something he hadn't always done so, especially in a moment of crisis.

A moon-rise can be even more spectacular than a sunset, especially when it's a full moon. The yellow cresting the horizon, spills out on the water like honey flowing from a mason jar. The swath of light spreads wider with each minute as the moon pushes above the horizon in slices until it hangs in full view like a grapefruit ready for the picking. It's simply breathtaking, no matter how many times you've seen it. Romantic and eerie at the same time, breaking the darkness with a hint of what is to come — another sunrise, another day, a repeating cycle that is never exactly the same. The differences were subtle, a few seconds each day, a slightly different location, another season, but predictable and persistent, not unlike the General's life.

The run got his endorphins charged up and kept him awake for a few more hours, long enough to grab some dinner at the hotel. He hoped he'd run into Amelia but assumed she'd probably figured out the finer eating opportunities by now and was smart enough to avoid the hotel food. It left a lot to be desired in his opinion, but then he wasn't here on vacation. Nor would he ever be. No wonder this place had so little tourism. It was in the middle of nowhere, had no decent hotels, and was not very traveler friendly. The landscape was spectacular, the ocean amazing, the plants and trees of all species made it visually stunning. But, the beauty had been invaded by the block buildings, lacking in interest and appeal, the garbage on the streets, even the lack of decent streets, and a general sense of untidiness.

The Mars and Venus apparently wasn't the hot spot, but he had to wonder whether any place on this sleepy little island was. Surely there must be, there always is. At least he could get a beer here. The General had heard that some islands were "dry" or required a drinking permit. Yes, a drinking permit. He wondered how you qualified. Was there a test? The thought brought a laugh, something he needed after this long day and very long trip. Tomorrow he had to get serious, very serious and so did Amelia and Justin. They were going to have to make some decisions, life-saving decisions, to wind their way out of the maze they'd unfortunately wandered, or perhaps charged headlong, and headstrong, into. He didn't know their motives, didn't really care, he just needed them to give up on this quest and soon, before someone got hurt.

The morning light didn't bring much relief from the jetlag. He felt as if life was being lived in slow motion. A hot cup of coffee at the hotel, though lacking in flavor and only slightly warm, gave him enough "pick me up" to figure out his next move. As he had his Danish—he missed an excellent opportunity by foregoing the local poi usually served for breakfast—the General contemplated the best way to approach these two. Should he go for the direct route, appeal to their sense of patriotism and moral compass, or should he play the role of a spy, hiding his true identity and using his subversive skills to manipulate the result he needed? He decided better to do a little reconnaissance first, try to see what they were up to, observe their demeanor and interactions with others. He fancied himself somewhat of a pop psychologist, able to determine the character and moral leanings of people based on certain behaviors they exhibited. More than not, he'd been wrong. But, he'd never admit it.

The General decided to follow them or at least try to end up in the same place at the same time. Perhaps he could overhear some conversation, figuring out what they were up to, or even better, discover a budding romance. It couldn't be too difficult to find them in this little fishbowl, there were only so many restaurants, public places, and beaches. The lab Justin had been running for several years now should be easy enough to find. That might prove a little too direct. What reason could he have for simply showing up there? In a place this small, he felt sure the gossip mill must be at full tilt. No doubt most of the island knew he had arrived, they just didn't know *who* he was, he actually hoped they didn't. The General wanted to keep the element of surprise on his side. Word of some U.S. military guy questioning local folks wouldn't stay quiet long or likely win him any friends. It could bring a screeching halt to his ability to find out what he needed to know.

The General decided to chat up the desk clerk, a rather unattractive young woman with long black hair, curled into a twist at the back of the neck and held into place with what appeared to be a set of chopsticks. Her wide set eyes and flat nose were made only more obvious when she smiled an ear-to-ear grin.

Despite her shy and retiring manner, the desk clerk was most helpful in providing information about the local hangouts — few as they were. She highly recommended the Jesus Saves Diner for their fish sandwich and taro fries. He wasn't sure what taro was, but figured he'd find out soon enough. The clerk recommended a side of wasabi mayonnaise dipping sauce. The wasabi sauce sounded right up his alley, but on further reflection he suspected it's powerfully hot nature was necessary to cover up what was sure to be the unpleasant features of taro. Well, whatever taro was, maybe Jesus would indeed save him from it; although, he doubted that was the point of the name.

He thanked the clerk for her advice, giving her a quaint nod and a toothy grin, his glance lingering a little longer than she was comfortable with. The general was a charmer at heart, a fact appreciated only by those who knew him intimately. To most others, his inferior officers in particular, he was a no-nonsense field solder with little tolerance for anything outside of his comfort zone. And it was a fairly limited zone. He saw no need to change or tolerate the view of others in a world, his world, which was perfect enough for him.

As he wandered along the litter-ridden streets, he wondered why people would tolerate garbage like this. Were they incapable of operating a pick-up service or did they simply not care? The bacteria, the potential for disease, especially with children playing everywhere. Did anyone consider this? Cleanliness was next to Godliness in his world. The concept of the island paradise had surely been lost in this place. What a shame, it had potential with its abundance of flora and fauna, an almost uninhabited coastline where gentle waves of lapis blue licked the sandy shore, soft and white with hardly a rock in sight. They had a gold mine on their hands and they were using it as a sewer.

He wandered into a small shop to kill some time before checking out the lunch crowd at the Jesus Saves Diner. The shop seemed to be a knock off version of the U.S. Dollar stores, combining substandard goods, most of which had no real purpose, with economy. How many corn cob holders did one need in this life? They offered an interesting variety of canned food products. Of course, there was your typical Charlie of the Sea tuna, even Vienna sausages, but the collection and variety of fake ham products was unrivaled by any he'd ever seen. No wonder so many locals were overweight. The jar of pickled eggs, the color of dirty bath water and most likely circa 1999, was more than he could bear.

"Can I help you?" the clerk asked, at long last.

Not likely he thought.

"Well, yes I've just arrived for a little vacation, somewhere off the beaten path you know," the General replied with great confidence.

"Well, this place isn't on any path, that's for sure. We don't get a lot of tourists. Any particular reason you choose to come to Panzau?" she inquired.

Typical nosey small town people, the General thought, but he had enough common sense to know better than to piss off the locals. As he was trying to formulate a quick, and believable, response, he saw a macaw land on a tree limb outside the window.

"Birds," he said, "I'm an amateur birder of sorts."

"Lord knows we got 'em around here, every size and color you can imagine. Of course, you need to get inland to see the best ones. We've scared a lot of them off with our development in the city."

Development—that was taking liberty with the term, he thought, trying not to laugh at the well-intentioned woman.

"Yes, so I understand. I'll definitely be heading inland to check them out."

"Need some binoculars?"

"Huh?" he asked, not catching what she meant.

"For your bird watching. "

"No, thanks, I brought my own." And a pair of night vision goggle for that matter but that would be too much information to share with her.

"Do you need a driver, because I've got a guy, a cousin, he would be glad to help you out."

Of course she did, there was always a cousin around the corner ready to offer the "special" price for unwary foreigners.

"How kind of you to offer. I'll let you know if I need him but I believe everything has been pre-arranged for me," he replied with that charming smile.

"As you wish, but here's his card just in case," she said, as she pulled out a yellow stained business card from underneath the equally stained jar of pickled eggs.

With a quick thank you he darted out the door just as a pack of dogs rounded the corner of the building. They were a mangy homeless looking bunch, but fortunately he remembered reading that rabies was non-existent in this part of the world. They couldn't pick up the garbage but they'd manage to stamp out, and keep out, rabies; a feat yet to be achieved in the U.S. Nonetheless, the prospects of a dog bite was not a happy thought, so with a bit of quick thinking he picked up a nearby rock and gave it a good long toss that sent them chasing after it as if it were a tasty bone. They'd be very unhappy when they realized it was only a rock, but by then he'd be gone.

The General took a quick stroll through what was, in fact, a book store with a very limited selection on offer, most of which was used, some of it severely used. According to signs posted on the walls, you could trade in old books on your "new" purchases, no doubt a result of the limited supply of decent reading material. The selection ran the gamut from John Grisham thrillers, to religious books, to Japanese comics. There was a small children's selection with English alphabet books and a few Barney selections. Dora seemed conspicuously missing for some reason. Perhaps she was sold out or maybe singing purple T-Rex dinosaurs just weren't as popular as fearless Latinas.

No self-help section, usually so popular in the U.S. bookstores; although, the General found them obnoxious and thought the entire section could exist on the basis of one book—*The Little Engine that Could*. "I think I can" was motivation enough for him and as far as he was concerned, should be enough for any self-respecting human being. Apparently, folks in Panzau weren't very interested in the seven steps to being king of the world. Maybe they were smarter and saw through shameless attempts to take their money for something they already knew or maybe self-help books were just in short supply.

He checked his watch, 11:45 a.m., by the time he found Jesus Saves the lunch crowd should be gathering. The General tried to help out the local economy and the book store in particular by purchasing some bookmarks made by local artisans from palm fronds. It gave him a chance to get directions to the restaurant from the clerk.

"Oh that's easy to find," he said, "Just go straight on up this street until you come to the roundabout and take a right. It's two blocks down on your left. You'll see the sign; although, it needs painting."

"Excuse me," he replied.

"The sign—it needs painting, been hanging there for a lot of years, getting faded because of that hole in the ozone." The General wondered where the clerk got her environmental information, maybe she needed to read some more recent books.

"I'll be sure to look carefully."

"Well, you can't miss the smell of grease. You'll know when you're at the right place."

Just the mention of grease caused a sharp pain in the General's chest. If you could sniff the place out from the smell of grease, that didn't bode well for the quality of the food, or his longevity. The clerk wasn't kidding—let your nose be your guide—there is nothing quite so pronounced as the smell of burned grease. He was sure he'd eaten worse, in the jungles of Vietnam, but at least that wasn't fried. Come to think of it, frying would have probably improved the army mess.

The General found the place soon enough. The décor inside was consistent with the greasy spoon concept. In fact, most everything was coated in a layer of grease, except for the tabletops which, thanks to the turnover of customers, were washed on a regular basis. The place was already filling up, mostly with locals, but that was to be expected, Panzau didn't get many tourists. He grabbed a table in the center so he had a full view of the place and could keep an eye out for his "friends."

He noticed a couple, perhaps American, maybe British— but he'd have to wait until they opened their mouth to be sure—check the accent and the condition of the teeth. Haven't they discovered fluoride yet in the old country? The pair was older than Justin and Amelia and the fact that they were reading a large map, wearing safari hats, and had a rather large digital camera, was confirmation enough that they were a couple of tourists. Or perhaps they were paleontologists hoping to discover something that might actually put them, and this island, on the map.

"What'll you have?" he heard a waitress ask, snapping him out of spy mode and back into reality. He almost responded with "anything NOT fried," but instead asked for a coke and a menu.

"We only have Pepsi, is that OK?" surprised she bothered to give him the option. "Sure," he responded. Although he much preferred Coke, he wasn't in a position to be choosey.

"Mahi and grouper are our fishes of the day. They come fried or grilled, if you prefer." Yes, he did prefer — the latter, obviously. This was welcome news indeed, but before he could respond she had disappeared, presumably for the Pepsi. His eyes wandered around the room. Nothing out of the ordinary here, and no Justin and Amelia.

Ten minutes later the place was packed with people and bubbling with raucous conversation. She returned with the Pepsi, and only the Pepsi. She stared down at him waiting on an order from the non-existent menu. Her mind was somewhere else. He could see the faraway thoughts of a young woman in love, and not in love with working at the Jesus Saves. In love, most likely with an island guy who probably wasn't even aware of her or, if he was, he'd been too shy to make his move, waiting for that perfect opportunity that might never come.

He decided it wasn't worth the trouble to ask again for a menu and opted for the Mahi, grilled.

"You want taro fries or slaw with that?" she had rebounded back to reality.

He almost gave in to the taro fries, but decided to save that treat for another day. The slaw sounded like a safe bet, unless mayonnaise was involved. He didn't ask. That was a judgment call he'd make when it got in front of him. With his order taken, she moved on to another, busier and much more vibrant table, to see if they wanted taro fries.

Another scan of the room was a bust, no other foreigners and the place was packed. The noise level ranked up there with a rowdy bar filled with drunken Marines. These folks had some lung power.

Ramsey had been too busy in the kitchen to notice a newcomer in the packed house. When he peered out through the kitchen port hole he saw money — not people.

Always the businessman, and today, business was good. But his nosey nature could not be denied and as soon as he spied the General he bolted from the back and helped himself to a seat at his table.

Ramsey threw out his big brown hand as a sign of welcome, offering a vigorous handshake that lasted a little too long. "Welcome to Panzau and the Jesus Saves. As you can see I've got quite a successful business going here."

"Oh, so you're the owner?" the General asked.

"Sure am, that's me. CEO of Jesus Saves, the diner — not for Jesus himself, though I am a religious man. Are you a religious man?" Ramsey inquired.

What an odd start to a conversation, going straight for the jugular. What happened to the rule of not talking about politics or religion with strangers, or family for that matter, at least if you wanted to stay on good terms? Apparently it didn't work that way in Panzau or at least not with this guy.

"Where are my manners? My name is Ramsey Treetop and we're very pleased to have you dining with us today. Did you just arrive? Are you staying at the Venus and Mars? On vacation?" he peppered the General with questions.

The General wondered whether he'd ever get a chance to answer and jumped in at the first pause. "Yes, I've arrived last night and the clerk at the Venus and Mars highly recommended your place."

"Well, well, I'll have to thank Betsy, maybe send over some of my taro fries. I'm glad to know she's getting the word out to visitors."

The entire island must be on a first name basis, at least those in the so-called hospitality business. This was going to be like shooting fish in a barrel.

"So why did you come here?" Ramsey asked, cutting to the chase, fearless with his nosiness.

"Bird watching," the General replied, figuring he'd better be consistent since gossip was likely to travel fast.

"Hmmm, bird watching, is that right? We don't get a lot of people here for that reason, but we should, we've got quite the collection — macaws, parrots, cockatiels — you name it."

"Yes, you do indeed. I did my homework and discovered the wide variety you have and besides, I wanted to be somewhere off the beaten path." Trying to stick to the storyline he already started developing.

"Well you've certainly found the place. Most of the world doesn't know we exist. They certainly are not beating a path to our door. We'd like to keep it that way. No offense to you, you're welcome, of course. We just don't want to be overrun with vacationers."

No danger in that, but the General didn't want to offend so he was careful to keep that sentiment to himself. "Well, I haven't seen many ex-pats around town, so doesn't seem like you need to be worried."

"Nah, we don't get a lot of tourists, only the hard core divers, hikers and the like. Probably a few folks running from your IRS or a bail bondsman."

"Any long-term residents here?" the General inquired hoping to get the answer he needed.

"A few, but after a while they just become one of us. Take Justin for instance, he's been working here for more than two years now," Ramsey said, looking around as if to point him out. "Doesn't seem to be here today, but he's pretty regular around here. Perhaps he's off having fun with that lady friend of his."

"Justin?" the General prodded.

"Yea, he runs the marine biology lab and is always trying to save our little ocean critters. Not sure exactly what he's up to over there at that lab, but he's a likable sort and always tips well, so we're fans."

"And he has some lady friend with him?" This was too easy.

"She only arrived about a week ago, but it seems she's trouble. Maybe trouble just follows her. Since she showed up strange things have been happening, not sure if they are connected, but they've even been shot at."

Well, the information just got more and more interesting. "Shot at? Really?" the General wanted details but Ramsey wasn't giving many, mostly because he didn't have many to give. The long and short, mostly short, of it was that someone took some shots at them while they were out checking traps and the police chief had not made any progress in finding out why or who it was. Not likely that he would.

About that time someone came in that caught Ramsey's attention, someone apparently much more interesting or important than the General. So, he welcomed him once again and was off to greener pastures before the General could prod him for valuable information on Justin. At least he now knew that Justin was a regular at the Jesus Saves and given the limited opportunities for dining, it was only a matter of time until he showed up here again.

Even though the crowd was thinning, the General hung on, eating slowly and hoping that he still might glean some information here. Besides, he had nowhere else to go unless he really did plan to take up bird watching. The waitress wasn't bothering him, the concept of service wasn't stellar, and in any case, she was probably day-dreaming again about her make-believe sweetheart. She'd not even bothered to bring the check, let alone offer a refill on the Pepsi. But he couldn't hang around forever so he headed to the cash register, still without a check. Since he was one of the few people left in the place, surely they could figure it out.

He paid his bill and headed out into the heat of the day, made tolerable by the consistency of the ocean breeze. The foreign couple was at the corner, lost in their map, and most likely lost in general. At least they had those safari hats to keep them from burning that pasty pale skin of theirs, definitely British.

The General decided to have a look at that lab of Justin's. It couldn't be too hard to find, especially based on the intelligence reports he had received and the size of this place. Everything was within ten minutes of everything else. He might just have a chat with them now—time was wasting, and he certainly didn't want to spend any time unnecessarily in this so-called tropical paradise. He could easily ask for directions to the lab from one of the infamously nosey citizens of Panzau. No doubt, they would not only point him in the right direction, but probably escort him there, with a side of taro fries. But wanting to remain under the radar, he was trying not to call attention to himself or his illustrious bird watching tour.

It wasn't hard to find, located next to the beach for easy access to the pier and ongoing experiments. He watched from the shoreline, a disinterested sun bather enjoying the ocean's hum. Around three o'clock the General saw, what he suspected were the three staff members, locking up and heading out for the day. No burning the midnight oil here. The sticky humidity was turning his cotton shirt into a wet towel, so he had just decided to head off himself when he noticed an old pickup truck pull up to the side of the building. And voila, there they were, the two of them looking no worse for the wear of this past week and actually giggling like a couple of teenagers as they attempted to unlock the door.

He'd give them a chance to get inside and not ambush them at the door, no sense in scaring them. They were bound to be jittery after all that had happened in the past few days. The General had gone over his appeal at least a dozen times on that never-ending flight, sure that he could convince them of the merits of what he had to say, to offer. He didn't think they had a lot of options here. He hoped he hadn't underestimated their good sense.

About ten minutes later, the General tapped confidently on the door, but opened it without waiting for an actual response. Justin was peering through the lens of a microscope and Amelia was engrossed in whatever was on her computer screen. They both looked up at him at the same time, slightly startled, but not as much so as he might have imagined. People never suspect the devil will show up at their door and even when he does, they don't recognize him.

"Can we help you?" Justin asked.

"No, it's me who can help you," the General proudly proclaimed.

Justin immediately pegged him as salesman, though they didn't get cold calls very often, so he was intrigued as to what he might have on offer. No gun was visible, so it didn't dawn on Justin that it had anything to do with the maimed marine life.

"You must be the bird watcher," Justin said to the startled look of the General.

"Wow, word does travel fast."

Justin chuckled as he let the General in on the secret, "We just came from the Jesus Saves Diner, enough said I suspect."

"Yes, indeed," the General laughed and said, "the joys of life in a small town, it's the same in most of them."

"So it seems. But it also seems you're not much of a bird watcher, so what are you selling?"

"Selling?" the General asked, puzzled. Although he did have something to sell, it wasn't at all what Justin was thinking of.

"I assume you're a salesman, maybe some new microscope, computer tracking system, what've you got?"

"Well, you're a very perceptive man. I'm not a bird watcher, or a salesman for that matter. But I have a matter of some urgency that I need to speak with both of you privately about. Are we alone?" the General's tone had turned serious.

That's when it began to dawn on Justin that this man was somehow connected to the events of recent days. A twinge of apprehension fell upon him. Should he reach for a weapon? Was this man here to harm them as others had tried? But before he could make a move, the General raised his hands in a sign of peace and said I'm just here to talk, to help you, to protect you. Justin looked puzzled but not nearly as much as Amelia, who couldn't begin to fathom what was about to happen here. She was afraid.

Even though the General had rehearsed his spiel several times, at this moment he didn't know where to start, how to begin to woo these two into a complicated labyrinth, much of which he couldn't divulge now, or ever. The sell was just as important as the information, he had to make it believable, compelling, prey on their fears as well as their hopes. So he began.

Fifteen minutes later he'd hit the high points and made his incredulous offer to have them work for the U.S. Government. He assured them they'd be doing a great service to their country and appealed, with great aplomb, to their sense of patriotism and selflessness. Lives could be lost, but they had a chance to save them. Their expertise was essential, especially given their recent discovery as to the source of some of the chemicals.

It was the Chinese, he told them. "They are trying to develop a chemical weapon beyond any every imagined. It's gone awry already, as evidenced by the damage to the marine life and thanks to you good folks, it's been discovered. Of course, they want to keep it quiet and that's why they've already tried to kill you, and why they will try again." That news quickly got Amelia's attention. Justin was a little more suspect of the General. How did they know if he was legitimate? Yes, he'd offered some identification but that could easily be forged. This guy could be the one here to kill them.

"We know the basic configuration," the General continued, "and we know it's dangerous for its intended use and even more so if it falls into the wrong hands. We need an antidote and you two are the ones to develop it."

They were both in shock, never imagining that it was an intentional weapon developed by another nation. Their theory had been toxic waste, courtesy of an unscrupulous corporation. The General made a compelling story, but the facts didn't add up, at least not in Justin's mind. Something was missing, the General wasn't telling the whole story. Not that Justin had every trusted the Government to be straight with the public, especially in covert matters such as this one.

Amelia, like a deer in the head lights, sat stunned, wondering where this would go next. Could she believe it, should she? It sounded reasonable. At least it was an explanation, beyond the wild guessing and speculating they'd been engaging in over the past few days. But there were questions, a million of them, racing through her mind at once. And yet, none of them seemed to bubble to the surface, she couldn't vocalize any of the specifics.

Fortunately, she didn't have to since Justin had plenty of his own. How would this work? Where would they work? Were they sure of the stage of development and the composition of this chemical weapon? He threw them all out at once, his brain firing off in rapid succession. Amelia still sat stunned, waiting for the answers.

The General, fearing it was too much for them to digest at once and knowing quite well they might not like the answer to some of these questions, put them off until the morning. "Let's meet for breakfast, after you've had time to sleep on it. I'm at the Venus and Mars, as I believe you are also Amelia." Amelia was a bit taken aback at first but then realized she shouldn't have been. If this guy was who he said, he knew a lot more about her than her current address.

"No," Justin replied, "I've got to have some more facts. At the very least, just how far advanced is this chemical weapon and how dangerous is it?"

"Mr. Gibbs, I think you probably already know the answers to those questions, given what you've discovered. We have every reason to believe it's basically complete and highly dangerous to humans, in addition to the harm it's already done to your little marine friends. I assure you this is most urgent and we have only days to turn this ticking time bomb, no pun intended, around. "

Justin looked deflated, hearing firsthand what he had already feared. Amelia, finally able to speak, asked whether their exposure to the chemicals, given their handling of the marine life was dangerous. The General couldn't say for sure, but suspected the chances of contamination from this limited exposure, especially this far removed from the actual source, were slim. She had to wonder if he was being honest, given her background in toxic substances. But she wanted to believe him, so she did.

"I'll give you time to think about it and let's meet somewhere for breakfast. Hopefully, not the Jesus Saves. I doubt we can get any privacy there," the General said with a bit of laughter, trying to lighten the somber mood in the lab. He'd been in funeral homes that were more cheerful.

"No, you're right about the Jesus Saves, it's too busy and too loud. Let's meet at the terrace café at the hotel. Almost no one goes there, you'll see why, but at least we will have some peace," Justin responded.

They agreed to meet at 7:00 a.m., hoping to avoid other guests and in any case, they weren't likely to sleep much with this situation hanging over their head. With plans made, the General excused himself and headed off along the shoreline towards the hotel.

Justin and Amelia sat in stunned silence for probably ten minutes before they began to discuss the believability of what was happening. Should they agree to help? Was this the truth? Was it as bad as it sounded? And the biggest question of all — what were their alternatives? What if they said no, would they be forced, could they outrun the danger if they went it alone? Amelia wanted to cry, but she wouldn't, she couldn't, she had to remain brave. Her life, not to mention perhaps millions of lives, were at stake.

Justin, on the other hand, was more focused on the mechanics of it all and how they might actually be able to effectuate a so-called antidote. Sure, he was worried, mostly about Amelia, but bigger thoughts of how the world might be affected were at the forefront. He just knew something didn't feel right. He believed some of what the General had to say, but he was sure there had to be more to the story. Whatever it was, it didn't bode well for them.

Amelia wasn't up for dinner. She wanted to get room service and take time to mull over the details that had been laid out, in the peace and relative comfort of the Venus and Mars.

Her immediate reaction was to say no. Why was it their obligation to undo the stupidity of government? There must be another solution. If they knew the chemical, why couldn't government scientists find the antidote? She understood his explanation of the need for secrecy and limited involvement, but why should this burden fall to her and Justin.

Justin offered to drive her back to the hotel but she wanted to take a walk on the beach. She wasn't sure whether she was safe, but she suspected if the government wanted them, needed them, that they were being carefully watched and, therefore, had some modicum of protection from the Chinese. Justin insisted on driving Amelia, for her safety, but she made it very clear that she wasn't having it. He realized his continued insistence was going to be futile, so he gave in and let her go, also assuming they were being closely watched; although, neither could bring themselves to say it out loud.

CHAPTER EIGHTEEN

Morning came not a minute too soon. There had been little sleep, for all three of them. Justin and Amelia were awake most of the night pondering their options. The General was also awake pondering what option they might choose and contemplating how to proceed if he didn't get the response he wanted. Things could turn ugly, but he hoped it wouldn't come to that.

Justin was the first to arrive and ordered a cup of coffee. The Terrace Café was one of the lovelier spots on the island; unfortunately, the food and the service left much to be desired. Both were unsavory. Amelia arrived before the coffee did, glad to see the General wasn't around yet. She wanted a chance to find out what, if any, conclusions Justin had come to. It seemed they both were at a loss as to how to proceed, but in agreement they needed more information, and assurances, should they decide to get involved.

The General arrived looking no worse for wear, despite his restless night, orchestrating various alternatives and trying to figure out how to cover his own tracks. He knew this wasn't going to be an easy conversation, these two were intelligent, savvy people and not likely to fall for the limited information he'd given them. He'd provide them with plenty more, no one said it had to be the truth, especially if it got the results he needed.

After the pleasantries were exchanged and coffee was ordered, which was no small feat given the poor service, they got straight to business. Justin wasn't a patient man and he made it clear that neither he, nor Amelia, were willing to jump on the bandwagon without a lot more details. The General acknowledged that he'd expected as much, in fact, he'd planned a more extensive presentation than the one he gave yesterday afternoon. But after seeing the rattled look on their faces, he'd thought better of it and decided to dole it out in smaller doses, doses that might be more easily comprehended and dealt with.

The General proceeded to lay out the problem. The Chinese had surreptitiously hired a lab in Taiwan to test and develop the chemical weapon. Even the folks working there weren't aware of what they were actually doing. The Chinese knew that if things went wrong they'd have an easy scapegoat. The General said he wasn't even sure the Chinese realized the extent of the contamination. It was quite possible this was a disposal problem was caused by the ineptness of the lab. However, they knew there had been some leakage since Justin and Amelia had discovered the deformities in the sea life.

Only a few high level folks in the Pentagon were fully aware of the circumstances, it was imperative this situation be kept quiet. He needed their complete discretion, assuring them he would get them off the island and back safely to an undisclosed location in the U.S. Even though it was a ploy, he suggested they would work to further figure out the chemicals involved and how to counteract them. They couldn't be sure of the extent of the contamination that had already occurred. The U.S. must be able to keep the contamination from spreading—Justin got the distinct impression this wasn't out of benevolence for the creatures of the sea—as well as being prepared for possible usage of the chemical by the Chinese in an attack on the U.S.

For their complete safety, they wouldn't be able to tell anyone where they were or what they were working on. They'd really stepped into an unfortunate dilemma here, the General explained, and he knew it would be hard for them to give up their lives and go into, what amounted to, a witness protection program. But if they didn't, it was only a matter of time until the Chinese took them out.

Took them out, that's exactly the term he used, and Amelia didn't like the sound of that. "How long?" she asked.

"Today," replied the General, "We need to leave Panzau today."

"No, how long would we be in this so-called protection program?"

"Until we are sure you are safe. Realistically, it could be for the rest of your lives," the General offered, his voice trailing in full anticipation of the horror that would bring to her.

"No, that can't be. I won't do it, I can't live like that. My mother, what would she think, what would she do? She didn't even want me to come here."

"Well, actually," the General continued, pausing for effect, "you can't tell anyone about this. It would also put them in danger and I know you wouldn't want to do that to your friends or family."

Justin could see the tears forming in Amelia's eye; although, she bravely fought them back as she choked down a sip of the lukewarm coffee that had been delivered. No menus or offer of food had been made yet, so Justin called for the waitress to break up the tension and it wouldn't hurt to have a full stomach for this conversation.

The General painted a rosy picture of the nice accommodations the government could provide and the money that would be at their disposal, not to mention the inestimable service they'd be providing for their country, the many lives they were likely to save. Somehow this opportunity to "save the world" didn't sound as convincing as he had hoped. If he wasn't feeling it, he was sure it fell flat with the two of them. While he also wanted to put enough fear into them to make them comply, he hoped he wouldn't have to resort to threats. Just in case, he had a contingency plan for that as well.

While they waited for what would no doubt be a lack luster breakfast, made edible only by copious amounts of butter and jam, the General provided more details on how it would all happen. He seemed confident, every step provided for. He'd learned through the years that confidence sells, people need to believe in you, your faith will become theirs. They peppered him with questions, and rightly so. He wouldn't want to be in their position. Hell, he didn't want to be in his position. Time was not on their side, they were being pressured to make a decision and it was no easy decision.

No one was very interested in the food, lucky for them, since it was not only unappealing, but tasteless as well. At least there were no taro chips being served for breakfast. Forget the cuisine, Justin and Amelia were interested in details, the future, and most of all staying alive. The General was interested in saving this operation and most of all, his own precious hide. He desperately needed Justin and Amelia to help him do just that. So far, they weren't convinced.

Despite his elaborate explanations, and what by all appearances was a serious and most generous offer, these two weren't coming around to his way of thinking. Rushed for time and owing to a significant loss of sleep, not to mention jetlag, the General decided to raise the stakes. He tempered it as a hypothesis rather than a threat, but Amelia was quick to see it for what it was. His suggestion that all of this could easily be blamed on them didn't leave a pleasant taste in their mouth. They understood that someone, the General and his cohorts, could easily make it appear they were the guilty culprits. With technology anyone could be set up and the General would easily make it appear that Justin and Amelia had the opportunity, if not the motive. The General pointed out that it would be easy enough to generate speculation as to what these two had been doing in a lab on a remote island that almost no one had ever heard of. Who was to say they weren't the ones experimenting with chemicals, testing it on marine life. They were certainly the only ones to have found the deformed creatures in close proximity to their lab. And the nail in their respective coffins: they were working, allegedly — the General used the word with great emphasis — for the Chinese; unpatriotic Americas who'd sold out to the highest bidder. When given a chance to come clean, to come back to "their" side and put a stop to this deadly weapon, they had declined. Surely such a response would be taken as evidence of guilt.

Justin and Amelia could hardly have been more stunned. How naïve could they have been to think they could walk away unscathed? Either path they chose, they were doomed. Their lives as they knew them were over.

It was a risk, a calculated one that the General had made. But it was a mistake of a rookie poker player, raising his bet, too much, too soon. He saw it in their eyes, he'd lost them. His choices were quickly becoming very limited.

They were both very confused, Justin and Amelia, not knowing what to do, what to believe, even how to respond to the thinly veiled threat the General had offered up. It was pretty clear, they had to cooperate or else. The else being an unacceptable alternative they felt sure he could turn into a reality. The goal post had been moved. The stakes were very high, perhaps too high, for all of them.

They sat in stunned silence, but it gave them a moment to reflect. Glances were exchanged, their thoughts in apparent harmony. The look didn't go unnoticed by the General, but he wasn't sure what to read into it. The silence was deafening.

Justin was the first to speak, "I think we need some time to mull over these new details. Can you give us a day or two?"

"I wish I could," replied the General. His fake nicety angered Justin. He wanted to pound the General into the ground and afterwards throw him to the sharks. "As I told you, you are in danger and we must move fast."

"I'm afraid you'll have to wait. We can't make a decision such as this over stale toast and runny eggs. Besides we'd have to pack," Justin replied.

"No need for that, you'll have everything you need where you're going."

And that was the comment that made up Justin's mind. "Ok," he replied, "just give us until tomorrow morning."

"This isn't a negotiation," the General quickly retorted.

"I thought we were free to make our own decision," Justin noted, "so I am not sure you have a choice and in any case the next plane isn't until day after tomorrow."

"There are other ways off this island," said the General.

Indeed there is, thought Justin, indeed there is, as he starred into Amelia's teary eyes.

CHAPTER NINETEEN

Given that the General was on his own — a fact that would have been useful for Justin and Amelia to know — meant his options were limited as well. Short of blowing his cover, the only way out of Panzau was commercial service, which operated only three times a week, a fact Justin had so correctly pointed out; meaning the next flight was Friday morning and today was only Wednesday. He'd waited this long, he'd just have to wait forty-eight more hours. But to make the arrangements tickets would have to be bought tomorrow, so he gave them a reprieve until 7:00 a.m.

With that news and a plan to meet, hopefully with tickets in hand, they parted ways, leaving the General with the bill for this loathsome breakfast, much of which had gone untouched.

Amelia still teary eyed and no less confused, blindly followed Justin away from the café, not knowing or caring, where they were going. All she knew was that she had to get away from this despicable man, the General. She wished she'd never laid eyes on him. Life had suddenly become a blur and she needed to clear her head, so did Justin. They both headed for the beach, walking side by side, wondering who would break the silence first.

They knew what they had to do, there was no disagreement between them. Justin and Amelia sat on the beach and developed their plan, watching the waves rock back and forth as the sun beat down on their skin. It wouldn't be easy, but what choice did they have? They discussed the details, they ignored their fears. Within a couple of hours it was set in stone and they headed over to the lab for some more work, if only to keep their mind off the situation and wile away the day. After work they packed, managed the logistics, and hoped for the best.

When they awoke the next morning it was to the rolling waves, a welcome sound to drown out the noise in their head. The cool breeze and light ocean mist would have made it a perfect morning, under different circumstances. The sun still barely above the horizon, welcoming what was sure to be a day like no other.

This place made the Venus and Mars look five star, at least the V & M had running water. So did this place, if you counted the ocean. But Justin and Amelia were the ones running now, from exactly who or perhaps how many different people, they weren't quite sure. Maybe the Chinese, surely the U.S. military, at least the General, and perhaps others they didn't know, or care to know about. It was too frightening to contemplate, especially after the getaway they'd just made.

Luckily Justin had friends, friends with tight lips and boats, boats they were willing to lend despite the earlier shooting episode. He had used the excuse of romance, something the good folks of Panzau found hard to resist, especially for a nice fellow like Justin. He'd concocted quite the story of how he was going to woo Amelia. There may have even been a suggestion of a marriage proposal to secure the boat that led them onto a path of no return. This was hardly a romantic adventure and by no means how he'd seen this visit turning out with Amelia. But he had to protect her, as well as his friends in Panzau. It was a complicated situation, but his first thought was to protect those around him.

Amelia was a trooper, thinking quickly to bring some necessities without leaving a trail, all the while making it appear as if she were still a guest at the Venus and Mars. The General was going to be livid when he found himself having breakfast alone, not to mention losing the key players in his plan. Justin prayed they had actually escaped unnoticed, he was pretty sure they had. They left at 1:00 a.m., under the low light of a new moon. They kept the boat on a low idle until they were a safe distance from shore. Once they were far enough away so as to not arouse suspicion, Justin ran the boat as fast as he could, for the two hours it took them to reach the shore of this tiny un-named island. Thank goodness for GPS or they'd have never found the place in the pale moonlight.

They were safe for now, but they had a lot of work to do, a lot of plans to make. At least the first step had been taken. It wasn't going to be easy to find a solution, one that would keep them alive. But they'd been thrust into what was fast becoming an international dilemma and there was no easy exit.

CHAPTER TWENTY

The Lieutenant was having another slow day at work, his project on Afghanistan complete. The day dreaming was tempting him, he'd been hoping for a chance to take out some Al Qaeda enemies in an exotic location, where afterwards he'd lounge on a beach and dream of good times with Amy. The clatter of footsteps headed his way didn't serve to deter his adventure. He'd prided himself on having developed a certain knack for looking busy, lost in analytical thought, when in reality he was pretending to be a sniper wielding an automatic rifle on the roof of some dilapidated building in a third world country.

Today, it was Yemen. A place that had been in the news recently, given the public demonstrations and fear of a downward spiral into a civil war. Al Qaeda had a presence there, the U.S. was concerned. But he was just the man to put a stop to all that. He'd been air lifted in, along with three other colleagues, on a specially outfitted Black Hawk helicopter. Dropped in a strategic location, plain clothed with a thick beard, he'd easily made his way to the designated location and now sat atop an abandoned apartment building, able to see only by the light of a half moon and a very futuristic pair of night vision goggles.

They'd been given an adequate description of the target and had good intelligence on his movements, thus their ability to hopefully be, in the right place at the right time. The Lieutenant didn't know much about the background or status of this target, but felt sure he was a high ranking Al Qaeda figure, at least in the Yemeni branch. The facts, the history, it didn't matter to him, orders had been given and the Lieutenant would complete the mission as charged.

Curious as to the whereabouts of his colleagues, the Lieutenant bobbed his head just far enough about the roofline for a look. He spotted one, then both of the other snipers, strategically placed on nearby rooftops, ready to shoot to kill and then, get the hell out of here.

The night was still, but not quiet. The sound of protestors could be heard in the distance, their chants and songs wafting across the city in a rhythmic dance. At least they weren't yelling 'death to America,' or burning the U.S. President in effigy. No, this one was about their own country, the repression, the poverty, the lack of freedom. They'd had enough and as long as they stuck together, they just might be able to do something about it. But the Lieutenant didn't really give a rats' ass about all that. Let them do as they pleased, his only concern was for his own country and the safety of its people. Since 9/11 he'd developed a callous attitude toward supporting other nations. He wasn't without a sense of empathy, actually he felt quite bad for the conditions they lived in. The Lieutenant just didn't see why it was his responsibility, the U.S.'s, to be the world's police.

He needed to focus, forget what was happening in the distance, or even what was going on at home. He loved Amy and preferred to be in her arms, but at this moment his country, its people, needed him more. There were times, fairly often, when she had to take second chair. The Lieutenant was sure she understood this, except, he was wrong. No wife wants to play second fiddle to the husband she loves, especially when it comes to her protection.

The receptor in his ear brought him back, announcing that the target was en route. He arrival was expected in front of the building in approximately two minutes. It was a very long two minutes. He feared something had gone wrong, maybe this guy had been tipped off, perhaps plans had changed as they are prone to do at the last minute. But finally, two cars pulled up, one appeared to be a Fiat, the other a Mercedes CL class sedan, long and black, almost melting into the night. Thank goodness for the mellow light of that half-moon.

The ear piece spoke to him again and all three queued up, scopes following the opening doors of the sleek Mercedes, ready to bring an end to this fateful meeting on an obscure street in Sanaa. The Lieutenant saw him first, just as described, laughing and prancing about with an indignant air. It would be his last laugh.

Pop, pop—the sound surprised even the Lieutenant. What happened to the high tech silencer? Again—pop, pop—and fear set in, they were going to be discovered and have to shoot their way out.

"Lieutenant, where are you? Hello?" and that's when he realized the pop, pop was the rapping of knuckles hitting his desk. The knuckles of his superior officer, no less. So much for his alleged multi-tasking skills. But, quick thinking saved the day when he looked down and saw the report in front of him. He lifted it up and droned on about how he was deep in thought analyzing the latest data so he could prepare a summary, which he, of course, would finish before he went home today.

"Have the classified's been delivered yet?"

"I was just about to take them over, they only arrived here a few minutes ago," and with that the Lieutenant was off, quick to avoid any reprimand and wanting to show his eagerness. Today the load was light and as he pushed the cart to the "secret room," he finished up his mission in Yemen. He took the guy out, well actually the team did, no one was sure which shot actually laid the fatal blow. For good measure they took out the whole lot of them, no need to risk return fire. The job done, they were quickly whisked away aboard the Black Hawk and on their way to safety, which was more than one could say for Amy.

Amy had done pretty well this summer with her jewelry sales, better than last. She was beginning to make a name for herself and locally made jewelry was in vogue these days. Supplies were low so she planned to hit the craft store at Pentagon City Mall, maybe make a stop at Costco, and then meet the Lieutenant for lunch in the Pentagon.

As she left the apartment, the heat rising quickly on this mid-summer day, Amy almost ran headlong into Mrs. Heverstein and her Corgi out for their morning walk.

"Excuse me," Amy said jumping back to avoid plowing the fragile, elderly woman into the sidewalk.

A bit startled but no worse for wear, Mrs. Heverstein was pleased to see Amy. She wanted a chance to tell her how lovely that "tuba" sandwich was and also to apologize again for the naughty behavior of her beloved Gepetto.

"I'm glad you enjoyed it," Amy replied, adding, "the next time I make some, I'll be sure to bring you one." Although, she was still justifiably ticked off at the little busybody dog for gnawing on her jewelry boxes, she was gracious. She once again assured Mrs. Heverstein that it was no problem. She had repaired them already with some scratch cover and polish.

"Do you know that man?"

"What man?" Amy asked, a bit surprised and wondering if Mrs. Heverstein was losing her grip on reality.

"That one, "she said pointing to the corner of the next building where he'd apparently already disappeared from view. "I thought I saw him at your table at the street fair."

"I didn't see him, so I'm not sure who it could be. I imagine it's just a coincidence," Amy replied, recalling the odd man and feeling a bit concerned. Out of an abundance of caution she decided to go back and make sure the front door was locked. She excused herself from Mrs. Heverstein, wishing her and the Corgi a pleasant day and encouraging her to stay inside, avoiding the intense heat.

The door was locked, but as she was about to continue on her way, Amy decided she better check the back door as well. Rather than unlock the front door and go back through the apartment, she walked around the building and into the back courtyard. She found the back door locked as well and the courtyard in need of some attention. The grass was growing wildly through the cracks in the patio brick and everything was in disarray. She'd remind the Lieutenant to take care of it this weekend.

As she turned to leave, there he was. It was the guy, the same guy, the one both she and Mrs. Heverstein had seen at the fair.

"Mrs. Ansley, please come with me and no one will get hurt," he said in a soft, rhythmic tone.

"Who are you?" she asked as she tried to step around him, to no avail. She thought she saw a gun protruding from his jacket pocket or was it just her imagination. She was scared and rightly so.

"It doesn't matter who I am, just come along."

"I'm not going anywhere with you," she boldly proclaimed, despite feeling as if she were about to faint and melt between the cracks in the patio bricks, joining the stray grass.

That's when she saw the gun in plain view, directing her towards the alley behind their apartment building. It crossed her mind to run but she was afraid he would shoot her. She wanted to scream, but no sounds would come. Her voice had already fled the scene, Amy wished she could join it.

She had attended safety training for women and she well knew that she shouldn't get into the car, but fear takes away your good judgment. Self-preservation seemed more important and given there was a gun pointed at her, she decided it was best to comply.

He walked behind her, gun concealed in his pocket, but pointed at her back. For Amy it was a surreal scene, unfolding in slow motion. She felt like a character in a spy move, helpless and fragile, willfully obeying her captors and fearing this might not end well, particularly if she offered resistance. Her foremost thought was — don't cry, don't cry, the Lieutenant will save you — she felt sure he'd never let anyone harm her. So she went, quietly and cooperatively, as cooperatively as one could under the circumstances, into the back of a black Lexus Sedan with California license plates. She wasn't sure why she thought to look.

Back at his desk, the Lieutenant had to get down to business. After promising that summary, he now had to deliver and before the end of the day. He wondered how he'd be able to fit in lunch with Amy. It would mean staying late again. He was just about to call and cancel, begging off because of his work load, but decided she'd be too disappointed. No doubt she was already at the mall and while he could most likely reach her on her cell, he didn't want to bail on her. So he got down to work, leaving the day dreaming behind, and moving full steam ahead on the summary. The Lieutenant put everything else out of his mind — Amy, daydreaming, spying — and focused on the task. He knew if he stayed too late, yet again, that would also piss her off.

It wasn't so hard for him to focus, the report was intriguing and, in fact, he got so caught up in it that he didn't notice when she was late. Enamored with the details of the Afghan operation, he couldn't seem to tear himself away, eager to find out the future of military operations there. It was the rumbling of his stomach that brought his attention to the time, 12:45 p.m. It wasn't like Amy to be late. At first he assumed she'd gotten carried away with the shopping or perhaps there was a delay on the metro, a common occurrence. He checked the metro website but no delays were listed. He'd give her until 1 p.m. before calling to see what was up.

When one o'clock came and went, he began to get nervous. A call to her cell got the voicemail, "Its Amy, you know what to do, so do it now," be-eeep. She thought her message was so very clever. But today it wasn't funny at all, now he was officially nervous.

CHAPTER TWENTY-ONE

The mysterious Asian man from the street fair had little to say as the car drove out of Arlington and into the Virginia countryside, not that Amy could see where they were going. The windows were tinted black, so black she would have sworn it was night rather than mid-day. She hurled repeated questions at her dubious captor. What did he want from her? Who was he? Who was he working for? Amy also made plenty of threats that her husband, a military man, would come to her rescue with the full force of the U.S. Government.

To that last comment, the kidnapper did reply, "We know very well who your husband is."

That's when Amy realized that the Lieutenant himself was the reason she'd been taken. They wanted something, some kind of classified information that her husband had knowledge of or could obtain.

"He'll never betray his country, you'll get no information from him," Amy proclaimed indignantly, hoping, even praying, that he would indeed do just that if it meant her freedom. She hoped they weren't after a handsome ransom, they didn't have any spare funds or the means to get them. Their family and friends were all in the same boat, financially speaking, basically living paycheck to paycheck.

"What do you want from him, you bastard?" Amy surprised herself with this tacky language, but, under the circumstances, she felt completely justified. Of course, there was no response, no reaction whatsoever. The ride continued in a hopeless silence.

The Lieutenant tried her cell again, called home as well. Nothing, no response. He wasn't sure what to make of it. It was still entirely possible she'd lost track of time while shopping, maybe she'd even forgotten about their lunch plans, but that wasn't like Amy. And why didn't she answer her cell? Yes, something must be wrong. The Lieutenant feared an accident on the metro, which wasn't unprecedented, the place was falling apart after all. He checked the metro website again, the local news as well, but no reports of accidents or even delays. Another call to her cell, again no answer, but this time he left a frantic message for her to return the call.

He debated whether to leave work, go look for her, perhaps even call the police. He knew the police wouldn't do anything, not yet. She hadn't been missing long enough and besides, he wasn't even sure she was missing. Such a call would only peg him as a hen-pecked husband, who not only wouldn't get any assistance, but who would be mocked. Given his recent run-ins with superiors, he was cautious of asking to leave early, fearing they would think it was a made up story. Even if they did buy it, he'd be seen as a quack husband, jealous of his wife's every move.

No, he'd wait a while longer. He was sure there was a reasonable explanation. There had to be one, there was one, just not the one he was hoping for.

In reality her ride lasted only about an hour, but in Amy's mind it was forever. The only thing she saw during the entire ride was her kidnapper and the black leather seats of this expensive car. In fact, the leather still smelled new. There was a Plexiglas divider so she couldn't see anything ahead of her. She had no clue where she was being taken, but given how long they'd driven, she suspected they were still in Virginia.

Amy was blindfolded before being allowed out of the car and led into a comfortable and spacious home; although, she didn't realize that at the time. She was quickly locked in what appeared to have been built as a wine cellar, sans any wine. Too bad, now she couldn't get boozed up and wile away the hours in drunken oblivion. What thoughtless kidnappers.

She was afraid, very afraid. But her tough character was serving her well, she put on a bold face in the presence of her kidnappers. The only one she'd actually seen, the Asian man from the street fair, seemed almost sympathetic, sensing her fear and strength of character.

"We mean you no harm. As long as your husband gives us what we want, you'll be fine," the man said in a meager attempt at comfort.

"And what if he doesn't?" Amy snapped back.

"Let's not discuss that possibility now. I'm sure he can be convinced," the reply came.

Amy knew the Lieutenant loved her, would do anything for her, well almost anything. He was such a "boy scout," but she wasn't completely convinced he'd betray his beloved military, and thus his country, even for her. She wanted to cry. She'd be completely justified under the circumstances, but she couldn't for some reason. She was apparently in shock, fully aware of what had happened but unable to grasp the repercussions. It didn't feel...real.

Reality for the Lieutenant meant he had a report to finish before he could leave work and his concentration was waning. Every hour he'd tried Amy again on the cell and at home, but still failed to reach her. With each passing hour he'd grown more frantic, fearful of her fate, while trying to convince himself there was a simple explanation.

Somehow he managed to plow through, analyzing what would be most important to his boss and organizing the pertinent facts from the report in a logical sequence, all the while hoping and praying for Amy to call. Every time the phone rang he jumped with hopeful anticipation, his voice practically shrieking hello as he answered on the first ring.

By five o'clock he was truly panicked. Normally she'd be home and cooking dinner by now. The report almost finished, though lacking in polish and proper formatting, he decided he couldn't wait any longer. His boss had left already for a meeting and was unlikely to return to the office tonight. Even so, he wouldn't be looking for this report if he did. It wasn't that critical.

The Lieutenant grabbed his back pack and sped toward the exit in a gallop, almost plowing down a two-star general on his way out. The metro, as usual, was a sea of people on a mass exodus back to the suburbs, mostly brain dead from another mind numbing day in front of a computer screen. On the platform, he noticed the man he'd seen several times before. He appeared to be lurking behind one of the columns or was the Lieutenant imagining this in his panicked state.

All the way home the Lieutenant couldn't help looking over his shoulder. He was sure he was being followed. Get control of yourself, the voice in his head kept saying. Sometimes even he was afraid that the lines were blurring between his imaginary spy adventures and reality. A dozen scenarios were running through his mind, the many possibilities of what could have happened to Amy — she could be hurt, run over in the street, fallen down the escalator at the mall, a heart attack — surely not, she was young and healthy. Maybe she ran into a friend and was having coffee and then a bigger fear hit him, maybe she ran away with another man. She couldn't, she wouldn't, do that to him. He was showing his arrogance about his own self-worth.

The Lieutenant couldn't fathom that Amy would ever leave him. She loved him, took such good care of him. And he was so good to her — wasn't he? He began to wonder now if she felt the same. A world of doubt suddenly flooded in, he began to imagine a smorgasbord of inadequacies he might be guilty of. But Amy had never complained, she always showered him, maybe flattered him, with praise.

Had she merely being suffering in silence or perhaps, making up the difference, elsewhere, with someone else?

Stop, he told himself, this is insane. She's at home cooking dinner. To try and keep his focus, and avoid a trip to the mental institution, the Lieutenant decided to imagine what she might be cooking tonight. Perhaps a roast, with those little "new" potatoes he loved so much or the ravioli she filled with a variety of fragrant cheeses. He realized now he'd skipped lunch and this line of thought wasn't helping the rumbling noise in his tummy. The Lieutenant almost missed his stop lost in confused thought, wavering between his fears of her demise and the anticipation of another fragrant, tasty gourmet meal. If he didn't keep his portions small and stay on top of his exercise regime, he'd easily put on ten pounds before Amy went back to school in the fall.

The Lieutenant sprinted from the metro to their apartment, taking every possible shortcut, anxious to solve the mystery of Amy's whereabouts and put his mind at ease. His heart was beating so fast he thought it might burst out of his chest onto the sidewalk, running ahead of him, daring him to catch up.

There weren't any lights on in the apartment, at least none that he could see from the front entrance, which only added to the nervousness. He did have a quick thought that perhaps Amy was playing a seductive game on him and when he opened the door she'd slither across the floor in a snake suit or perhaps be serving him dinner in a French maid uniform. The Lieutenant caught himself wondering how such things could go through his mind at a time like this. Perhaps it was wishful thinking, both that she was safe and that he'd be getting some relief from all this stress.

He hastily grabbed his keys from his uniformed pocket, finding it difficult to locate the keyhole due to the shaking in his hands. But finally he hit the mark and as the door bolted open he felt the presence of someone behind him. When he turned to look, it was too late. He was shoved inside the apartment, barely avoiding falling over the table beside the door where Amy kept her ceramic turtle collection. The Lieutenant bounced back quickly and came up swinging but this guy had the advantage on him, the advantage of a gun.

The events of the next ten minutes or so were a whirlwind, a blur that he'd try to remember for years to come. You kidnapped my wife? Where is she? Is she ok? What could you possibly want from us? And that's the question he got an answer to, an answer and a demand. A demand he found almost impossible to live with, but this was his wife, his Amy, the love of his life. However, he also loved his country and his country's army, his army. It was his entire world, well almost.

Of course, he was told not to go the police, not to tell anyone—and that meant *no* one—or else. The else didn't need to be explained further. He understood the stakes. What he didn't understand was, why him. There were plenty of other people at the Pentagon, many of them with a higher security clearance who could get what they wanted, assuming they would give in to their demands. Perhaps these folks thought the Lieutenant was an easy mark, that they'd have no trouble getting what they needed from him. But he wondered who wouldn't do as told, in this situation?

Perhaps he should be flattered, in a perverse sort of way, that he was chosen for this mission. But, the 9mm Glock pistol the kidnapper was pointing at him negated those feelings rather quickly. Now he had a real spy mission to complete, but this one didn't quite fit with the elaborate twists and turns, not to mention the exotic locations he usually imagined. Most unfortunately of all, it was for the wrong side. How could he steal secrets from his own country, the one he'd sworn to protect and defend, from the very organization that had given him his entire working career? If he was caught, his career—his life, as far as he was concerned—was over. How could he do such a thing? To save his Amy, that's how.

The Lieutenant listened carefully to the instructions, he was good at retaining those types of details, especially given that Amy's life depended on it. They not only wanted the Lieutenant to obtain information, but to replace it with misinformation, presumably to throw the U.S. off course. "Duplicate" documents would be left for him in the apartment while he was at work, the next day he'd make the switch, bring them home and leave the real ones in the same place on the coffee table. Someone would pick them up the next day; again, in his absence. It was made clear he wasn't to be at home during the daytime, he wasn't to see the "deliveryman."

"Where is Amy? When will I see her? How do I know she's ok?" he asked furtively.

The man, clad only in black — pants, shirt, shoes, a leather jacket, expensive Italian leather — moved toward the computer. Before the Lieutenant could protest, for what little good that might do, the man had a video stream running on the screen and there was his beloved Amy, looking tiny and helpless, pacing back and forth in a small dark room, oblivious to the fact that she was on camera. Just as the Lieutenant moved in closer for a better look, the man cut the feed.

"As you can see, she's fine. Let's hope it can stay that way," he noted in tart reply.

"When will she be freed?" he asked, the desperation clear in his quivering voice. He wanted to cry.

"When we are done with you," came the rather emphatic reply, "That's enough questions for now. I'm sure I don't need to tell you, that your every move is being watched, so don't think you can escape us."

"Who is us?" the Lieutenant inquired, ignoring the command for no further questions.

"I told you no more questions. Besides, it's of no relevance to you."

Relevance, all things were relevant. The Lieutenant wanted to know who he was spying for, what world catastrophe he might be causing or adverting, what dastardly deeds he would soon to be guilty of. His heart sank to his stomach, and then to his shoes. How could he get caught in this position? How could he let himself be compromised? How could he let Amy be put in harm's way?

Thoughts of harm, serious harm, were at the forefront of his mind, but not for Amy. The Lieutenant wanted to beat the crap out of this man, the messenger, tearing him limb from limb, before throwing him in the Potomac. Physically, the guy was much smaller, the Lieutenant was sure he could take him, but size didn't always matter when it came to a fight and this was no time to find out. Besides, it wasn't a risk he could take, at least not right now, he had to get Amy back. He had to get his head around what was happening, figure out how to respond, decide if there were any other options.

With a final admonition about the very real threat to Amy's personal safety and doing exactly as he was told, the man was gone. He moved like a svelte tiger prowling in the night, so much so that the Lieutenant didn't even hear him close the door.

How could this be happening? Why me? Why me? The Lieutenant said over and over again in his head. In a desperate and hopeless act, he spent an hour on the computer trying to find that video feed of Amy. But, he knew better than to think this guy would leave a trail. The Lieutenant wondered who had this type of technology, could it be a clue to who was involved, who was destroying his life. His heart was torn. On the one hand he so wanted to see the video of Amy again, but on the other hand, he couldn't bear the thought of watching her locked away somewhere on account of him, of his career. The guilt was almost too much for him to handle, but he knew he had to pull himself together and figure a way out of this. Now was the time to put his day-dreaming spy adventures to a real purpose. He had to devise a way to rescue Amy from this wretched box she was locked away in before a worse fate could befall her.

CHAPTER TWENTY-TWO

Thank goodness for 4G technology. Under the branches of a coconut tree on this un-named island, with a gentle breeze blowing through his wavy locks, Justin sat in the sand, laptop perched on his extended legs and connected to the outside world. What he needed now was some luck and a few favors. Fortunately, he had some friends he could count on to help them out of the quite delicate situation he and Amelia had found themselves in. The question was how to enlist their support without getting them ensnared in this labyrinth and more importantly, how to avoid leaving a digital trail that would expose their whereabouts. With modern tracking devices he knew they would need to change locations, at least every few days, to avoid being caught.

They'd both taken all the money they could withdraw from every ATM on Panzau before they departed in the middle of the night. Justin had even liquidated the lab's grants account despite knowing it was a federal offense to misuse government funds. Given this desperate situation, they had no other choice. Who knew how long they might be on the run, moving from place to place, living in backwater locations with sketchy accommodations and finding cash work, just to keep themselves alive.

Their current accommodations were in many ways, quite superb. What high quality resort could offer the beauty and tranquility they had here? When their food supply ran out, they'd be surviving on mangoes and breadfruit which would get old pretty fast. For now this place, this island on the edge of the universe, offered them a peaceful, serene existence and, but for the fact that they were on the run, quite literally for their lives, it would have proven an idyllic setting, especially with Amelia there. Without the distractions of life and death they were facing, he'd very much enjoy getting to know Amelia better, much better.

But romantic notions, perhaps aspirations, aside, it was time for the two of them to get to the bottom of this story and most of all, live to tell about it. They'd found themselves in a dilemma of biblical proportions and they had a lot of work to do to unravel the mystery. Amelia was making herself useful, if not as a spy, at least in the domestic arena. Nervous energy Justin suspected; he was pretty convinced she wasn't normally a domestic diva. She'd managed to scrounge up some mangoes to go with the jerky and stale bread they'd wisely thrown in the boat at the last minute. But the kicker was the coffee she somehow had managed to brew using one of the Bunsen burners they'd brought from the lab. Justin thought she was crazy for bringing it, but now he appreciated her foresight.

"Any luck?" she inquired.

"Well, I'm getting a signal, a weak one, but enough to surf the web. I've done some searching to see who has recently purchased thalidomerta. At least they might narrow the field of culprits."

"What about Skype, can we call out from here?" she asked with a hopeful refrain.

"Yes, I think we can definitely get out, not sure how long we might hold the call so we'll have to be strategic on who we call and what we talk about. No calling your mother," he added with a laugh.

Amelia appreciated the attempt at humor, but she knew, as well as he did, there was no way they could call family. They were both painfully aware their loved ones were being close monitored for contact. She never thought she would hope to hear her mother badger her about getting married. How she would love this juicy scenario of her daughter on a faraway, deserted—well almost deserted, island with a handsome single man. The mileage Amelia's mother would get out of this one, especially with a little harmless elaboration. She'd be telling her friends the story for years to come. Amelia wondered, given their current predicament, whether her mother would ever get a chance to know about this island, this adventure — if one could call it such a thing. She realized they were in serious danger, how could she not. It was hardly a time to be thinking about her mother's meddling ways. It's funny the inane things that stress can bring into your mind.

"Let's have some breakfast first, we have a tough day ahead of us I suspect," Amelia said.

"I guess beggars can't be choosers, at least it beats the Terrace Café at the Venus and Mars," Justin said, adding, "Do you think our pal, the General, is enjoying his breakfast alone?"

"I suspect he's not enjoying anything and, if it's within his power, he'll have the whole Pacific command looking for us."

"Well, here's the thing," Justin started, obviously having put some thought into the situation, "I think he's working alone, or pretty much alone. There wasn't anyone else on the island, it's too small, someone would have seen them. Besides, it seems he's gotten himself into a bit of a pickle and at this point I think he's trying to drag himself out before taking it higher and risking his career. The Pentagon doesn't look too favorably on failed operations, especially something as big as this."

"I hope you're right," Amelia said, passing the mango.

Breakfast finished, the summer sun was beating down on them like a couple of pizzas thrown in a stone oven, so they moved inland under the cool shade of the palms. The 4G coverage was better near the beach so they'd have to alternate their online research time and their reading, to manage both the heat and the internet reception. Thankfully, Justin had invested in a solar charger some months back when the electricity on the island was on the fritz; otherwise, they would be powerless, literally. They certainly felt powerless, hiding on a remote island, fearing the weight of the entire U.S. military, perhaps the Chinese government as well, to come bearing down on them at any second.

Justin and Amelia weren't sure how they were going to outrun both, they were caught in a triangle, one in which they could quickly get squeezed out. It was bad enough when they thought some rogue person or company was shooting at them, now with two of the most powerful governments in the world on their trail, they were truly in the crosshairs.

They had to find out who was making this toxic cocktail that had upended their lives. Some days Justin wished he was sweeping floors in a factory; the stress would be less, the safety much more. But that wasn't him, he wouldn't be satisfied with that kind of life. His goals were different, he'd long ago decided that work had to matter, and not just for him. Justin felt bad disappearing suddenly from the island. Even though they were in danger, he felt he was deserting his trusted staff. Given the recent events, not least of all the shooting, he knew they'd be worried to find him missing today, not just from the lab but from Panzau. He couldn't tell them, couldn't leave any clues that might risk their safety as well. Still it pained him to put them through the agony of wondering what happened, whether he and Amelia were safe, and if they would ever see him again. He wondered that himself.

There was no time for self-pity or speculation about what the future might hold. Right now their future was looking particularly bleak and the two of them couldn't seem to agree on the best way forward. Justin was gung-ho on acting like a couple of CIA agents, chasing leads all over the world, if necessary, until they got the answers they wanted or else. The else being that someone put a stop to their investigation, or them. Amelia, on the other hand, wanted to take a more conservative approach. What she really wanted was to get on a plane and go home, pretend none of this happened, and go on with life as usual. While she knew she was kidding herself that this could be done, she thought there must still be a way to get back to the states and remain safe. Justin was less optimistic and less naïve.

Justin spent twenty minutes scurrying about the island trying to get decent reception for a Skype call to some friends, friends who could keep quiet, friends who wouldn't ask too many questions. He knew some well-placed people in both the government and internet technology circles that had access to, or could hack their way into, the information he needed. The time difference complicated things, but those IT guys were up all hours of the night anyway, he wouldn't worry about waking them. Besides, this clearly classified as an emergency, it was hard to imagine more dire circumstances.

Technology was an amazing spy tool. Within a few hours, Justin's friends had put together a short list of locations where high levels of thalidomerta had been shipped. Now, the trick was to figure out the "right" location, if there even was a right location. This process could be happening simultaneously at multiple locations. Justin and Amelia poured over the list, there were four in China, but they needed to find out if factories or military installations were near. One was in Mexico, almost certainly for manufacturing, so they ruled it out. There were a few in Europe but the concentrations were small and the supply inconsistent. One was in Taiwan and two were in the U.S.; although, in locations far removed from one another.

Amelia suggested cross checking with other chemicals they suspected. If a location had purchased both, it should be top priority. A second call to friends, Justin didn't want to wear out his welcome, but it had to be done. This time it wasn't so easy to fend off their questions. The first time he'd pretended it was part of his research and that all was well in his island paradise. They were none the wiser. But this time, they were starting to wonder what was up given the questions about obscure combinations of chemicals, not the type of thing Justin was usually working with. He told them it was a special project that the he had been asked by the government to undertake, that it was hush-hush and he'd really appreciate their discretion. That was good enough for them, they were ready to jump to his assistance, anxious to be part of a secret mission for the U.S. Government. If they only knew.

In the meantime, Justin was contemplating how they were going to travel unnoticed. Should they get fake passports, or should they go with the old eyeglass and mustache disguise, pull some comedy routine and hope they could laugh their way to safety. He thought of suggesting to Amelia that he go it alone, not because she wasn't up to the task, but because of some misplaced sense of chivalry, a noble gesture he was sure she wouldn't appreciate. Besides, she was pretty amazing with the logistics, not to mention her technical expertise in ferreting out the chemical background.

In a matter of hours, Amelia's suggestion of cross checking chemical purchases had significantly shortened the list to a manageable number. The only places left on the list were in China and Taiwan. Now they'd just head over to the nearest Chinese embassy for a visa and book their ticket with the Travelocity gnome. If only it were that simple.

Getting to the next level didn't prove as easy. Trying to determine if there were military installations, some type of government lab, or perhaps even a manufacturing company in those locations, took some ingenious research. Amelia knew that information on these types of facilities existed, even within the EPAs information systems, but her security clearance didn't give her access to that level of detail. She debated the possibility of contacting someone who could get to the information, but Justin quickly dispelled going down this route. First, it might blow their cover if she made contact with someone in her office. Justin was sure that by now the General had a team of CIA agents looking for them. And second, no one was going to risk their job handing out classified information. Where are those WikiLeaks folks when you need them? No, it was too risky and too unreliable for Amelia to call her friends. They'd find their own way or Justin's guy might have to do some creative hacking.

Surprisingly, it wasn't that difficult to find some of the military bases, or at least the ones they wanted you to find. A couple of bases in China matched up with the location of the chemicals and were kept on the list. But the location that stood out was in Taiwan. They couldn't pinpoint the exact location but large amounts of chemicals, and a variety of types, had been sent to this mountainous area, consistently over the past few years.

Sitting on the sandy shores, Justin felt as though he never wanted to leave this place. Maybe that was his best option. He was easily distracted by the beauty, the sounds, the tranquility it inspired. He felt safe here, but it was a false sense of safety and he knew that. Eventually someone would find them, even here in the remotest of locations. It was most unlikely, given what they knew, that they'd be left alone, no matter where they went. Justin couldn't forget the veiled threat from the General, that they could easily be arrested and put on trial for espionage. The two of them would make the perfect scapegoats the General needed.

Justin's thoughts were interrupted by the sound of two black pelicans, fishing about twenty feet offshore. They flew, floated really, just above the surface of the water looking for their prey—their lunch. He watched them dive headlong into the crystal blue water, occasionally scoring a fish but more often than not, coming up empty handed, or empty beaked, as it were. What gorgeous creatures they were, long necks, graceful and elegant, even longer beaks, slender and pointed.

"Earth to Justin," he heard Amelia saying, "What's so interesting?"

He needed only to point toward the water for Amelia to see the pair flying, diving, sailing along on the ocean as if they owned it.

"How beautiful," she gushed, "the poor fish won't know what hit them, swimming along in peace, when suddenly some huge billed creature swoops in on top of them and they're done for."

"That may be exactly what happens to us." Justin duly noted, bringing them both back to the ugly reality that haunted them in the midst of this scenic paradise.

"Can't we just stay here?" Amelia asked in a sad whining tone, her face that of a puppy dog trying to charm its owner.

If it were up to Justin, she could have anything she wanted. Standing next to him on the beach, the golden rays of sunlight sparkling on her fair skin, he'd never been more attracted to her. His gaze lasted into an uncomfortable moment, when she decided to break the lingering silence and the longing look by heading into the ocean for a swim.

The water was a pleasant, lukewarm temperature, probably eighty-two degrees, a welcome respite from the sun and the worries of the day; although, even the pelicans playing and feeding couldn't help Amelia escape her fears. She wondered if her mother had called the Venus and Mars, only to find her missing. Was she now furious or frightened—Amelia wasn't sure which one it might be. Her mother would never imagine Amelia embroiled in such a sticky situation, she wouldn't expect danger and was more likely to be furious—furious she couldn't keep tabs on what was going on with her life, her love life in particular. It pained Amelia to leave her mother hanging, unable to communicate directly, or even indirectly, for fear of blowing their cover. She wanted to send an e-mail, a call was clearly not an option, and Justin reminded her that email traffic could just as easily be traced. Even if she opened a new "fake" account, it was most likely they, whoever they were, had her family under surveillance and she'd be putting them in danger.

In fact, she feared whether her family, especially her mother, might be interrogated or worse, in the hunt to find them. Amelia began to cry, tears drizzling from the sides of her eyes like a well-worn faucet incapable of holding back the drip. She tried to stop, or at least muffle the sound, but the tears keep coming until suddenly one of the pelicans dove mere inches from her, startling Amelia out of her melancholy. The pelican had scored a clownfish, which it swallowed in one gulp, the same way local folks down oysters in seafood restaurants all along the Gulf Coast.

Justin laughed furiously when the Pelican almost roosted on Amelia's head. "I think he likes you. You really have a way with these creatures. First the dolphins, now the pelicans."

"Well, I wish they'd like me a little less," Amelia said, wiping away the tears as if they were water, splashed on her face by the pelican's broad wings.

"It's really a compliment, they feel the calmness in your soul," Justin replied.

That comment made Amelia laugh. Her soul was anything but calm today, maybe these big birds were dyslexic in their people reading skills. If anything, she thought they were very gentle and kind and trying to pass their calm on to her. Neither Justin nor Amelia would dare admit their fear to one another. It was an unspoken truth between them.

"Perhaps they could feel it a little further away," she suggested and it was as if the Pelican heard her, understood exactly what she had said, and thus, took its flight. Maybe these birds were smarter than she had given them credit for.

"Hey, come look at this," Justin yelled from the beach.

Amelia hurried out of the water and plopped herself beside him and his computer. "What are we looking at?"

"We are looking at the place we need to be," he said with an air of emphatic confidence.

"Which is where?"

"Zhushan, Taiwan. A small village in the mountains."

"What, and give up this glorious find?" Amelia asked, gesturing with her arm towards the sandy beach and green fragrant coastline as if she were Vanna White, bringing your attention to the Wheel of Fortune letters, which now seemed to spell B-I-N-G-O.

"I think we are on to something here," Justin proudly proclaimed. He explained to her, the high volume of chemicals, of all types, that had been shipped there during the past five years — thalidomerta, in particular, over the past two months. As far as he could tell there were no military installations nearby, but there was a small lab. A lab that appeared to be one of the few sources of employment in this village. There had to be a connection, they needed to find out for sure.

"How do we get there?" Amelia asked.

"That's the million dollar question," Justin sighed.

CHAPTER TWENTY-THREE

In the silence of his office, door tightly closed, the window open for some modicum of ventilation, Mr. Kao was devising plan B, and just in case, Plan C. He wasn't the brightest star in the sky, but he could see this operation turning out badly. He didn't want to be a victim of the fall if it should happen. Sometimes he amazed himself, when he thought of how he got caught up in this. However it ended, he planned to walk away with plenty of cash, and he just had to figure out how to exit Taiwan unnoticed. Perhaps one final explosion would provide the cover he needed.

Given the number of explosions at this place, no one would be surprised at one more, and he surely had the resources to make another happen. It was also a good way to ensure that the truth never saw the light of day. He'd blow up the entire lab if necessary, leaving no trace of what had happened there or the records that could prove it. Never mind that the explosion might kill some of the good citizens of Zhushan, or leave them in jeopardy of exposure to highly toxic substances. It wouldn't affect him, he'd be long gone.

Kao gave some thought on whether to take his wife should he need to make a quick departure from this peaceful village. For most people, this would have been an easy decision; of course, you'd take your spouse. But not Mr. Kao. He didn't have a magnanimous bone in his body and the only reason he could conjure up for taking Mrs. Kao was for the limited assistance she might be to him, the domestic skills she could bring to taking care of him. His selfishness was boundless.

But whether or not to have Mrs. Kao in tow, during an imminent departure, was one of the easier decisions in Plan

B, and Plan C, for that matter. The way things were going he might need a Plan H. When he started working at the lab, things were easy, he was simply the manager of a small operation working for the Taiwanese government. But things turned complicated when Taiwan decided to rent their services to both the Chinese and the U.S. Taiwan didn't trust either country but they needed the support of both, just in case. They needed leverage to maintain their independence.

A cooing sound caught Mr. Kao's attention and upon further inspection he saw a couple of pigeons on his windowsill. They flapped nosily, brooding and pooping, leaving their calling card. Their cooing was maddening, the low continual lull, the sound of death he was convinced. They were hapless creatures with no real purpose in life, except to, apparently, harass him, and of course, leave their droppings on his window.

Enough of this bird chatter, back to plan B and his eventual escape. He knew he needed a lot of cash to set him up well, in the fashion to which he hoped to become accustomed for the rest of his life. He'd put a lot on the line, taken significant risks, and he wanted to be duly rewarded. Never mind that he hadn't delivered the final product; although, that could be problematic, he surmised. What a genius. He would definitely need plan C and D. He'd have to find a safe place to hide out, maybe a remote island paradise somewhere, where hopefully neither of his "customers" could ever find him. Of course, the logical conclusion would be to finish what he'd been engaged for, deliver on his promises, collect a big bonus and move on to that life of luxury he was sure he deserved.

His next decision was when to make his escape for a better life. This was the bigger dilemma for him—not a moral one, of course—but rather a financial one. If he could in fact deliver the final product, it would mean considerably more money for him and for Mr. Kao, more money was definitely a welcome addition.

The trouble was whether he could in fact deliver. The lab had been experimenting for almost five years and only succeeded in not burning the place to the ground, which was no small miracle given the cocktail of chemicals they'd been mixing. At least he'd know how to destroy the place and the evidence of the lab's work on his way out of town. Certainly no one would be surprised if the lab went up in flames, least of all the fire department. The lab had been their primary source of business for years now.

Mr. Kao felt sure they were close to perfecting the mix for a successful product that would meet the requirements he had been presented with. If he could actually achieve this goal, then he would have to decide when, where and who to deliver it to. Should he sell out to the highest bidder, sell it to both of them, or choose between them? Financially, he'd do well to sell it to both sides, assuming he didn't get caught by the other, in which case he'd only need enough money for a casket — his own.

On the other hand, if he skipped out now, he was much less likely to get caught or to bring harm to himself. If he didn't have the final formula they were much less likely to care where he went. He was a nuisance to them, but not much more. In fact, they'd probably be glad he was gone, except that he did know too much. But his customers were savvy, sophisticated people and they also understood human nature. They knew Mr. Kao appreciated the risks to himself, if not others. They'd picked the right guy, he was happy to keep his mouth shut, for a price.

He took the file from its secret location on the bottom side of his desk and reviewed the details. He'd kept a very accurate accounting of the payments he'd received, from both sides, on separate ledgers of course. Never the twain shall meet. It had all been in cash, no one would ever be able to trace it. He smiled at his good fortune, how he'd managed to be in the right place at the right time. He could have never imagined that being born in this loathsome village would one day prove to be a benefit.

Frankly he was amazed that he'd been able to keep all of this from Mrs. Kao. If she had discovered what he was doing, she would have left him, or worse, she'd demand half the pie. Mr. Kao was nothing if not selfish and he had no plans to share his good fortune with anyone, least of all his un-beloved wife.

A knock at the door sent him scrambling to hide the evidence before opening up the door. It was Lin.

"Mr. Kao, I believe we have good news."

"What is it?" he barked, never imagining her response.

"I believe we have a successful formula. No explosions or other adverse results. The chemicals seem stable, the mixture is odorless just as requested." Lin proudly reported, not knowing whether this was really the news Mr. Kao was hoping for.

"What? Are you sure? But you only mixed it yesterday, we have to wait and see what results may develop."

"Yes, I know," said Lin, in her deferential employee tone, "but so far so good and it's been more than twenty four hours. This is the formula which came in two days ago."

Two days ago, he thought, hmm. Yes he remembered which side it came from. He almost laughed, now he knew for sure who the winner was in this current "cold war." It wasn't surprising, he'd have bet money on this result. In fact, he wished he had, then he'd been ever richer.

Well, let's not get too excited. Let's see how it looks tomorrow. Go back and mix another batch. We'll need to try it several times to be sure."

"Yes sir," she replied, bowed and was gone before he could even blink.

On her way back to her work space it dawned on Lin that this success could mean her downfall. If this formula was the ultimate goal, their work was complete, job done. Would she soon be unemployed? What would become of her family? What about the opportunities for Bingwen's future? Would he ever become a doctor? She knew her husband, Gang, would never earn a sufficient income to support them, let along to send Bingwen to college. Lin had such high hopes for Bingwen, to make something of himself and, more importantly, to do something that would change the world, or at least this corner of it.

Lin wondered again today, as she had on many occasions over the past few years, whether the lab was developing a cure, a life-saving product. But Lin knew this was wishful thinking. She feared that what they were doing here would have quite the opposite effect on the world. Lin had a feeling in the pit of her stomach that this project was up to no good.

She poured the first two chemicals into the beaker, no adverse results, no reaction at all. Lin was no chemist, she didn't know what to expect. As she reached for the next chemical, Lin realized she had a choice, a choice that could change the future, her future, perhaps the future of the world. She could always change a substance or the amount, she could alter the results. If this was an important cure or drug of some type, she would feel guilty for the rest of her life for interfering. But if it was a dangerous substance that could hurt or kill thousands, maybe more, Lin would be the one changing the world—although she'd be the only one who knew it. Lin stood silent, but the noise in her head was growing louder as she pondered her next move.

Mr. Kao was pondering his next move with even more vigor now that he imagined success could well be at hand. If Lin was right, it would mean he could wrap this project up soon and be on his way to better times. But given the dashed hopes of the past few years, he expected to see the place blow sky high before the afternoon bell rung, sending his employees on their way, back to their meager homes and shallow existence, none the wiser as to the fruits of their labors.

He knew better than to count his chickens before they hatched. He'd been close to this dream before, only to have it thwarted by failure or the occasional, unexpected intervention of the suits. He was surprised that'd he had the patience to wait it out this long, but the payoff was too big, he had no choice if he wanted to get out of this remote village and live the good life.

For now, his focus was on his departure, his imminent departure, and how best to not leave any incriminating evidence. He was done with this lab, this village, the people of this town, and not least of all, Mrs. Kao. He knew that he was a different sort, a worldly sophisticated man such as himself didn't belong here with these naïfs. They didn't appreciate him, his foresight for not only making the most of opportunities that presented themselves, but for making your own opportunities, his head for business. Maybe one day they would appreciate his cunning, once they realized he'd made himself wealthy and was living a life they could only dream of. His days filled with lavish food and entertainment in the confines of a mansion most of them could only imagine. He'd again be the talk of the town, but this time he'd also be the envy of them all.

Mr. Kao sat arrogantly behind his desk, the king of this small universe, papers scattered about, pigeons still cooing at the window, his rice bowl at the ready. The rumble of his stomach reminded him that lunchtime was approaching, and he was left to wonder what Mrs. Kao had prepared for him today. What, besides rice? There was always rice, everywhere in Taiwan, in China, there was always rice. He made a silent vow to himself that once he was rid of this place, he'd never eat rice again.

He'd eat steak, yes steak, every day and maybe lots of pork. There'd be French pastries and fresh fruits, the imported kind, like kiwis from New Zealand and grapefruits from Florida — the best ones, the ones from Indian River. These were the good things he expected to learn about in his new life. Now he was making himself hungry, hungry for things he couldn't have, at least not today, so he decided to see what meager rations Mrs. Kao had allotted him for lunch.

There was rice, of course. Exasperated, he wondered whether she might even consider serving a meal without rice. She'd never have the imagination, this was Taiwan after all, and things were nothing if not consistent. Today there were bean sprouts, plenty of bean sprouts, and a small serving of chicken; fortunately, a very tasty chicken with peanut sauce. At least she'd included some dessert, a pudding, creamy but not too sweet. He liked his sugar, but she worried about his weight and kept the portions small. What she didn't know, or least he hoped she didn't, was that he frequented the local bakery, imbibing in pastries, puddings, and the vast assortment of cookies they were famous for. He even kept a small stash in his desk drawer for those moments, late in the afternoon, when his sugar level began to wane and he needed a burst of energy.

Mr. Kao reached into the filing cabinet, moving aside some old Chinese poetry books, and found the bottle of homemade rice wine. Today was special, his plan was complete, perhaps his work as well, so he was going to celebrate. He poured a gracious portion into the handle-less, porcelain tea cup that sat next to the dated black telephone, with its rotary dial and startling loud ring. He quickly returned the bottle to the filing cabinet, this wasn't a bar after all, he'd save the real drinking for later.

CHAPTER TWENTY-FOUR

Danger was their business at the Chinese Ministry of Defense, a business they knew well and were inclined to perfect. Being a superpower brought a lot of challenges, one could never rest on their laurels, the enemy was always a step ahead. But they had plans to stop their enemies in their tracks, bring them to their knees and win the new cold war, which was heating up fast. It was a different war now, one not fought with the threat of missiles, or even nuclear threats, but something just as serious, something lethal — chemical weapons. Easy to produce and easy to deploy, this was the way they'd chosen to go, the path to prosperity and peace, but peace at an enormous cost.

Taiwan had always been a balancing act. China beat its chest and demanded their return to the fold, knowing that in practical terms this could be difficult to achieve, especially given the U.S. support for Taiwan's independence. And that was why they'd chosen this path, it wasn't just about Taiwan, it was about the U.S., their arrogance and bullying, thinking they were so superior and could continue to run the world. China decided it was time to show them that there was a new sheriff in town and this sheriff had an iron fist.

General Peng decided it was time to call a meeting, let the suits bring everyone up to date, giving them the official version of the story. It had taken no small amount of finesse to make sure the truth would never see the light of day, that folks in the Ministry always believed this was solely the work of Taiwan in a misguided attempt to protect themselves, aided by the U.S., leaving sufficient grounds for retaliation against both. The U.S. was always the ultimate target, how convenient that their liaison with Taiwan would provide that validation.

They met at four that afternoon, an elite group of brass, the fewer who knew the better. Even fewer knew the actual truth. The suits were all in attendance, having been well-schooled by the General as to the facts appropriate for consumption by this particular group. The room was dark, no windows and low lighting as well. Shadows danced about the room as if they were the ghosts of meetings past, of times when other sinister events were discussed and planned in this room. Individual lives were of no consequence here. The greater good, as they determined good to be, was the ultimate goal.

The suits laid it all out, in power point no less, presenting a version of the facts that satisfied the needs of those positioned closely around the round bamboo table. This table had seen a lot of discussions and weathered the toil of many a conflict, internal and international. As the suits saw it and, more importantly, presented it, Taiwan was up to its usual no good. They had sold out to the Americans on the promise that they would be protected should China attack. Of course, China was never supposed to find out they were developing this chemical weapon. But then Taiwan had double crossed the U.S. making basically the same agreement with China. The suits failed to mention that important piece of information.

The suits estimated it would take two weeks to acquire the relevant intelligence. Two weeks—who were they kidding? Even under significant pressure, the chances of the Lieutenant coming through in that timeframe were significantly low. He started to ask, actually suggest rather vigorously, that they were wrong, but he quickly thought better of it. Others in the room might not be so pleased with his challenging them, he had his own career to worry about. They'd made the promise, let them deliver—or, suffer the consequences. Other, smaller, much smaller failures had been tolerated. But now, the stakes were too high.

The reports were handed out, no questions were asked, and the group disbursed as if the meeting had never occurred. Officially, it never had.

CHAPTER TWENTY-FIVE

When the General realized that Justin and Amelia were gone, it was too late. How could he have been so stupid, thinking there was no way off this island? Obviously Justin had friends, smarter and better friends than the General imagined. They were gone, he might as well accept it and put his other plans into motion. He should have arrested them when he had the chance.

They couldn't have gone far, but given their apparent sense of curiosity they weren't likely to let this go. Justin and Amelia would surface and he'd be there to find them. But then what? Where was he going with this? The General hadn't anticipated the situation playing out in quite this way. He knew there was a good chance they might not cooperate, but for them to disappear overnight was a bit of a blow. As he saw it, he'd played fair with them, given them a way out—sure, he was lying to them, but in his mind his means justified the end.

A greater good was at stake and the General saw it as his job to bring that good to its' rightful conclusion. Doing it his way would have saved their honor and quite possibly, their lives. But now, with them on the run, there were no guarantees. They were caught in a triangle, one they didn't even know existed, and all the angles were dangerous. That danger gave the General options. He could do nothing and let someone else take care of them; although, he couldn't be sure the Chinese or the Taiwanese knew and if they did, whether they would deal with Justin and Amelia. Surely, they must be keeping tabs on them, or worse, maybe Justin and Amelia were working for one of the other sides of the triangle. Could they actually be traitors or was the General trying to convince himself to make it easier to do what he knew he must?

He had to get back to the Pentagon and move quickly to contain this situation. A situation that, if not handled properly, might bring a rather unceremonious end to his otherwise stellar career. If handled properly, he could exit the stage as the hero he'd always dreamed of being.

The General called the front desk and told the receptionist he was checking out and needed a taxi to the airport.

"Seen enough birds?" she asked.

"Huh?" in the ire of the moment he'd quickly given up his bird watchers badge.

"I thought you were here to see our birds," the receptionist responded.

"Oh yes, and lovely birds they are, but there's been an emergency back home and I'm needed urgently."

"Sorry to hear that, I hope you'll visit again soon."

"I'm sure I will," he replied, knowing the chances that he'd ever be on this island again were even less that his chances of winning the lottery.

He hoped against hope that he could get a seat on today's plane. The good General could practically hear the ticking from his Swiss watch, a gift from his wife more than twenty years before. The ticking was only in his mind, a subtle reminder that time was running out to handle this precarious situation.

Fortunately, he was able to change this ticket — for a fee of $300. These airlines really had you over a barrel. They would charge for seat belts if they could get away with it. People only put up with this kind of treatment because they really had no choice, except not to fly, which was not an option for him at the moment. In a mere thirty hours or so, he'd be back at home. In the meantime he had a lot of thinking, planning, and scheming to do. He couldn't help but wonder how it had all gone south so quickly. But it didn't really matter now, it was his job to make it right, whatever right was.

Back at the Chinese Ministry of State Security, they had their own issues to deal with, several of them. General Peng was well aware that Justin and Amelia were on the run, but he wasn't sure where they had gone. He pondered whether they were out of the picture for good, but he doubted these two determined Americans would give up so easily. He didn't understand their motivations, it was hard for him to imagine they were so concerned about the environment or about people they didn't even know being injured. Perhaps, they didn't care, maybe they were actually spies. The CIA seemed to be very skilled in farming out covert work to those you would least expect, hiding the obvious in plain sight. The MND couldn't be sure who Justin and Amelia were working for; although, at this point it didn't matter whether it was for themselves or for some rival government, they had to be dealt with.

Now the Lieutenant and Amy had fallen into the mix, quite possibly offering the best, and fastest, solution to achieving their goals. The good Lieutenant would never risk his wife's life. That was another thing about the Americans — anything for love. The Lieutenant was putty in their hands as long as they had control of his beloved Amy. The conundrum was how to manage the situation to get what they wanted in the shortest amount of time. Complications were not welcome. There'd been enough of that already, on several fronts. The Lieutenant had to provide the intelligence, but without getting caught. In their estimation, that would be no easy task.

A plan was already well underway, according to the suits, to get the intelligence they needed. But General Peng never trusted the suits, who appeared confident and well informed, filling him with lavish details, as if they were mind readers anticipating every move. They laid out masterful plans, always one step ahead of the enemy, always anticipating his next question. But no one was that good. Their apparent perfection belied their faults, the cracks in an almost seamless operation. He wasn't paid to trust them. Nonetheless, he was forced to rely on them to some extent, often to a large extent; too large for his liking, when delicate situations could lead to his demise. Their failures had been few. He didn't doubt they were skilled, in fact, that was what kept him awake at night, wondering whether they were actually outsmarting him.

They were right to believe in the eagerness of the Lieutenant to comply with their requests, as if he actually had a choice. His beloved Amy was in harm's way and being the Boy Scout that he was, he would fall on his proverbial sword for her if necessary. Fortunately, a sword wouldn't be warranted, but betraying his country felt like one, no less. The struggle in his mind was epic—can I do wrong to make this right? The life of someone he loved was in jeopardy and it was within his power to change that, to save her. But was there another way, one in which he could have her back, unscathed and still keep his honor, and his job?

It was a frightful dilemma, the likes of which he could have never imagined despite his wild and colorful daydreaming episodes. In all of these years at the Pentagon, he'd never thought of this scenario presenting itself in quite this way. Sure he'd imagined himself captured in some secretive undercover operation, facing torture and yet resisting, repeatedly, any opportunities to give up classified information. But this, this was different. If they'd taken him, he was sure he would not have cooperated, risking and maybe even losing his life. His stubbornness alone, never mind his sense of loyalty, would have likely been his downfall. Of course, he'd die for her but that was not a choice he'd been offered. With Amy he had to take a different approach, he couldn't bear her suffering because of him, because of what he did for a living.

The Lieutenant would give them what they wanted — he didn't see any other choice — assuming he could get his hands on it. It was going to be no small feat to smuggle this kind of information out of the Pentagon without getting caught. It wasn't as if he could just make copies, tuck them under his arm, and walk out the front door. Of course, he couldn't, he wouldn't have to. They would have some high tech way of collecting and delivering the information, technology he'd probably never heard of, let alone seen. He prayed he was right, that the level of sophistication would be beyond even his imagination, offering him a way out of this nightmare, allowing him to keep his job and reputation in tack. But more importantly, to get Amy back, safe and sound.

The Lieutenant was worried sick about her. He wondered where she was being kept and how she was being treated. He couldn't bear to think about it. She looked to be in pretty good shape on the video, pretty good under the circumstances. Amy was brave, in her own way, keeping her fears inside and putting up a façade that camouflaged the feelings she held so closely within. Feelings that were gut wrenching and sometimes even debilitating. She'd never admit it, but he'd seen her get physically ill in a frightening situation. She was fragile inside.

The Lieutenant still had not figured out what kind of Operation this was, despite his vivid imagination. Sure, he'd conjured up plenty of potential scenarios but none of them were remotely accurate. The Lieutenant wondered what kind of details they were looking for, but he wasn't sure he even wanted to know. That knowledge could only bring more danger. The real story didn't matter one way or another to him, all he wanted was his Amy back, back at home, back with her school children, and back in the kitchen trying new recipes.

CHAPTER TWENTY-SIX

The General had a lot of time to think, between short naps and a few glasses of chardonnay, bad chardonnay, on a torturous flight that lingered on and on like a bad Latino soap opera. But the trip gave him some time to piece together some options. Option one: just shoot them, or shoot himself. In either case he was done, quick and simple, but perhaps not the best way to go. Option two: have them kidnapped, threaten torture and see what he could find out. At least keep them locked away somewhere, preventing them from causing trouble or gallivanting about the world stirring a pot already about to boil over. But that option could be costly and very labor intensive, too many people would need to be involved. The better option was to arrest them, charge them with espionage and try them in one of the secret security courts that few in the U.S. knew about, or at least tried their best to forget. This was clearly his best bet with the only kink being that he had to find them first.

As soon as he got back to the Pentagon, he'd start building his case, planting the evidence and jumping through the not-so-legal hoops. He knew Justin had a grant from NOAA. Some well-placed documents would easily prove that he was diverting funds to help the Chinese develop secret chemical weapons. Espionage was a winner, everybody hated a traitor. He was sure to keep it all secret, but if some reason it did leak, he'd still have the tide of public opinion on his side. As for Amelia, the picture was even worse—a U.S. government employee assisting this traitor when he ran into difficulties finishing the job he'd conspired with a foreign enemy to complete. To seal their fate—they ran, after he generously allowed them an opportunity to come back into the fold. Wasn't flight a tacit admission of guilt? The General felt sure the public would see it exactly that way.

Once again, the General believed he had it all figured out, a grand plan that would, in the end, make him the hero. The plan was actually very do-able, assuming he could find these two would-be spies. Once he made his case to the powers that be he was sure to have a plethora of resources, capable of tracking them down quickly. He would spearhead a worldwide manhunt for them. There would be nowhere for them to hide, almost nowhere.

Still ten hours from home, the General began to reminisce about his life in the military and how much warfare had changed. In Vietnam he'd been a foot soldier, prowling the jungles in what often resulted in hand to hand combat, kill or be killed, and just hoping you could survive the god-forsaken place one more day. But at least they were backed up with some air power, helicopters and airplanes always at the ready. He couldn't imagine how it must have been at Gettysburg, Antietam, Manassas. How brave those young men must have been, marching to an almost sure death, face to face, with their enemy—their own countrymen—in a battle that was in the end a loser for everyone. A nation divided, more U.S. dead than killed in all wars since, and feelings so bitter and deep they lasted for another hundred years. Young men blindly following orders, serving their country, standing up for what they believed in. Was that really what it was all about or were they just young and impressionable, egged on by others with much less to lose, forced into a battle for a way of life that most of them never got a chance to live?

Is it any different now? Young men, well intentioned, brave and strong, standing up for a way of life that only benefits others. No, he couldn't believe that. It was about doing what was right, standing up when others chose to sit down, defending God and country above all else, no matter who the benefactor. We were all in this together and for those who betrayed their country, he had no pity. They were the lowest of the low, they deserved to die.

It was this kind of thinking that had, at times, gotten the good General into trouble. When he mounted that proverbial high horse, he was at risk of falling off, usually in a rather open and unceremonious fashion, bringing ruin not only to himself but also to his beloved army; a failing that was not taken lightly. He'd luckily been forgiven in the past, but his chances had all been used up. The General knew it wouldn't be tolerated again, which made it all the more imperative for him to redeem himself in what he considered one of the biggest coups of his career.

He fell asleep imagining another flight when he could bring Justin and Amelia back to the U.S. to stand trial on the charges he was concocting. The more he thought about it, the angrier he got, causing him to lose what little objectivity he had left. Now it was a matter of pride, they'd spurned him and then they'd escaped his clutches; it was too much for his fragile ego to handle. So he faded off to sleep with high hopes of being the victor in the end. It wasn't just about winning, it was about being right and he was sure that he was right this time.

But isn't that always the case, both sides in any conflict always think they are "right." But justice is in the eye of the beholder and usually one side is more right than the other; although, it doesn't mean they will win. If justice were always served, there'd be no conflict. Unfortunately, there just isn't enough justice in the world to bring us peace. Human nature would never allow it. There will always be wars and rumors of wars, leading men, and sometimes women down a primrose path to nowhere. Not nowhere actually, but rather to their untimely death. How could we have not, in all of these thousands of years, found a better way to live and let live? Maybe we just haven't evolved all that much since more primitive times.

Back at the Pentagon, the General began concocting a story, complete with written evidence, that Justin and Amelia were traitors of the worse sort. He'd fabricated invoices for the lab alleging purchases of dangerous and little known chemicals at the expense of the U.S. government grant. He already had pictures of the inside of the lab from his reconnaissance on the island. With a little photoshopping, he had added some equipment that would incriminate them. Doctored cell phone records confirmed calls to high level Chinese official on several occasions.

Sure it was all circumstantial, but that was all he needed for the secret U.S. Security Court. The Court quickly issued a warrant for the arrest of both of them. Given that Amelia was now significantly AWOL from her government job at the EPA, tacit guilt seemed a given. Now, he only had to find them, but that was a task that would prove much more difficult than he imagined. He couldn't imagine how they had disappeared so quickly and so effectively. They couldn't have gone far, but finding someone on all of those remote islands in the Pacific can prove elusive, like looking for a needle in a haystack. And who was to say they were still in the Pacific, for all he knew, they could be in Paris or Timbuktu by now.

CHAPTER TWENTY-SEVEN

Back at the lab in Taiwan, it was hijinks as usual and Mr. Kao was getting quite ready to make his escape. He spent most of his time now daydreaming of the life he planned to live in grand style, never denying himself any possible luxury. His hopes were high. Sure he was worried about making his escape, but now he'd thought through the whole process and felt sure he'd covered all possible hurdles. There was no time like the present, he needed to get out while there was still time. He knew no one in Zhushan would miss him anyway, especially not his employees. But then he wouldn't miss them either. He'd made a deal with the devil, but in the end he'd be the one to land in heaven, while these poor village saps suffered in tyranny. Well, perhaps he was being dramatic, but their possibilities were limited on this mountain and he knew for sure there was a better life, out there.

The next question to resolve was how to destroy the evidence. His was still considering the option of blowing up the lab. It was really a perfect plan. In addition to destroying all the physical evidence, it would create chaos, allowing him to escape unnoticed. Of course, people could get hurt, they had before. But he couldn't be worried about that minor detail, he had to look out for himself and his priority was getting out and moving on to the great life he had imagined for so long.

In the end he decided to give Lin a new formula that was sure to result in a significant explosion. He'd plan to be away from the lab when they were mixing it and escape in the ensuing chaos. Just for good measure, he'd add in something slightly toxic that would engage the attention of the entire town and keep the focus on their own self-protection. Not toxic enough to kill anyone, but enough to raise concerns and quite possibly send a few people, those in the nearest vicinity of the explosion, to the hospital.

Just yesterday, Lin had once again reported positive results with the newest formula. She seemed very surprised and quite anxious that the formula had worked with no adverse reactions. The poor soul, if she only knew what she was involved in, Mr. Kao was sure she would resign. As desperate as she was for the money, he knew her conscience would get the better of her. Lin would never willingly be a part of this experiment.

But Lin was smarter than Kao realized. She knew something wasn't right, and whatever it was, she was sure the final outcome could prove dreadful, if not for Taiwan, surely for other countries, most likely enemies of China. She didn't want to be a part of harming people, even those she had never met or never would. She, too, had some important decisions to make, some that could come at great personal costs but she knew she'd never have peace if she didn't do what was right. What kind of mother would she be, what kind of world would Bingwen have to grow up in, if she didn't do the right thing?

Mr. Kao took the most recent formula and added a chemical to the list—thalidomerta. He knew it was highly toxic, and when combined with the others in this particular formula would create the chaos he needed to get out. Meanwhile, he'd been working furiously with his contacts on the coast to line up his escape, to have a boat that would whisk him away to safety. Money talks, no matter the country. Mr. Kao couldn't just walk into an airport and get on the next plane, he would need an exit visa and while money could buy that, too, it would take more time and he could easily be tracked. No, simple was the way to go and skipping out in the hidden hull of a fishing boat was no problem given his financial resources.

He couldn't believe that this was his last day at the lab, in Zhushan, in Taiwan for that matter. This was the only home he'd ever known, but he wouldn't be sad to leave it, he'd been dreaming of a better life for many years. Most of all he wouldn't miss these imbeciles who worked for him, including whoever was knocking at his door now.

"The formula seems to be working," Lin proclaimed, not sure what kind of reaction she would get.

"Thank you for letting me know, but we need to make a slight modification to it tomorrow, as one final test." He threw that little falsity in for good measure, as he handed Lin the new recipe.

"Sure, I'll start on it first thing in the morning." She wanted to ask about the change, but she knew better. Lin knew Mr. Kao wouldn't tell her anything, so she simply took the paperwork and backed out of his office, bowing as she went.

Mr. Kao pulled out the books, both sets, as well as his statements from the offshore account. He'd like to have more cash, get that final bonus for finishing the job, but it was enough, and not worth the risk of having this house of cards cave in on him. Just for extra insurance he decided to take the records, the documents that could indict all three sides of this triangle. He wondered how one didn't know what the other was up to, or maybe they did. Maybe he was just being used, but he didn't care, it had been profitable.

Taiwan agreed to participate in this project, believing that they themselves could gain access to the chemical weapon, in which case they had an easy threat against other. But even if they didn't actually have the formula or the ability to deliver the weapon, Taiwan could use the leverage of their knowledge against the Chinese and the Americans. All three of them were in so deep, they couldn't blow the whistle. It was a classic web of deception, where enemies were equally complicit, unable to rat the others out without exposing themselves. And if that weren't enough, the off the books financing by these three governments would certainly mean that heads would role and men with great hubris, are loath to let that happen.

Mr. Kao decided to knock off early, it wasn't as if he feared being fired. It was his last day, regardless. He found his drinking buddy, Changpu, and they were off to their favorite watering hole to start happy hour early. Today he truly had something to celebrate, even if he couldn't share that news with anyone else.

CHAPTER TWENTY-EIGHT

Justin and Amelia were amazed at the information they'd been able to gather. It helps to have friends who can hack into government computers. It probably saved them a trip to Taiwan; they'd been trying to figure out how they were going to sneak in. Seriously, Justin was considering it, but Amelia knew their chances were slim, not only of getting in, but of getting out alive.

It was quite a puzzle, actually more of a maze, with lots of twists and turns, most of them ending up at a block wall. Justin and Amelia were still sorting out the useless information, filling in the gaps, and putting together a clear picture of what was going on. Some of it was their personal speculation, but it wasn't much of a leap to figure out what had happened, at least from the U.S. perspective. A couple of hacked reports had laid out the background.

From what they could determine so far, the U.S. had indeed made a deal with the devil, the devil being Taiwan. The U.S. military wanted a chemical weapon that could easily be delivered through a variety of mechanisms. The hope was that the threat alone would be a sufficient deterrent, but they couldn't count on the Chinese or anyone else for that matter, to be afraid. It had to work; it had to be more dangerous than anything ever developed. The military knew there was no way to develop a weapon this lethal within the borders of the U.S. It couldn't be kept quiet, not in an environment where everyone has a camera, hackers run rampant, and where, if it were found out, protests would quickly ensue. Apparently the decision to work with Taiwan had been extremely contentious. The U.S. had been in a delicate balancing act for many years, careful neither to recognize nor deny China's claims to Taiwan. Some felt engaging Taiwan in this operation was ingenious, making them complicit, providing deniability if necessary, while others felt it was buying friendship. But when was the U.S. ever adverse to buying friends? They'd done it all over the world, for much less of a return, assuming the plan worked.

Amelia was astounded as she read the reports and pieced it all together. Maybe she was a Pollyanna, actually she knew that she was, but this was too much. Taking this kind of risk with the lives of people — those involved in the development and testing, and even more so the potential exposure from the leaks.

"But how did the chemicals end up in the ocean and cause this much damage. Is it really that toxic?" Amelia asked, not even wanting to know the answer to her question.

"They had to dispose of the excess chemicals from the unsuccessful formulas somewhere and I doubt Taiwan is all that concerned about the effects on the environment," Justin replied.

Amelia, still filled with her Pollyanna hopes, tried to rationalize the situation, tried to imagine another scenario than what the facts before her offered. Was it possible that the U.S. contemplated such a plan and chose not to pursue it? Could someone else be to blame? Who's to say that Taiwan wasn't developing this weapon on their own, maybe it was their leverage against China. A million thoughts were racing through her head and she had no way to definitively confirm or dispel any of them. She wanted to believe that something like this couldn't happen. But here she was on a deserted island, on the run, because of what they had, or what someone thought they had, discovered.

Who was shooting at them? Who broke into her room and into Justin's lab? Was that the work of the General or had they aroused the suspicions, and unwanted attention, of a lot of people. Neither she nor Justin wanted to discuss the issue, but they didn't know who to trust, where to go, or most of all, whether they could ever go home again. If the General was as upset as they imagined, there was either a contract out on them or an arrest warrant. Either way their future was looking bleak.

They'd taken in a lot of information, disturbing information that made their heads ache from trying to process it all. Justin and Amelia decided it was time for a swim, time to clear their minds, and try to figure out what they were going to do, where they were going to go. They couldn't stay here forever, although today they both wished they could. But practically speaking this was a deserted island and after two days here, their limited supplies were starting to run low. Justin had heard of an island only a few hours away where there was some semblance of life, at least some food and shelter and a legendary bar run by an ex-pat that was a bit of an urban legend. Some said he was a CIA agent, others said he was in the witness protection program, some even said he'd had a complete identity change. Justin suspected he just owed a lot of alimony and back taxes and the gossip mill had tuned it up a few notches. Maybe he didn't even exist.

The sunset was up to its usual spectacular display; colors dancing across the sky that would never show up in a box of crayons. Before she arrived in Panzau, Amelia anticipated a chance to see the green flash, although given the way things had gone so far, she'd completely forgotten to even watch for it. Most people had never heard of the green flash—a visual phenomenon seen at sunset or sunrise, lasting only for a second or two. You had to have a quick eye, and be in the right place at the right time, to catch it. She'd seen pictures of it, but had never experienced it herself.

"Have you ever seen the green flash?" Amelia asked.

"The comic strip," Justin responded, oblivious to the reference.

"I thought for sure you would have seen it after all this time with such a clear view of the horizon."

Justin realized what she meant, "Yes, actually twice, it's really amazing, but you have to watch a lot of sunsets to make it happen." He was wondering how many more sunsets he might get to see, given their current predicament. Time could be short and right now it was feeling extremely precious. That reality inspired him to swim over to Amelia, take her in his arms and before she could speak, press his mouth to hers, but this time he wasn't going to apologize for it. Even though his eyes were closed, he was sure he saw his own version of the green flash. What happened next was far better than the green flash.

CHAPTER TWENTY-NINE

The Lieutenant wanted nothing more than for this to be over. Most of all, he wanted to have his beloved Amy home again. There were so many things he missed about her, things he didn't bother to appreciate before this happened. He missed her cooking more than ever, even though he wondered how he could even think of food at a time like this. He would gladly cook for her every night for the rest of their lives if he could only have her back, safe and sound.

The Pentagon was a very secure place and one not easily infiltrated, even by those on the inside. Security clearances existed for a reason and obviously, that made his mission a difficult one. But failure wasn't an option so he had to do as he was told; that is, if he ever wanted to see his Amy again. He still hadn't considered what they might do to him, whether or not he gave them what they wanted. All of his thoughts were on Amy. The Lieutenant considered telling his commanding officer, in the hopes of being able to provide disinformation that appeared legitimate enough to get Amy freed, but he feared his superiors wouldn't be willing to go that route. He couldn't take any chances with Amy's life. The black ops had the potential to extract her from the captors, assuming they could find where she was being held. But he knew the risk was still high, a potential firefight, one mistake and it would all be over.

So the Lieutenant set about his task with the earnest fervor of a man whose life depended on it, his wife's life at least. Amazingly, the process proved easier than he had anticipated. Through some electronic snooping and overheard conversations — some might say eavesdropping — he quickly heard speculation about a project that fit the profile. Getting the documents they wanted proved a bit more elusive, however. In the meantime, he fed them some low-level classified information, easily plucked during his report deliveries, stringing them along to buy time.

Amy's captors weren't pleased with the results her husband offered. They wondered if the Lieutenant was playing them. The Lieutenant, unable to provide what the captor demanded, was going crazy without his Amy. He was afraid her days were numbered and much as he hated to admit it, he needed help if he was going to save her. His plan of feeding misinformation wasn't working out so well. There were only so many useless documents he could hand over, without seriously pissing these folks off. He hadn't had any sleep in two nights trying to figure a way out of this, worried sick about whether Amy was safe, and he was starting to get delirious.

As much as he hated to take the risk, he decided he had to run this one up the ladder; otherwise, he might end up fired and Amy might end up dead. But deciding who to approach was the big dilemma. He was sure that it was a small circle of folks who actually knew anything about this operation and he wasn't going to risk expanding that circle. If he told the wrong person, he might get others fired or simply be told that no such operation existed, just after he was advised to clean out his desk.

The Lieutenant had been observing some of the Generals, to see if he noticed any unusual angst, strange schedules, or high-level visitors that might indicate they were in the know. But, of course, it was a guessing game, there were always a lot of unusual things going on at the Pentagon, so much so, that was in fact normal. General Foley had disappeared for a few days but he was back and in a bad mood, but then he was always in a bad mood. It didn't mean he was involved. General Joseph was working late almost every night, and lots of people, including the Vice-President had been to his office, but the Lieutenant knew he was working on Afghanistan so that was a likely explanation.

The Lieutenant found it hard to keep his focus on work, his mind was on Amy. He missed the sound of her voice, the smell of her cooking, the feel of her body next to his at night. Most of all he feared the danger she was in and decided it was time to seek help. The Lieutenant planned to stay late and talk to General Foley, he certainly didn't have any reason to hurry home.

The day seemed as if it would never end, there were no reports today, the halls seemed quiet by comparison, or was that the Lieutenants' imagination, *not* being overactive today. All of his co-workers had gone, some asking on their way out if he wanted to join them on the walk to the metro, but he feigned important tasks to complete before he could leave.

Finally, the Lieutenant decided it was time, his heart was in his throat. He didn't know whether he was on a path to save Amy or whether his world was about to come crumbling down. The first time he went to General Foley's office he was nowhere to be found, so he headed down to the break room to check the television. Nothing interesting was going on in the world today, at least nothing he found news worthy. Out of the corner of his eye he caught the General walking briskly toward his office, so he gave him a few minutes and then went to see if he was there.

"What do you want?" the General barked when he knocked at his door. He wondered who the General thought was there. He actually seemed surprised and not nearly as troubled when he saw it was the Lieutenant opening the door. At first, the General denied knowing anything about such an operation. What else could he do? There was no way someone at the Lieutenant's level should know anything about this. But when he explained that Amy had been kidnapped by what appeared to be, Chinese nationals, his interest was piqued.

The Lieutenant failed to mention the previous classified documents he'd passed on in attempt to buy time, He saw no need to admit guilt that could land him on the street, if not in jail. The General was suspicious, naturally, but the Lieutenant was able to offer enough inside information for him to know this was legitimate. When the Lieutenant finished explaining his version of the truth, the General put his head in his hands and looked down for what seemed like minutes. The Lieutenant wondered if he was about to cry, which didn't exactly inspire hope, but finally the General spoke, trying not to reveal any more than he had to. What he told the Lieutenant was *his* version of the truth.

The General claimed that the Taiwanese were developing their own chemical weapon. China found out, not surprisingly, and Taiwan's response was to claim they were working on behalf of the U.S. According to the General, Taiwan was trying to create a diplomatic situation, pulling the U.S. in to defend them and risking a potential international conflict with China. The General seemed convinced that the Chinese already had a workable formula, but were looking for an antidote to reverse it if used against them. Whether the Chinese actually had the ability to deploy the chemical weapon, was still up for debate. Although that story didn't jive with what the Lieutenant had figured out on his own, or been told by the kidnappers—he clearly couldn't trust them—he didn't really care what the truth was. The truth is relative after all, and the only truth he was interested in at the moment was what it would take to get Amy back. That was no easy task, at least not without involving people that the General didn't really want to know about this situation. But a woman's life was at stake, a wife no less and the General couldn't let that go. Maybe he did have a heart after all, or maybe he had an ulterior motive.

The General told the Lieutenant to leave the planning to him. They planned to meet again in the morning. The

Lieutenant didn't completely trust him, he didn't trust anyone these days, but this was his country, his General, so he had to go on faith. Feeling a little more hopeful for Amy's future, he left the Pentagon and headed for Alexandria.

The kidnappers were waiting at the apartment and they were clearly running out of patience. The Lieutenant told them he was close to getting what they wanted, that, in fact, he hoped to have it for them by tomorrow night. Just for good measure they roughed him up a bit and told him Amy was next if he didn't produce. He didn't even bother to fight back, he was too tired and he knew they had the upper hand, for now. But that was all about to change.

When the Lieutenant appeared in General Foley's office the next morning, after delivering the day's reports, he almost turned and left. He had company, high level company. But the General yelled at him to come in, the door was closed, the mood somber. The Lieutenant had a bad feeling.

The Lieutenant was interrogated heavily, peppered with one question after another in attempt to see the depth of his knowledge about this operation. It became quickly obvious that he had been feed a lot of misinformation about Operation Jungle Juice, a fact for which they were thankful. To his amazement, the group included a five-star general and the Secretary of Defense, who asked the Lieutenant to come back in an hour. The told the lieutenant they were devising a plan. There was a lot of nervousness in the room and not only from the Lieutenant.

When the Lieutenant returned, General Foley wasn't there. When he asked why not, the question wasn't answered, but that wasn't the Lieutenant's problem, all he wanted to know was how they were going to rescue Amy. The five-star general laid out the plan in as little detail as he could to convince the Lieutenant they were on top of the situation. The Lieutenant's head was spinning and he couldn't quite take it all in, this was not how he thought this day would go. According to their — *yet another* — version of the truth they'd known for days about Amy and they'd been following the Lieutenant. They had hoped General Foley would resolve the situation, but, as on other critical occasions, he failed to respond. The Lieutenant wondered if they fired him. They knew where Amy was, a plan was already in motion to rescue her and if necessary, take the kidnappers out, though they preferred not to do that. This was already on the verge of an international incident; having two Chinese nationals killed by special agents was going to escalate the situation.

Beyond their plan to rescue Amy, the Lieutenant wasn't given any more information about Operation Jungle Juice. The details were highly classified. He wasn't cleared for that kind of information, even now that he and Amy were involved. What happened next was a surprise and under other circumstances would have been a dream come true. The big brass had plans for his future, plans he couldn't have anticipated just a few weeks ago, plans he wasn't so sure were in his best interests. Was he trading one kind of danger for another? He was told that, he and Amy — assuming they were able to rescue her — would be relocated to Cuba, where he would work undercover for the government. Their cover would be a restaurant, how apropos, now Amy could make Cuban sandwiches for real. Luckily the two of them had been taking Spanish classes at night for the past six months.

But what if — he couldn't even think about the possibility — they couldn't get Amy out alive and unharmed? If not, he'd be expected to go to Cuba without her. He'd fallen into an ugly web, and while he wasn't sure of the truth, he knew he wasn't going to be allowed to simply walk away. News of this operation could never get out, they had to make sure he was kept quiet. He realized that now. Could he do it, did he want to, did he have any choice? The Lieutenant quickly thought about his options, which were limited, very limited.

He could bolt, make a run for it himself, but not until he got Amy back. Where would they go, how would they survive, was there anywhere they could hide? He saw the fallacy of even considering the possibilities, besides, he was hard wired as a G-man and he couldn't desert them.

"Lieutenant, are you with us?" someone in the room asked, he wasn't even sure who.

His head was spinning, it was a lot to take in. "Do I have any choice?" he asked, not meaning it disrespectfully. It was a normal reaction given his stress.

"Yes, but I don't think you would like the options. We need you son, you have a chance to help your country." They always played on the desire to help your country. The Lieutenant wasn't sure he believed their pitch, but he had to find a solution that would keep him safe, him *and* Amy. It wasn't the end of the world.

He walked down the hall in stunned silence, grabbed a few important things from his desk and left, as if he was simply headed out for lunch. He'd never be back in the building again.

While he was packing a few clothes, the television roared in the background. A familiar voice caught his attention, and when he turned to look, he saw General Foley tendering his retirement notice. He offered the usual—family obligations—as his reason for leaving now. No one cared anyway, he was hardly a favorite and the public would never know, or question the real reason. General Foley was looking tired, yet confident, always defiant to the end that he had served his country with every measure of devotion he had. The broadcast was interrupted by his cell phone, the news he had hoped for. Amy was free, his heart almost stopped beating.

On the way out of the apartment, the Lieutenant almost ran over Gepetto. Mrs. Heverstein was out for her usual late afternoon walk.

"Hello Philip, how are you? How is Amy? I've not seen her in a few days," Mrs. Heverstein said.

The Lieutenant had to do a bit of quick thinking, "Yes, she is visiting her sister for a few days and I'm going to join her."

"Well, tell her how much I enjoyed that tuba sandwich. I look forward to having another one soon."

Tuba sandwich, the Lieutenant almost laughed. He needed a laugh. But seeing Mrs. Heverstein and Gepetto only reminded him of the good life they'd lived here, this apartment had been their only home and now they were leaving it without a word to anyone. He wondered what Mrs. Heverstein would think when she never saw them again.

"I'll be sure to tell her. Have a nice life, I mean a nice night, Mrs. Heverstein," the Lieutenant said as he quickly headed for the black car that was waiting at the corner; the car that would take him to Amy and eventually away from the life they'd known.

CHAPTER THIRTY

General Peng was not happy when the word came. Failure was not an option and heads were going to roll. How did this situation unravel so fast? Mr. Kao was missing, most likely a good riddance, and the lab had another explosion. But none of that was as upsetting to Peng as the fact that Amy was gone, along with her husband, and his men were on a plane back to Beijing. Although he suspected they were lucky to escape with their lives, he wasn't sure why the Americans didn't kill them. He never would understand their perverse logic. Given the situation in reverse, China would have never let the kidnappers out alive. Perhaps they had turned them, trying to make double agents out of them, but the Americans should know better than to think they could ever be trusted; besides, the Chinese would take care of them in their own way.

And the icing on the cake, that couple in Panzau had gone missing with no clue as to where they might be. It was a glorious day. He sat in his office contemplating how it all went so wrong and what he was going to do to clean it up, figuratively and literally.

"The Director is here for the meeting," Lt. Liang announced.

"What are you talking about?" General Peng barked, even more coarsely than normal.

"The Director from the Institute, Mr. Houng, is here." The General had forgotten that Mr. Houng promised to come to his office this week. This was just what he needed today. He checked his watch, the Director was only five minutes late. It was a miracle.

But the meeting turned out to be the bright spot in the General's day. Much to his surprise, Mr. Houng was actually well versed in Operation Red Panda, even up to the current events, and more importantly, he had some critical information. He should have been more candid with him last week and some of these complications could likely have been avoided. At least Mr. Houng had some viable options for moving forward; the suits weren't going to like it, but he didn't care what they thought. They'd made a mess out of it so far, so they didn't have much standing to complain.

When Mr. Houng had gone, the General pondered the possibilities, how he might turn this around and make a success of it after all. The situation had presented an interesting opportunity. What could make a better cover than a Chinese restaurant, every city has one. No one would expect anything sinister to be happening over an order of Kung Pao Chicken. The General needed to look at a map and now they had this new computerized satellite system that he didn't know how to operate. He liked it much better when he could just unfold a piece of paper on top of his desk. He called for Lt. Liang to come help him, these young folks were useful for some things.

Liang was at the General's desk in minutes, opening up their high-tech satellite mapping system. He loved this tool. He could see almost any place in the world in real time, giving him a chance to travel to places he'd never have a chance to visit.

Once he had the search engine opened he asked the General, "Where do you want to go?"

"Havana."

CHAPTER THIRTY-ONE

No one was surprised by the latest explosion at the lab, but this one was the worst they'd seen. A rather large toxic cloud was forming over the top of the building and employees laid scattered on the ground, coughing and wheezing, some with significant burns, as the fire brigade once again lumbered up the mountain. Mr. Kao was nowhere to be found, how convenient. The employees were trying to determine who, if anyone, might still be inside, taking an informal head count of their departments. It quickly became apparent that several people were still inside, and to make matters worse there was a fire burning at the side exit of the building.

Fearless, though untrained, members of the fire brigade ran inside to rescue their fellow townsfolk. They managed to pull several to safety, dousing them with the water hoses to relieve the stinging and itching, their skin quickly developing bumps and unusual rashes. Others who came to watch quickly realized the severity of the situation and helped get the injured to the local hospital. Changpu was pulled from the building, barely breathing and severely burned. When he succumbed to his injuries, one of the fireman attempted CPR, but it was no use. Changpu was gone, his buddy Mr. Kao wasn't here to protect him now.

Lin lay coughing, and burned, under a table in the middle of the lab. She attempted to yell but the sound wouldn't come. When she tried to move, her limbs wouldn't cooperate. It was as if she were paralyzed, a very strange feeling permeated her muscles, or was she just delusional from the fumes. She thought of Bingwen, what would happen to him if she should perish. Was Gang up to the task of raising this child, would he even try? Lin knew her parents would help, but they were older and had limited means to feed another hungry mouth. She began to weep and tried once again to yell, but still nothing and then, only darkness.

Once the scene was under control, Mr. Kao had still not materialized, so the fire chief ordered the lab closed. It was the talk of the town, the explosion and the disappearance. Everyone wondered where he had gone, including Mrs. Kao. Not that anyone really cared, in fact they were glad to be rid of him, but there was plenty of fodder for gossip. In the end, everyone assumed that he left to avoid being fired; for where, they couldn't imagine. When the suits appeared and began to question his wife, they all knew there was more to the story.

Poor Mrs. Kao stood by while they turned the house upside down, looking for what she wasn't sure. They only thing they found was the rice wine hidden in her closet. Thank goodness she'd bought a new bottle, she was going to need it today. The suits did the same at the lab, but it was clear that whatever records had been kept were now long gone, no doubt on vacation with Mr. Kao.

When Lin awoke in the hospital the next day, she had no clue how she got there. She only knew she was happy to see Bingwen sitting at the foot of her bed, her mother in a chair at her side. Gang was not there, she hoped he was at work; someone needed to be earning a living. The pain was intense, her limbs felt heavy and tired, but at least now she could move them slightly. Burns on her arms and face were covered in a local salve, but the stinging and itchiness remained. When she tried to scratch her arm, her mother stopped her. It would only prolong the recovery. Lin was thankful to be alive, and especially thankful to the fireman who managed to pull her from the building before some beams fell that could have crushed her small frame. She was getting the details of her rescue from her mother, but she would definitely want to talk to and thank the fireman as soon as she felt better.

A few days later, back at home, and now able to move about, the suits showed up for a chat. Based on their last meeting, Lin obviously knew a lot about the operations at the lab, even if she didn't know the truth. Lin was very afraid, she knew what she had done; she wondered if they did, too. Thankfully Gang wasn't home, so far he was still working at the bike shop, but no doubt he would have complicated the conversation. Lin hoped he'd stick with his work, it looked like they were going to need the income.

Most of all, Lin wanted to know if she still had a job, whether any of them did. Was this the end of the enterprise that had kept so many of the villagers in food and clothes for the past five years? But she knew the suits were there to get information from her, not to answer her questions, so the conversation was mostly one sided. Reading between the lines, it was clear that Mr. Kao had been up to no good. She wondered who the suits worked for, but this was one detail she would never know. In the end, she was just happy not to be taken away in hand cuffs, how terrible it would have been for Bingwen to come home and find his mother gone.

After they left, Lin felt a great sense of relief, she'd dodged a bullet. She wasn't used to disobeying orders, but in the end she may have avoided more deaths and destruction. Lin poured herself a cup of the oolong tea and sat, taking in the peace and tranquility that surrounded her. The mountains spoke to her, giving her a sense of comfort, a feeling that somehow all would be well. She had a simple life, it was enough.

Lin imagined those folks on the other side of the world, toiling away in jobs they hated, some greedily chasing more money so they could have more things. She wondered about their life, their happiness. Lin wasn't quick to judge, especially those lives of which she had no first-hand knowledge. She'd never know someone like Amy, live the privileged life she did, enjoying street fairs and gourmet cooking, teaching children and touching young lives. Nor would she ever meet Justin and Amelia, know their passion, both for their work and for each other. But she was happy, she hoped they were, too.

Lin took a deep breath, a light breeze blew her hair in her eyes, obscuring the view that brought so much meaning to her life. As she wiped her long back locks behind her ears, she noticed a Formosa tree starting to bloom, its beautiful red flowers dancing in the breeze, as if laughing away the cares of the day. But her tree gazing was interrupted when Bingwen dashed into the house, full of energy and thrilled to have his mother at home.

"Momma, come outside and watch me play," Bingwen begged.

At first Lin felt too tired and distracted, she almost told him no, but she realized how uncertain life is, especially now after this explosion, so she decided to do as he asked. Lin knew what was important in life, the lab was just a means to an end, yes a means of support, but at what cost. Despite many materials differences, what Lin had in common with those folks on the other side of the world, on the other sides of the triangle, was that desire to protect the ones she loved, and she, like they, would do whatever was necessary to keep them safe.

CHAPTER THIRTY-TWO

Justin and Amelia's tender moment was interrupted by Skype, that sound so obvious, the familiar vintage ring of a 1960s telephone. Justin jumped up from the blanket where they lay, wrapped in the warmth of each other's arms, and grabbed his computer just in time. His buddy was about to give up on reaching them.

"Man, I was afraid I'd lost you guys. It's good to hear your voice. What have you guys done, are you telling me the truth?" His friend asked, and Justin knew it wasn't good news.

Amelia joined him in front of the computer to hear the latest, her head still spinning from what had just transpired between them. She was happy but confused, her heart skipping a few beats, her mind cloudy, but she had to focus, quickly, they were in danger lest she forget, and the clock was ticking, almost as loudly as the Skype ring.

Justin was amazed at the information his hacker friend had uncovered, it really made him wonder about the ability of governments to keep secrets. There was a warrant out for their arrest, allegations of misappropriating U.S. grant funds — well, that much was true — espionage, and the kicker, treason. They were alleged to be spying for China, they'd sold out and were a danger to their country.

Although he didn't have time to offer a full explanation, Justin made it clear they were trying to undo something very dangerous, not only to the environment but to humanity. Justin tried to take solace in the fact that maybe, just maybe, they had put a stop to this particular operation. But in the end, he knew there would be another, whether it was China, Taiwan, the U.S., or some other country, for that matter, it was only a matter of time. Clearly, they couldn't put a stop to the development of all chemical weapons, but they wanted to be a part of preventing them from harming the environment and innocent people. But how were they going to do that now? They were wanted, pegged as criminals, possibly being hunted down by several countries and if that wasn't enough they had limited resources to protect themselves. Figuring their way out of this one wasn't going to be easy.

Justin wanted to return to Amelia's arms, but now was not the time. They had decisions to make so romance would have to wait. But Justin knew it was something he wanted to pursue, he hoped Amelia felt the same. Given what had just happened, he was pretty sure she did.

CHAPTER THIRTY-THREE

Otis was wiping down the tables at the bar, trying to clean away the grunge from last night's crowd. He hadn't even bothered to turn on the television today, it wasn't time for the Andy Griffith re-runs, and as usual, the news had been slim in recent days. Did it really matter anyway? Precious little that happened in the real world affected his life.

His cleaning spree was interrupted by a local fisherman bringing in the catch of the day. Otis always had the freshest fish around, straight from the ocean to his tables. Today there were grouper, mahi, even some lobster. He always inspected every piece, these guys were forever trying to rip him off and thank goodness he took the time to check, especially today. In the bottom of the bin, Otis found several severely deformed fish.

"Where did you find these?" he asked holding up a grouper that was missing a tail and covered in yellow bumps.

The fisherman tried to convince Otis it wouldn't affect the taste, even going so far as to suggest that Otis cut away the deformed parts and cook it, the diners would be none the wiser. But Otis knew something wasn't right and even on this tiny island, where no one ever heard of a food inspector, he wasn't going for it. He rejected the bad ones and paid the fisherman for the rest.

"Don't bring me any more of those freak fish." Why these guys thought they could scam Otis, he'd never know.

Figuring he couldn't pawn them off on anyone else, the fisherman threw the deformed fish in the ditch on his way out. Even though he'd tried to sell Otis on their safety, he wasn't taking the risk himself.

While Otis was packing down the catch in fresh ice, the new couple appeared at the bar. They'd been on island for several days now and in the bar a couple of times. He'd not had a chance to interrogate them yet, but was looking forward to finding out "their story." The guy, handsome with wavy hair, was holding one of the deformed fish in his hand, the woman, looked angry and scared all at the same time.

"Excuse me, do you know where these came from?" he asked.

"The ocean," There's one in every crowd, today it was Otis.

"No seriously, do you know where it came from?"

"Well, a local fisherman brought them in earlier, trying to pawn them off on me with the good stuff. They looked kind of scary so I wasn't taking any chances. I guess he threw them out when he left," Otis responded.

"Do you know where he gets his catch?"

"He usually fishes up on the north side of the island. He has a small boat so he doesn't head too far out in the ocean. Do you know what's wrong with them?"

"Yes, I believe we do," the woman replied in a seemingly disappointed voice as she gave a curious, but knowing look at him—her husband, boyfriend, partner. Otis could tell there was something between them.

"Can I get you something?" Otis asked.

"How about a couple of fruit salads and some guava juice? We'll be sitting over there," she said, pointing at the corner booth.

While Otis was delivering their salads, a guy strolled into the bar with a young Asian woman on each arm, both of them taller than him; although, it didn't take much. Was he Chinese, Japanese, or what? He was loud and obnoxious, quite an attitude of entitlement. He yelled, loudly, for Otis to bring over three mai tais.

"Where does this guy think he is?" Otis asked, to no one in particular.

"Who is he?" she asked as Otis placed the salad in front of her.

"Not sure, but I'm going to find out. We don't put up with that kind of attitude around here, even if he does have money. He's certainly being throwing a lot of it around the past few days. And the women, it's a different one — or two — every day," Otis offered, before departing quickly to confront this nincompoop.

"Listen, Mr. 'whoever you think you are' we don't do mai-tais. This is not the Four Seasons, you're lucky to get one season here — summer, and you can have a beer or some whisky and maybe some milk for your, uh *daughters*. How old are they by the way? So what's it going to be?" Otis asked, with great confidence, as he leaned over their table.

"I expect you to treat me with respect," he retorted.

"You have to earn respect, and we don't hand it out easily in this place," Otis told him.

"We'll take our business elsewhere," was his reply.

"Fine," said Otis, knowing the options were extremely limited. There was no other bar in town.

Despite that fact, or perhaps in ignorance of it, the man jumped up, barked at the girls to follow, and started to walk out. But before he did, he pointed to the corner booth where Justin and Amelia were sitting and asked, "Who are those two?"

"Why don't you go over and ask them?" Otis suggested and walked away, but Mr. Kao was a bit paranoid today, as he would be every day for the rest of his life, with good reason. He found it very odd that this couple showed up on the island shortly after he arrived, but he decided it was just a coincidence, they didn't look like CIA agents, so he ignored them and walked out, his *girls* in tow, he had better things to do with his time these days.

CHAPTER THIRTY-FOUR

On his way out of the bar Mr. Kao almost collided with a guy on his way in. The man, clearly distracted, hadn't even noticed Kao or his girls. "Excuse me," he said to the group. These Americans, Kao thought, they are always so polite, even when they don't have to be. The man was obviously looking for someone and he quickly found them. When he slid into the seat beside Amelia she was visibly startled. Given the events of the past few days, it was justified.

Time was of the essence so he wasted none of it getting to the point. He knew a lot more about was going on in Taiwan than they did, including the cause of the recent explosion that had killed Changpu and sent Lin to the hospital. While he wasn't completely transparent with the facts, he closed a lot of the gaps Justin and Amelia had been trying to fill with their limited information. They were skeptical, naturally, given their recent confrontation with the General and the facts they had discovered on their own. They knew they had stepped into a tangled web of deceit and danger. The only good that had emerged was the fact that they had found each other. But was there any future in it, for them, were they doomed to a life on the run or worse? At this point they were weighing their options, limited as they were, and quite simply, just hoping to stay alive.

Now this stranger shows up and offers them another way out. But could he be trusted, could they trust anyone? The world of spies, espionage, and counter-intelligence is a place where reality is never real. It's a life filled with secrets, lies, and danger. They were scientists, not spies, this was no life for them.

Otis came over to check on them, see if they needed anything else, maybe some of his homemade hooch. He was startled when he saw they were now three.

"You again, I figured you were just passing through. Did you hear anything else about that mushroom cloud in Taiwan?" Otis asked.

The guy was a bit taken back, not quite sure what Otis meant, or more importantly, what he knew. "Huh, what cloud?" he asked as if completely unaware.

"The one we saw on the big screen when you were here a couple of days ago."

Relieved, when he remembered their previous encounter, he replied, "Nope, seems to have been much of nothing."

"Like everything else that goes on out there," Otis said, pointing to nowhere in particular. "Can I get you something?"

This was going to be a tough conversation, so he asked for the hooch. He suggested that Justin and Amelia do the same.

Most of what he told them was the truth, as much truth as will ever be told in these circumstances. General Foley had been diverting funds for special operations to the Taiwanese, a large chunk of it to Mr. Kao, for development of a chemical weapon. It couldn't be done in the U.S., it would be too controversial and no doubt, word would get out. The U.S. had not officially sanctioned it but, of course, there were those who allowed, if not outright condoned it. It was to be the best tool in a post-9/11 world, one that would give the U.S. a clear upper-hand, allowing them to quickly and quietly take out anyone they considered to be a threat. It could easily be administered, death would come quickly, and the cause would appear natural.

Unfortunately, the Chinese had a similar plan and the Taiwanese, Mr. Kao in particular, was most happy to provide services to both. They had the perfect location to make it happen, a small village, where no one would think to look or be bothered if a few folks died in the process. The glitch, in addition to the fact that a stable version had yet to be created, was the disposal of chemicals involved in the process. Mr. Kao, in his usual haphazard style, had sold the "leftovers" to a less than scrupulous waste disposal company who'd been dropping the sealed barrels in the ocean. When they chemicals met with water the barrels quickly busted, the mix of toxic chemicals flowing into the ocean, maiming and killing the marine life that had been washing up on the shores of Panzau.

They all took another drink of the homemade hooch — hot and sharp, burning from the throat to the stomach, but only for a few seconds before spreading that warmth throughout the body and providing some much needed relaxation.

"So, who was trying to kill us?" Amelia asked, hoping for the answer she wanted.

This was where the truth got a little blurry. He wasn't sure the General had ordered a hit on them, even though he knew it was almost a certainty. But it was safer to make the Chinese the culprit, so that's what he told her. Did it really matter who? Plenty of people wanted to shut them up, for good reason.

"Why are you telling us this?" Justin asked, with no small amount of trepidation, wondering if this guy was here to kill them.

"We need your help and your silence. It's the only way we can guarantee your safety," he responded in a rather ominous tone.

"Who is we?" Amelia wanted to know.

"Your government." Not being fully clear on what or who that meant.

Amelia and Justin looked at each other, knowing they'd heard a similar offer before. One they had been wise to decline, but now things were different. They couldn't stay on the run for the rest of their lives. They didn't have the financial resources or the nerves of steel they suspected it would take. They liked this island and Otis's little bar but this was no life for them.

They spent a couple of hours listening to the explanation of how it would all work. It sounded a lot like the witness protection plan. The government would plant reports of Justin and Amelia's death, killed in a boat at sea to ward off the continued threat of the Chinese trying to kill them. They would work for the government, the CIA to be precise, at least for a few years, to figure out an antidote. The genie was out of the bottle, but she could be contained. Otherwise, lots more marine life and eventually a lot of people were going to die. He appealed to their sense of justice and their scientific knowledge to help the government find a solution.

"When would we leave, assuming we agree to this, this plan?" Amelia asked with a trembling voice.

"Tomorrow," he said as he laid out two passports complete with their pictures but new names, along with tickets for the three of them on a flight from Bangkok.

"How do we get from here to Bangkok?" Justin asked.

"That's easy, we have our own boat waiting on the north shore. It'll only take a few hours."

"We? Our boat? Just exactly who do you work for?" Justin inquired, fully suspecting he would never get an actual answer.

A CIA identification was produced, it looked authentic, but then how could they know for sure. Regardless, this guy had found them. He wasn't likely to let them go now.

Amelia and Justin stayed on at the bar and had a couple more glasses of the homemade hooch after he left. They were understandably nervous about where this might end up, but wherever it might be going, they were going there together. They debated another escape, but doubted they'd shake the agent as easily as they had the General. No doubt there were reinforcements on the island or watching nearby, their chances of getting off this island alive were slim. Going with the agent was their best chance at survival, and hopefully a decent life, together.

When they boarded the boat the next morning, they were surprised to see another passenger. It was the loud mouthed man from the bar, sans the girls. His presence made them all the more nervous. Had they sold their soul to the devil? Were they going to make it to Bangkok alive? Maybe the cover story about them dying at sea wasn't just a fantasy.

The agent explained that Mr. Kao was the man who ran the lab. They'd tracked him to the island when he disappeared from Zhushan. He also had been given an option, join them on the boat or be shot. He decided to take his chances with the Americans, especially when facing down the barrel of a gun. Mr. Kao had been foolish and now it was catching up with him, but he was still convinced, in his infinite hubris that he was going to be the winner. Today he was on his way to the U.S. to be a double agent for the CIA.

Justin and Amelia went below board to a small living room. It wasn't safe for them to be seen on deck. Another agent on board offered them some juice and they settled back for the ride, hoping for smooth water. The time passed quicker than expected, despite their fears, and they were soon at a small chaotic pier in Bangkok, a kind of floating market, where food and wares were readily available. But there was no time for shopping, they quickly disembarked and headed for the airport.

The plane was ascending, now 10,000 feet about the Pacific Ocean. Amelia asked the agent where Mr. Kao was. She realized she didn't see him get off the boat, but she had other things on her mind and thought he left before them.

"He's enjoying a cocktail."

Amelia looked around the cabin but couldn't see him.

"No, down there," the agent said pointing out the window to the hazy blue water below. "He's enjoying a chemical cocktail. At least he won't be able to further endanger the marine life, or anyone else for that matter."

Amelia was startled, but somehow relieved to be rid of this sinister character, this person in large part responsible for her current predicament. She reached over and took Justin's hand as she gazed out the window. The Ocean looked so peaceful, clean and clear, the beautiful place she'd come to love as a child. But like our lives, it holds many secrets, some better left untold.

ABOUT THE AUTHOR

Teresa Cannady is an international development consultant who has traveled to more than 60 countries, living long term in several including Egypt, Serbia, Kazakhstan, the Philippines, Sri Lanka, the West Bank, and the Federated States of Micronesia. A graduate of the University Of Alabama School Of Law, Teresa was an attorney in private practice in Alabama before moving to Kazakhstan in 1998. In Kazakhstan she worked as a volunteer lawyer with the American Bar Association Rule of Law Initiative, planning to stay for one year and return to private practice. But 17 years and many countries later, she still works in international development, assisting countries as they develop legal systems, conducting training, and advocating for women's rights. Teresa now lives in Vero Beach, Florida and continues to complete short-term assignments in developing countries such as Moldova, Sri Lanka, South Africa, Ethiopia, and Haiti.

Teresa began writing poetry as a small child from her playhouse on Drum Creek in Albertville, Alabama. During high school some of her poetry and a short story were published in the high school literary magazine. But creative writing fell by the wayside with the constraints of a busy work life that required a lot of "uncreative" writing. Teresa moved to Vero Beach in January of 2011 to work as a consultant and devote more time to writing. This is her first work of fiction with high hopes for many more.

You can follow Teresa on twitter @tlcannady, at her website, and on Facebook.

.